MURDER IS A SHORE THING

A CAPE MAY MYSTERY

MILES NELSON

WORKING STIFF PRESS
www.MilesNelsonAuthor.com

www.MilesNelsonAuthor.com

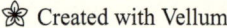 Created with Vellum

1

Traffic was light on the stretch of Ocean Drive that left Wildwood Crest, passing Two Mile and cutting through the marsh on its way to the toll bridge and Cape May. It was a crisp and clear Tuesday morning in early November, and Jason Kane was glad that most of the tourists and other seasonal visitors had retreated back to their homes up north. There were no other cars in sight, and he kept to the speed limit as he savored the sunny morning and the unusually warm air that rushed in through the half-open window. It was fifty-five degrees at 8:00 a.m. in November at the shore. *And there won't be many more days like this,* he thought to himself.

The jarring sound of a ringing phone coming through the car's speakers startled him, as it always did. He scooped up his phone from the passenger seat and stole a glance at the screen to see who the caller was before punching the button on the steering column to take the call from his twin brother.

"Hey Erik," he said, "what's up? Don't tell me you're bailing on me."

"Wow, thanks for all your faith in me. No, I'm not bailing on you, but I'm running fifteen, twenty minutes late. I'm just working on shaking off a slow morning. I'll be there."

"No problem, take your time. I'll tell Jo you're on your way. What does she want us for anyway? Moving furniture or something like that?"

"Ugh, I hope not, but whatever. I think she wants help with getting boxes brought down from the attic, or up from the basement, or one of those. She told me she's determined to finally go through the last of Dad's stuff. You know— since she found grandpa's old papers and got all excited."

"You're right," Jason said, "she probably wants to talk about that. Silly stuff most likely, but I guess it can't hurt to dig into it some more."

"Agreed," Erik said. "Most likely nothing, but hey, worth a look. Who knows, crazier shit has happened. Alright, well, let me get it together here and I'll be on my way soon."

"Sounds good, see you there. Over and out."

He hit the button to end the call as he passed the Canyon Club condos and smiled at his lucky timing as he breezed through the green light and up onto the bridge to Cape May.

Five minutes later he pulled up in front of the big old house on Kearney Avenue that the three siblings had inherited from their father. He got out of the car and stood for a moment, looking up at the house. A classic northeast beach house. Cedar shake shingles, weathered gray by years of blazing sun and wind-driven salt air, with white trim all around the windows and doors. *Yeah, I guess I can't blame her for thinking of moving. This is a lot of house for a single lady. Her golden years should be easier.*

Eight cement steps, ten feet wide and beginning the same distance in from the sidewalk, led from the brick walkway up to the house at the center of a wide wrap-around porch. A central banister of lightly-rusted iron pipe ran up the steps as if to divide them into two lanes. As Kane took the steps one by one, memories of long-gone summers flashed past and through him. He could smell the beach two blocks away – *or was that just a memory?* Endless summers of fudge and taffy, morning bike rides and skeeball at Frank's Playland on the rainy days.

He pocketed his keys as he found the front door to be unlocked. Going through and closing the door behind him, he looked around the large entry foyer which opened to rooms on either side. Directly in front of him was the stair-case up to the second floor. To the right of the staircase and parallel to it was the hallway leading to the rear of the house.

"Hey Jo," he called out into the house. "I'm here. It's Jason." He paused to listen, standing still. He was expected of course, and he knew his sister to be an early riser, but yet the house seemed oddly quiet. He called out a second time, and after getting no answer, a third time as he followed the central hallway past the staircase and towards the kitchen at the rear, pushing open the old-style swinging door. There was nobody in the kitchen and no sign of the typical break-fast activity—no toast plate, no margarine or jam out, no juice. And the coffee maker was cold. *This is very strange*, he thought, his pulse quickening as he felt the first hint of tightness in his stomach. He left the kitchen through the other door into the dining room and from there through the front sitting room and back to the foyer. He took a quick look into the other front room, which his sister used as a combined office and reading room, and called out again, louder, and then again with no reply. He backed into the foyer and looked up the stairs, noting that there didn't appear to be any lights on up above.

"Hey Jolene, you're scaring me. It's Jason. I'm coming up."

Halfway to the second floor was a wide landing where the staircase made a 180 degree turn back towards the front of the house. The light was dim, but as Kane approached the landing he noticed a shape on the floor at the base of the second run of stairs.

"Oh no, oh no," he said aloud as a human form came into focus. "Oh Jolene, oh shit." His head swam and he went blank for a few seconds before turning to look for the landing light switch, finally seeing it and shuffling to the wall to flick it up. And suddenly there she was, her brown eyes, lifeless but still clear, looking up at him. Her head seemed to be bent at an unnatural angle against the landing floor, as was one of her arms, which looked to him like a doll's arm that had been twisted around the wrong way until it came undone. Her legs extended up the stairs with her bare feet resting several steps up. She was wearing a quilted housecoat that had fallen open below the waist to reveal flannel pajamas. She was gone, and he knew it, but he knelt beside her, forcing himself to remember the training he had been through a lifetime ago to check for a pulse at both her wrist and her neck. He found none, and she was cold to the touch. *Oh Jo, what happened here? I told you to be careful on all these damn stairs.* He stood up, putting one hand on the banister to brace himself against a moment of dizziness.

"I've got to call," he said aloud. "Gotta call 9-1-1." As he patted his pockets, he realized he had left his phone in the car. Something hanging over the edge of the top step above him caught his eye. He stepped carefully over his sister's body and went up, finding the object to be a recent model iPhone in a colorful plastic case. One of his sister's return address stickers was stuck to the back. He tapped the screen and was relieved to find that the phone wasn't locked. As the screen lit up he saw that the phone's number pad was open, with "9-1-1" already keyed in. *That's weird,* he thought. *That was already there. Am I losing it?* He switched over to look at her recent calls, finding that the last one had been two days earlier. *Was she about to call for help last night, right before she fell?* He flipped back to the dial pad, confirming that the "9-1-1" was in fact there, keyed in but undialed. He shook his head and pressed the button to make the connection to the emergency services.

The conversation was brief. He gave the dispatcher his name and his sister's information, and told them that he had been trained as a medic in the service and was certain she was dead. The dispatcher told him that a patrol car should be there within ten minutes, and to please be sure to flag them down and let them in.

Back on the landing, he knelt for a moment to touch his

sister's cheek before standing and wiping his sleeve across his eyes. He went down to the foyer and opened the front door wide, pulling over a heavy iron door stop to hold it. Looking again at the phone, he brought up recent texts, and found a thread from the middle of the prior afternoon, between his sister and someone she called "Aaron", with a number that Kane didn't recognize. *Aaron,* he thought, *I've only ever known one person by that name.* The gist of the text conversation was that Jolene was looking forward to him coming over later, so they could talk about an old diary she had found and some research she had done that might be related. Aaron seemed interested and the conversation appeared friendly.

Kane's mind raced. *Could they have been talking about that? And why wouldn't she have called me or Erik instead? Did this guy come over and threaten her? Good God—did he kill her? It looks like she fell—could she have been pushed?*

He looked at his watch, noting that it had been four or five minutes since he had called the police. On the desk in his sister's office he found a small pad of sticky notes and a pen, and wrote down the number from the text thread. After a twenty-second mental back and forth, he tapped on the phone to delete the thread, set the phone on the desk, and started looking around for anything that looked like a diary. Just as he heard the sounds of an approaching siren, he turned over a legal pad and saw that there were a few pages of scribbled notes in his sister's handwriting with yesterday's date penciled in the top. He tried to read quickly. *Something about train tracks, something, something, 150 years, swampland... What is this crap? No sign of the diary.* There was a lot more material but too much for him to figure out quickly. No time to look at whatever might be on her computer. He tore the three pages off the pad, quickly folded them and shoved them into a pocket. The siren sounded like it had stopped in front of the house, and he could hear one or two more in the distance. He went out to the porch where he saw a police officer hurrying up the steps towards him. He gestured to the inside of the house.

"It's my sister. She's halfway up the stairs."

The first block of Kearney Avenue was empty of cars apart from the small crowd of vehicles clustered on both sides of the road near Jolene Kane's house. Cape May Police Chief Tate Saxby parked behind an ambulance from the local rescue squad and walked the half-block to the house, exchanging nods with a uniformed EMT who was standing nearby talking to somebody on a cell phone. He knew that several of his officers were already on the scene, including recently-promoted Sergeant Vicki Barstow and Deputy Chase Connor III, who was called 'Three' by many of his friends and co-workers.

As Saxby paused in front of the house, he saw Deputy Conner on the other side of the street talking with two men that he didn't recognize. All three men looked over at Saxby, who returned a wave from his deputy.

"Morning Chief," said Sergeant Barstow. Saxby turned to see her up at the top of the cement steps. Another EMT was behind her on the porch, leaning against the house to one side of the open front door.

"Good morning Vic," Saxby said, climbing the steps to meet her. With a slight turn of his head, he gestured across the street to the two men with Deputy Connor. "Family?"

"Right Chief," Barstow said. "Those are her two brothers—Jolene Kane I mean, the deceased. Jason and Erik Kane, twins I think. I asked Three to feel them out and try to get a preliminary statement."

"She lived here alone, right?" Saxby asked. "Seems like they got here fast."

"I only spoke with them briefly, but as I understand it, they both came into town this morning to help her move some things around the house. Boxes, furniture—I don't know. Jason Kane got here first and found her. It was him who called it in. I got here about eight minutes later with Newman and Redding on my heels in the same car. They're both inside. The other brother, Erik, showed up maybe ten minutes after that. Doctor Coyle got here just a few minutes before you."

"Okay, well," Saxby said, gesturing to the open door. "Who are we looking at?"

"Jolene Kane, according to the ID in her purse along with her brothers over there," Barstow said. "Sixty-six years old. She lived alone and this appears to be her house."

Barstow led the way through the door and into the foyer, where Saxby exchanged nods with Deputy Newman and a third member of the rescue squad, who both appeared to be guarding the bottom of the staircase. An aluminum stretcher stood nearby at the ready. Intermittent flashes of light bounced off the walls of the stairwell above.

"I asked Redding to start on the pictures," Barstow said, as they started up. "He does a good job with that. Just up here on the landing Chief."

Jolene Kane's body lay almost as it had been initially found by her brother. A man who was kneeling next to her stopped writing in a small spiral notebook and stood up as they approached.

"Tate, I'm not fond of this habit you seem to have of finding a body every time I'm in town visiting my aunt," he said. Mostly bald, and at least as old as Tate's mid-fifties, he had a distinctly boyish face that looked like it would try to smile even in the most terrible of circumstances. He was casually dressed in jeans and a heavy sweatshirt, and wearing blue nitrile gloves.

"I am truly sorry about that Mark, er, Doctor Coyle," Saxby said. "I'll try to remember to apologize to your aunt on behalf of Cape May." He had been leaning over to look at the body and then turned to look up the stairs to the hallway above. "So, what's your initial here? She tripped or stumbled on the top step up there, or near it, and twisted around as she fell? Probably tried to grab at the banister, right?"

"That's a good guess," Dr. Coyle said, "and exactly what my first impression was too, you know, just based on the visual here." He moved his arms in a sweeping gesture to indicate the overall scene. "Until I saw this. Here, grab her shoulder there and help me turn her a bit." With Saxby and the doctor on either side, they twisted and partly lifted the body so they could see the back of the shoulders and head. Dr. Coyle produced a small flashlight and directed the beam downwards. They could all now see that the hair at the back of the head was matted with partially dried blood. Blood had also soaked into the upper part of her robe, and more had pooled under her.

"Now, if she had simply fallen, like in our initial impression," the doctor said, "it makes sense that she could have smacked the back of her head pretty hard on this hardwood floor here, cracking the skull maybe. Unconsciousness and then death within, I don't know, a few minutes to fifteen or so. Sure, that could have happened."

"Yeah, that makes sense to me," Saxby said. "So what's your concern? What else do you see?"

"Actually, I think she did fall and hit her head on the floor here," the doctor said, "but that isn't all that happened." He pointed a gloved finger at the bloody back of the head. "When I felt around under her hair, I found what clearly feels like a depression—right about here. A dent. I guess this floor is oak, and really hard, but also flat and smooth. I don't see how it would cause that kind of wound."

"When I first got here, I took a quick run through the house," Barstow said, "and just up there in the hallway, it looks like a table was upset and a few things broke. Before you and the doctor got here, I was thinking maybe she banged into that table in the dark and that's what disoriented her and sent her down the stairs."

Saxby stood and went up the upper section of steps, passing Deputy Redding, who had taken a break from photographing the scene while the others were talking. He looked around at the hallway, noting that a narrow side table was clearly out of place, as though it had been kicked or bumped into. A small potted plant had fallen to the floor along with a lamp shade and other parts of a table lamp. He knelt for a closer look, using a pen to turn over the broken base of the lamp.

"That could have happened Vic. Not a bad thought at all," Saxby said. "Or else there was some kind of struggle. Something went on up here anyway. Did you see this lamp base Doc?"

"I took a quick look at it, just before you got here," the doctor said. "I'll need to get a closer look up in the lab, and compare it to the wound. We'll get it printed and see if there's anything on it." He paused, looking down at the body of Jolene Kane. He shook his head back and forth, slowly. "Any conclusion is premature at this stage, and you know that. But standing here right now, I'd bet that there was someone else here last night, or more likely, in the first few hours of the morning. A burglar, whatever—that's your department—but there was some kind of an encounter, and she got whacked on the head with that lamp base at or near the top of the stairs and down she fell. If the initial blow didn't cause her death, the impact with the hard floor certainly could have. Let's get her up to my lab and I should have a pretty good picture for you by sometime tomorrow."

"Right Doc," Saxby said. He had rejoined Barstow and the doctor on the landing. He paused to let out a deep breath and rub a hand over the back of his neck. "We'll do that." He raised a finger in turn to each of the deputies. "Okay. Vic, Redding, you heard the doctor. As of this moment, we will treat this as a crime scene until we know otherwise. Nobody who isn't here already gets into the house. The brothers need to stay out—I'll go out and talk to them in a minute. Redding—when you finish taking pictures, talk to Newman and make sure we have a complete list of anyone who's been here this morning. Get a few pictures of everyone's clothing and shoes while you're at it, including us and the good Doctor here. That could help eliminate false trails later." He looked at Doctor Coyle. "Thanks Doc, just let any of us know when you're finished here. The ambulance crew is waiting downstairs." The doctor nodded and turned his attention back to the body.

Saxby touched Sergeant Barstow's elbow and motioned to her to follow him back downstairs and into the sitting room.

"You're in charge of the scene here Vic, and if this turns out to be a crime scene, you can take the lead on the case. Are you okay with that?"

She was looking over Saxby's shoulder at the side wall. He turned to follow her gaze to one of the windows, noting that it was open a few inches. They both walked over to look through it to the rear part of the wrap-around porch outside. "Sorry Chief. I heard everything you said, but I'm just noticing this now. If there was an intruder, that could be where they got in. I'll check with the others and make sure none of us opened it this morning. And to your question, absolutely. Whichever way this goes, I'm on it."

"Good," Saxby said. "You'll do fine. Now, that doesn't mean that I'm not going to work on it with you, but it's your case. And I don't have to tell you that if this does turn out to be a suspicious death, you're going to need to check in with the county and they'll assign a detective to help us."

"Got it," Barstow said. "I know the process, whether I like it or not. Are you going out to talk to the Kane brothers?"

"Yeah, I'll do that now," Saxby said, "you know anything about them yet?"

"Not really, no. It was Jason Kane who found her, and he did mention that he was military way back when, but I don't know details. He said he had some medic training, which is why he knew different ways to check for a pulse. That's about all I know. Even less about the other one."

Saxby nodded at that before turning towards the front door. On his way out he stopped for a minute to talk with Deputy Newman and the EMT, both still guarding the stairs and the front of the house, as Barstow headed back up the stairs.

Outside the house, Saxby crossed the street towards where Deputy Connor was still speaking with the Kane brothers, who were both leaning against the fender of a late model Chevy pickup. Connor looked up as he approached.

"Good morning Chief," Connor said. "I'm just about finished here. Gentlemen, this is Chief Tate Saxby, and Chief, this is Jason and Erik Kane, Miss Kane's brothers." He pointed to the two men as he said their respective names.

"Gentlemen," Saxby said, shaking hands with each of them. "I am very sorry for your loss, and that goes for all of us here. I understand you've had a shock this morning, but we appreciate that you've been able to spend some time with Deputy Connor here—that's really very helpful."

"Of course," Jason Kane said, "we want to help any way we can. I saw the doctor go in a while ago, what is he saying? She didn't suffer, did she?"

"It's early to say anything for certain Mr. Kane," Saxby said, "but no, there's no indication of anything like that. On the face of it, she lost consciousness right away when she fell on the stairs. Though, there is something else I need to tell you, and again, it's very early in the investigation." He was about to continue when Erik Kane cut in.

"Investigation? What are you saying? Our sister fell down the stairs and hit her head in the middle of the night, right?"

"Well, whenever someone dies there is always going to be some level of investigation," Saxby said. "That's completely routine. But what I have to tell you, is that, in your sister's house, we see some indication that there may have been foul play. It's just a possibility, but it's something that we have to check out fully."

"Are you saying that someone came into the house and attacked my sister?" Erik Kane said.

"Please, Mr. Kane," Saxby said. "I can't stand here and say that right now with any kind of certainty. What I can say is that we found evidence that appears to point to a struggle of some sort taking place near the top of the stairs. I'd be happy to be wrong about that, believe me, but it's something we have to look at very seriously. So please, for the moment, that's all I can say. We'll know more within the next twenty-four to forty-eight hours and we'll share our findings with you. With that in mind, the medical examiner and my department are going to begin the investigation right away. Can you take a few more questions before you go?"

The brothers exchanged a look before nodding in unison. "Sure, go ahead," Jason Kane said.

"Great, thanks," Saxby said. "Remember, just covering bases here, but, can you think of anyone who might have wanted to harm your sister? Anyone she had fought with, who had threatened her, anything at all?"

"Sheesh, wow," Erik Kane said. "I really don't think so. I mean, she was kind of like your classic quiet, older lady. She didn't go out much but she wasn't a hermit or anything like that. He tossed the question over to his brother with a look and a shrug. Jason Kane scratched at his thin beard and shook his head slowly back and forth.

"No, I agree with Erik on that. At least there was never anything big enough for her to mention to us. She kept to herself a lot but she was friendly with people. She had a regular mahjong game with a group of three or four other ladies around her age. Every Wednesday or Thursday, I forget which. There were one or two of them she would hang out with sometimes. Dinner or maybe watch a movie —something like that. And the three of us would try to get together for dinner at least once a month. I gotta think she would have told us if there was anything to tell."

Deputy Connor made a few notes on his clipboard as Saxby continued. "Her driver's license shows her name as Kane. Was she ever married?"

"No, never," Jason Kane said. "She was engaged once, a long time ago, thirty years or more. Far as I know, it just faded out until they called the whole thing off. There was no yelling and screaming or anything like that. A few other serious boyfriends, but not for, I don't know, ten years or more. She was just happy being single I think is all."

Saxby turned to point across the street to the house. "I noticed that part of the front room there, on the left side, is set up as something of an office. Now, a lot of people have an office space in their house—I always have. Nothing strange about that. But I noticed a bunch of books and maps kind of stacked around. Was your sister working on some kind of project that you know of? Researching something maybe?"

The brothers again looked at each other before each giving a little shrug and shaking their heads. It was Jason Kane who spoke first.

"She was a reader, so a stack of books here and there was pretty common, but I don't know about anything special lately."

"Yeah, Jason's right that she loved her books," Erik Kane added. "She was always watching those nature shows, and stuff like that. About the universe or the rainforest or whatever. Something would grab her and then she'd be looking it up and going to the library looking for books about it. She was the smart one of the three of us." He started to laugh before catching himself, and Saxby could see that his eyes had started to well up. Jason Kane reached over to put a hand on his shoulder.

"What happens with Jolene's... I mean, with Jolene now?" Jason Kane said "And then, I guess, when are we going to be able to get in the house?"

"She'll be taken up to the Medical Examiner's office in

Courthouse, attached to the hospital. I know Dr. Coyle personally and I can tell you that your sister is in good hands. Exactly what happens after that will depend on his initial findings. As for the house, better plan on it being at least a few days," Saxby said. "The first thing is to determine if your sister's death was an accident, which will take a day, maybe two. If that's the case we should be able to wrap up soon after and you can do whatever you need to do. If it turns out that we're dealing with a crime scene though, then there's going to be a search warrant and all that could take several more days. My department will keep you informed.

"Okay, well look, tough morning for you guys," Saxby said, "and I think that's enough for now. Just make sure Deputy Connor here has your contact information and then you can go. We'll be in touch when we know more."

———

Within another half-hour, the doctor had finished his work, and the EMT crew had bundled Jolene Kane's body onto the stretcher and driven away with her. The brothers left shortly after that in their separate cars. After a brief meeting between Chief Saxby and his four officers, and after confirming that all windows and doors aside from the front door were secure, the two junior deputies had left to resume their daily routine. Connor and Barstow followed the Chief into the office at the front of the house.

"Check me on something, would you Three," Saxby

said, "Outside, when I was speaking with the Kane brothers, what was your impression?"

Connor thought for a bit before answering. Saxby could tell that he was playing the interview back in his mind, rewinding parts and picturing the moment.

"I think that they're fairly stoic guys. Shocked and sad for sure. I think there was some real emotion there, but no drama going on with them. At least the one was military way back—Jason. He might have been through some stuff. They're twins too, so they have some of that twin behavior going on, like looks back and forth, mirrored movements, you know that kind of thing."

"Good. Good. I agree with all that," Saxby said. "Anything else strike you?"

"There was one thing Chief," Connor said. "When you asked them that question about if she had been working on anything or researching anything specific. They gave each other a quick glance, and I don't know if I can put a finger on it—because they did that a lot—but it seemed like that time was something different. They didn't like that question. If I had to guess, I'd say, yes, she was looking into something, and they knew it."

"Yeah, that's what I picked up too," Saxby said. "I wanted to see if you'd come to that on your own. Good cop intuition there."

Saxby gestured to the long table that had served as Jolene Kane's desk. He picked up a large book and opened the back cover. "Cape May Library, same as those other two on the side table. Different New Jersey history books. This one was checked out a week ago. And here we have two, three—no, four different Jersey maps, and this one's a real antique. Probably early 1900s. She was digging into something, that's for sure."

"So, if you two are right about the brothers' reaction to your question, Chief," Barstow said, "and she really was looking into some obscure piece of New Jersey history, then why would they care if we knew about it? Or maybe, why would anyone care?"

"Good question Vic," Saxby said. "In fact, as the police, we only care what she was looking into to the extent that it might tell us who might want to do her harm. Well, that and curiosity of course."

"I get you Chief. We don't care what 'it' is," Connor said. "We just care *who* else cares what 'it' is. But anyway, aren't we getting ahead of ourselves with this? There's still a possibility that she just fell down the stairs and banged her head, right?"

"You're right Three," Saxby said. "Good points. If we end up with a warrant, we'll be able to look at her computer and papers, and that could shed some light. Even then, her research may well not have any bearing at all. We'll have to see. So, I think we're done here for today. Let's lock up and wait to hear from Doctor Coyle. You have the key Vic?"

Barstow held up the single key that Jason Kane had loaned her, and they went out, locking the door behind them.

3

O nce the two police officers had finished with them, and after they had watched the ambulance crew carry their sister out of the house and drive away with her, Jason Kane walked his brother Erik to his car.

"Man, I thought they'd never leave us alone. Where can we go to talk? I could use some coffee. How about you?"

"Yeah, me too," Erik said. "I haven't eaten anything yet, because, you know, Jo usually makes muffins or something. Dammit."

"Yeah, I know bud. I know," Jason said. "Okay then, let's try the Ocean View. It's big enough. Should be able to get some privacy."

They drove away in their two cars, and ten minutes later were seated at a table in a quiet corner of the restaurant. Through the picture windows, they could look across Beach Avenue to the cement seawall that separated the street from the promenade and the beach and the ocean beyond. The staff wasn't busy and almost immediately they had steaming mugs of coffee in front of them and had ordered breakfast.

"So, that cop cut us off back there," Erik said. "You were starting to tell me you saw something in her phone?"

"Right, right," Jason said. He took a sip of his coffee and proceeded to tell his brother about the text chain he had found on their sister's phone, and how it looked like she had been about to call 9-1-1.

"And you deleted all that, right?" Erik said.

"I did. Well, I deleted the conversation," Jason said. "And I called 9-1-1, which wiped out the other thing." He fell silent while the waitress served their food and topped off their coffee cups. As soon as she left, he took a bite of scrambled egg and then suddenly dropped his fork and leaned back to look at the ceiling. "I don't know. I should have told the police all about that, right? I screwed up, didn't I?"

"No, no you didn't" Erik said. "You did the right thing. You heard the police chief—they saw something that maybe says foul play to them. Something else that you didn't notice. You see—they have their own stuff to go on without those texts. And Aaron, you say, with the double 'a'. That's got to be Aaron Starr, don't you think? I haven't seen him or his brother since we were little kids. She must have called him about that book she found in Dad's old stuff. But why?" He looked around the restaurant, confirming that there was nobody else within earshot before leaning in across the table. "If Aaron Starr came over to Jo's house yesterday to meet with her, to talk about this book or whatever, did they have a fight? Struggle over it maybe? Did he kill our sister?"

"Maybe," Jason said. "Or maybe he knew something else that added to the story. He heard what she had to say, got worked up and tried to get the book from her. Or else maybe he left and came back later, like thinking to swipe it, and she surprised him. If that's anything like what really happened, you know what I'm thinking? I'm thinking that maybe what she was talking about wasn't all that crazy as we thought. People will do a lot for a chance at big bucks."

"This is some heavy shit," Erik said. "It's making my head hurt. And Jo's on a slab up in Courthouse. What are we going to do? The cops can't know about Starr yet, right? I think we need to have a talk with that guy. No. You know what—I'll do it myself. I'll have a talk with him and I'll find out if he laid a finger on her. That much I will find out."

"Come on man, don't go killing him and getting yourself in trouble," Jason said. "Can't we let the cops handle him?"

"They handle him or we handle him, what does it matter?" Erik said. "The thing is, if he hurt our sister, he's gonna get what's coming to him, you can bet on that. And if he knows something that makes this crazy land deal thing look more like it might be real, why blow that? I say let's not. If the cops already know about him and whatever he's up to, so be it, but if they don't, I want to talk to him first. Even if it's only a wild shot, losing a chance at a ton of money won't bring Jo back."

They ate in silence for a few minutes. The waitress gave

them a coffee refill and dropped off the check. Jason Kane counted out some bills and tucked them under the edge of the sugar bowl. "I guess you're right," he said. "The cops don't need to know about Starr or the land deal just yet. But how will you find him? He must be in the area somewhere, but I don't have anything on him."

"I still have some friends in low places from back in the day," Erik said. He fingered the slip of paper his brother had given him with the phone number from the text thread. "I'll find him. Didn't you say you saw some other notes?"

"I almost forgot—yeah," Jason said, shifting in his seat and reaching for a back pocket. He unfolded several sheets of roughly-torn yellow notepaper. "I only had a minute before the cops arrived. I didn't see the diary, but I did grab this. She really did have some sloppy writing, didn't she? Hard to make a lot of it out. It looks kinda like random thoughts scribbled down in a rush, like to look up later or something." He handed the wad of papers over to his brother, who squinted down at them, frowning. "Could it be something about the value of coastal swampland? And look at the bottom of the first sheet, right down there. She circled it. '150 years'. What the hell does that mean? A hundred and fifty years from what?"

"I'm with you man," Erik said. "She said she was trying to find out about some old land deal that never went through, so this could be about that I guess. The swampland reference. Aside from that, I don't see anything here that makes sense to me. Hmmm. But maybe something made sense to Aaron Starr. I don't know, but I'll find out. This must be something that goes way back, but our family hasn't had any business with the Starrs since forever."

"You're right, not in our lifetimes anyway," Jason said. He took a last bite of bacon and pushed his plate away. "The police chief—Saxby, right? That was his name. He said it could be a couple days before we can get in the house, but as soon as we can we need to turn it upside down and find whatever it was that Jo was working on."

"Yeah, that's right," Erik said, "we do. Whatever it is, the cops may have seen it too, but hopefully it won't mean anything to them. Meanwhile, why don't you see if you can find out anything about an old New Jersey deal. Somebody trying to sell swampland or marsh or whatever."

"Whew, I don't know where to start with that," Jason said, "but I'll give it a try."

"Let me know if you find anything," Erik said. "Maybe just Google it. You can find out anything that way."

4

T he clock on the dashboard clicked over to 7:30 just as Chief Saxby pulled his cruiser into the police parking lot behind the station. Just outside the building's entrance he stepped aside as Sergeant Roy Brody came out with Deputy Davis, one of the recently-hired patrol officers under Brody's supervision.

"Oh, good morning Chief," Brody said. "I'm sorry—I didn't mean to bowl you over there."

"No trouble Sergeant," Saxby said. He nodded to Davis. "It's good to see the energy. Where are the two of you off to this morning?"

"Deputy Davis is going to take me on a standard patrol route," Brody said, "and then we're going to circle around and go over the jurisdictional boundaries of the whole island. He's really starting to get a feel for the area."

"That sounds like a great plan," Saxby said. "A good part of the basis of police work is simply knowing where you are and feeling a connection to the place. And the people, of course. All that might sound obvious, but it's an important part of noticing when something isn't right, or when something doesn't fit. There was a movie I saw once where the police chief called it 'copley intuition'. I always thought that was a good way to put it."

"Do we know anything yet about the lady we found yesterday Chief?" Brody said. "The Kane woman?"

"I believe we know something," Saxby said, "but I don't know yet what it is. Vic told me we got something from Dr. Coyle overnight, but I haven't seen it yet. When I know something, I'll be sure to pass it around."

"Got it Chief, we'll let you get to it then. Have a good day," Brody said. He continued out to the parking area with Deputy Davis as Saxby went inside.

Entering the police station's reception area, he found Deputy Doreen Watson wrestling with an imposing pile of file folders that spread out across her large desk and threatened to spill out onto the floor. Several bankers boxes, also bulging with folders of various colors, sat on the floor beside the desk. Doreen was a licensed deputy, but mainly served as the primary dispatcher for the small Cape May Police Department, along with being the office manager and something of a 'mother hen' to Saxby and the other officers. She looked to him as though she had already been working on the files for hours.

"Well, what a sight to see. I hope that isn't destined for my in-box," he said.

"Good morning Chief," Doreen said. She let out a small laugh and waved an arm across the desktop. "No, this is mostly ancient stuff from the old file room in the basement.

I finally decided that I couldn't put off dealing with it any longer, so I've been steeling myself for the past few days. I think most of it's bound for the shredder. Coffee was fresh just about ten minutes ago and Vic's been waiting for you in the conference room."

Saxby left Doreen to continue her assault on the folder pile and went through to his office. He hung up his coat and checked the desk for any urgent memos before filling up a mug of coffee in the kitchen and joining Sergeant Barstow in the conference room.

"Oh, hey Chief," Barstow said, looking up from a legal pad that Saxby could see was full of notes in her special writing style that nobody else had ever been able to decipher. A laptop stood open to one side. "I just got off a Zoom call with Dr. Coyle."

"Oh, I'm sorry I missed that," Saxby said. He was a bit surprised and had been hoping he'd get to speak with the doctor that morning.

"I'm sorry Chief," Barstow said. "He said he had to run on to something else and he needed to meet earlier than I first thought. You did tell me I was in charge of the case."

"It's okay, no problem," Saxby said. "All I meant was that I'm sorry I missed it, and yes, you're the lead on the case. That is, if there is a case. So, let's hear it, what did he have to say about Miss Kane?"

"Looks like murder, Chief," Barstow said. "Or manslaughter anyway. Doctor says the base of that broken lamp we found in the upstairs hallway matched the wound on the back of her head. Apparently, the lamp was made out of a super-hard wood called 'black locust', and one of the corners actually bashed a dent into her skull. He thinks she was probably hit at or near the top of the stairs and then fell right down. Unconscious immediately and dead within a few minutes."

"Hmmm, so there was probably a struggle—a fight over something," Saxby said. "She must have surprised whoever it was. Maybe threatened to call the police or something like that. What did he say about the time frame?"

"He said probably between midnight and two, and no more than thirty minutes on either side of that."

"Well damn. I don't know about you," Saxby said with a sigh, "but I liked it more when people around here just died of natural causes. But hey, that isn't what we have today is it? So, at least now we know that we'll need a search warrant. That should help us fill in some blanks. What would someone have been after? Was she wealthy, or did she have some valuable collection that people knew about? Did she keep lots of cash in the house? Once we know more about what she had that somebody else wanted, that could point us to who wanted it. Let's not forget that it could have been some random break-in too. I'm really not feeling like that's what we're dealing with, but I hope I'm wrong and it's that simple. Okay then, what's your next move?"

"Two priorities at the moment Chief," Barstow said. "I need to jump on the warrant paperwork first, to get that moving, and then I need to check in with the county detectives and see if they can assign someone to 'assist'."

"Right, I like your priorities," Saxby said. He looked off at the wall for a moment and Barstow figured he was lost in thought. "Either you or Three should give the Kane brothers a call to let them know we've determined that their sister's death was a homicide—no details—and that we'll be searching the house. Go full speed ahead with the warrant, but if you don't mind, let me look into the county detective angle first. There's a guy I know up there who's really good to work with, and I'm hoping we can get him assigned. Not my call of course, but I know someone who might be able to help in that area."

"Mayor Torrance, right?" Barstow said. "I bet that's what you're up to. Good idea Chief. He probably plays golf with all the right people. Oh, I'm sorry, I didn't mean any disrespect."

"Just you and me here Vic," Saxby said, with a grin. "And I know what you mean, but everyone can play a role. He was quite helpful with the Parrish case last year. Handled that well. He's a politician but a good guy overall, I think."

Saxby left Barstow to her work in the conference room, and went to do his usual daily tour of the office, before checking for any messages, and then going off to find the mayor.

5

W hen Saxby entered the mayor's outer office, he found the ever-efficient Mrs. Davis sorting through a huge stack of folders not unlike the one Doreen had been wrestling with downstairs in the police department.

"What's going on around here?" he asked, "some kind of Old File Day in Cape May? I didn't see anything on the activities calendar, but it sure looks like fun."

"Oh sure, lots of fun Chief Saxby," Mrs. Davis said, standing with arms akimbo and giving him a scolding look over the top of her horn-rimmed glasses. "A regular barrel of monkeys, isn't it? Eh, it's really not so bad. Your Doreen's been talking about working on the old files for a while and I didn't think it was fair to just put it on her. Maybe I'm crazy but I volunteered to help out. A lot of this is seventy or eighty years old. And so dusty—I've already taken an antihistamine."

"Well then it sounds like a job that's long overdue," Saxby said, "and I thank you both for tackling it. I think a dinner out for both of you afterwards might be in order. I bet the mayor would agree."

"That's a nice idea Chief," Mrs. Davis said, "and I just might hold you to it. Anyway, speaking of the mayor, you caught him in time but he's heading out soon. Go ahead in."

"Well good morning Tate," Mayor Torrance said as Saxby entered the office. "I thought that might be you I heard out there." He gave Tate one of the broad smiles characteristic of a natural politician and waved him to a chair.

"Thanks Jack," Saxby said, "but I won't take long. Mrs. Davis told me you were on your way out."

"Headed up to Courthouse for a meeting, then to Stone Harbor for lunch," Torrance said. "The folks up there are meeting with—get this—a 'municipal parking expert'. How's that for an occupation? Anyway, maybe I can steal some good ideas without us having to hire him ourselves."

"Yeah, that's a funny one," Saxby said. "If the colleges in this state don't offer that as a major, they should. Guy probably makes a good living up and down the shore towns."

"You're right. I'd bet money on that," Torrance said. He shuffled papers around on his desk while he talked, putting some into a leather briefcase and setting others to the side. "So, what brings you here this morning? Is it about the woman you found yesterday? Any more on that?"

"As a matter of fact, yes," Saxby said. "And I did want to ask your help with something related. It looks like we probably have a case of manslaughter. Of course, that's pending an investigation that's only barely started. Dr. Coyle got back to us this morning."

"Oh geez, Tate," Torrance said. "Not again—damn. So, she didn't fall down the stairs after all?"

"No, she did fall down a flight of stairs," Saxby said, "or a half-flight, only it looks like someone helped her on her way. It appears there was some kind of struggle, maybe it got heated, and the assailant grabbed a heavy lamp and whacked her on the head. Coyle thinks she fell right down, out like a light."

"Well, I am sorry to hear that," Torrance said. "And a brother found her, right? That is terrible. You said you wanted to ask me something—how can I help?"

"I'm putting Vic in charge of the case," Saxby said. "I'm going to work it with her, but I want her to start getting more experience taking lead. Anyway, as you know, now we've got to call county and get a detective assigned, and I was hoping, since it'll be Vic's first time on point, that we could get a certain guy I've worked with before, name of Tom Dooley. He'd be a big help to her without trampling over everything. A big help to the case too, of course. Are you in good enough with anyone up there that you could put in a word?"

"Yeah, I think so," Torrance said. "The Chief of Detectives is still Jerry Dalton as far as I know. Jerry and I shared an apartment up in OC back in the day when we were both working up there in Margate. Long time ago, mid-eighties it must have been. I run into him every now and again. I'd have no problem giving him a call. I mean, if he says no, he says no, but I can ask."

"That would be great Jack," Saxby said. "Asking is all I'm looking for. And you're right—if he says no, he says no, and we move on with whoever we get and I'm sure we'll be fine."

6

L ater that day, just after Saxby had finished his lunch of a take-out sandwich and a bag of chips, Sergeant Barstow appeared in his office doorway, a coffee mug in one hand.

"Knock knock. Got a few Chief?"

"Sure Vic," Saxby said. "Come on in and have a seat. Just finished my monthly cheesesteak. Oh man, that was good."

"Only monthly Chief?" Barstow said.

"One a month is enough for something like that," Saxby said, patting his belly. "Believe it or not, I've reached an age where excess pounds tend to seek me out and then won't go away."

"You're not showing a whole lot of excess there Chief," Barstow said. "Don't worry too hard about that yet. So, a few things have happened on the Kane case. I guess you must have called county, because they assigned a detective and he called me a little bit ago. Guy called Dooley. Tom

Dooley. I haven't met him before but he said he knew you. I filled him in on what little we know so far, and I've sent Dr. Coyle's report over to him."

"Tom's a good guy," Saxby said. He made a mental note to thank Mayor Torrance. "I was hoping he'd be the one. He'll help out where he can and won't butt in when he doesn't need to."

"Yeah, I got a good impression of him when we talked," Barstow said. "And he's already helped out with the search warrant. Walked it over to Judge Zimmerman and got it signed. I was going to head over to the Kane house with Three in a little bit. I also got Brody to loan me Dunnigan and Lathrop, to handle the prints and help with the search. You want in on that?"

"Oh, you bet," Saxby said. "I've been looking forward to it. We could use the extra hands and eyes. Let me know when you're ready to go."

———

Three hours later, Saxby joined Barstow and Deputy Connor in the makeshift office at the front of Jolene Kane's house. An unfolded map covered half of the desk, with a stack of hard-cover books to one side. Several of the books were very old, with stiff spines and faded covers, while one or two appeared to be of more recent vintage. Two large and very dusty boxes sat on the floor next to the desk.

"It looks to me like whatever it is we're dealing with," Barstow said, "comes down to what's in this room. As for the rest of the house, nothing remarkable. A few trinkets here and there, some Hummels in a display case. A handful of stuff that a collector might like, or might sell on eBay, but nothing that looks really valuable. There's an Alice Steer Wilson watercolor in the other room, which would be desirable to some people who know what it is. Her purse had about a hundred bucks in it and there was the same again in one of her drawers, along with a box of old silver coins. There's a jewelry box on her dresser with a fair collection in it, but nothing that jumps out at me. No big hunks of gold or large diamonds. She had a vintage gold watch on her nightstand—an Omega—that just might be the most valuable thing in the house."

"Sounds typical for a lady her age," Saxby said, "comfortable, but not wealthy and not one to flash a lot of expensive stuff."

"But, whoever was here with her last night," Connor said, "probably the person who hit her, didn't bother to grab that watch or the cash from her purse. I mean, that's gotta be the minimum the average burglar would do, right? Look for the purse and grab the cash, quick look around for jewelry. Probably grab the jewelry box just to sort through later. Very strange."

"You're right Three," Saxby said. "That is an oddity, isn't it? If someone came in looking for valuables, they didn't try very hard, did they? Or, was it that the guy came in—let's assume for the present that it was a man—but then she surprises him. There's a struggle, or maybe she starts to dial her phone, in the heat of the moment he grabs the lamp and hits her. She falls and he panics. Runs out without spending the time to look for money or jewelry. So, where does that leave us? Or I should say, where does that lead us?" He looked at Barstow.

"Well, yeah," Barstow said. She waved her arms to take in the room and the boxes on the floor. "I think that leads us to whatever it was she was working on in this room. And let's not forget, we've been talking about someone coming in and surprising her—like a burglar. But it's also possible that she invited someone in, you know, someone she knew, for a visit or a meeting about something. They talked about whatever it was or she showed him something of value that set him off, but what?"

Saxby was leaning over the map on the table. "This must be from the very early 1900s. Route 9 isn't even here, and that was built in the twenties. What the hell was she looking for?" He straightened up and shrugged his shoulders. "Maybe she was just a history buff like her brothers said."

Deputy Connor had been looking around the expansive desk, leafing through the books and fanning the several pads of paper that lay about. As he opened a well-worn copy of 'The History of Southern New Jersey', a folded sheet of paper fell to the carpet and he bent down to pick it up.

"What's that Three?" Barstow said. "Anything interesting?"

"I don't know. It's a handwritten note. Something about voice memos. 'SE' is circled at the top, and below that it says 'open utilities' with an arrow pointing to 'voice memos'. What do you think the 'SE' means?"

"That's a recent iPhone model," Saxby said. "I looked at

them last year but ended up with something different. Who has Miss Kane's phone?"

"I have it, it's right here," Barstow said. She went across the room to where a large box loudly emblazoned with "EVIDENCE" sat by the door, and retrieved Jolene Kane's phone from a plastic bag. "So, utilities folder, right?" She swiped across the phone and tapped the screen a few times. "Here it is, wow, bingo. There are four messages, all from the last week. She must have just learned how to use it." Saxby and Connor came in to stand closer.

"Okay, let's hear 'em," Saxby said. "Be careful not to delete anything."

"This first one's from the 3rd. Last Wednesday, I think. Here goes." She pressed a button and within a few seconds they heard a woman's voice:

'*Testing, one, two, three. Testing, one, two, three. Testing out this voice memo thingie.*'

"Okay, that probably would have been the first one for me too," Barstow said. "Here's the next one. This is from last Friday, the 5th."

'*I need to remember that it's my turn to bring a cake to the next mahjong game with the girls on Saturday.*'

"And this is from Sunday evening, the 7th."

'*Don't forget to call Erik and Jason to get them over to help me on Tuesday morning. Also, need to tell them what more I found in the diary.*'

"And the last one—oh wow—this one's from Monday night at 9:25. Couple hours before she was killed. Here goes."

"*Aaron came over tonight and we had an interesting talk.*

He was very surprised when I told him about the diary, and I showed it to him. He said he had known about the document since he was a kid, but it had been for eighty years and had expired in 1951. I need to remind him to send me a picture of that if he has one. Now I don't know what to think because Aunt Mary clearly thought it was for 150 years. He just left and I'm going to try to do some more reading, but I'm really tired. At least now I finally know what it's all about. Can't wait to tell the guys about it when they get here in the morning."

Barstow played the last memo again and they all listened in silence. "Wait, what? So, this Aaron person came over for a while but then left her alive and well. I don't hear anything in her voice that says she was worried or alarmed."

"Agree with you on that," Saxby said. "She sounded excited that he had been able to tell her more details about whatever this thing is she was looking at. Still, he's certainly our prime person of interest at this point. I think the odds are slim to none that it wasn't him who came back later that night, but we can't rule out anything yet. Is there a contact in her phone for an 'Aaron'?"

Barstow tapped on the phone and scrolled through screens, reading for a moment. "I don't see anything Chief, but there are a few recent calls with no name. I'll see if I can get a reverse trace on them. And I'll need to talk to her brothers too. If she was on a first name basis with this Aaron, seems a good chance they might know him also."

"Just a suggestion," Saxby said, "but take Three with you. He spent some time with them yesterday and him being there might ease the situation a little." He knelt down next to one of the old boxes. "So, what else do we have here? Have you gotten a look through all this yet?"

"Only really quick so far," Barstow said. "This one box was shoved under the table here, and Three found the other under a pile of old junk in the basement."

"And they're the same type of box," Connor said. "About the same age, and both loaded with bundles of old letters, notepads, loose papers. Even an antique stapler and some pencils. Not very orderly at all. The box I found in the basement had a bundle of old business ledger books from the late 1800s to early 1900s."

"Interesting," Saxby said. "Like someone was cleaning out an office and grabbed a couple of boxes to dump things into without caring too much. Maybe they were moving in a hurry."

"Or maybe someone had died," Barstow said, "and someone else—like a younger relative—was going through their stuff."

All three officers turned to the doorway as Deputies Dunnigan and Lathrop came in from the hallway.

"We're finished with the prints," Lathrop said. "We did get some, but won't know whose they are until we get to work on them back at the station." Barstow and Chief Saxby nodded their approval.

"Also, I did a second sweep of the bedroom of the lady, er, the deceased," Dunnigan said, "and found something I must have missed the first time, stuck under the cushion of that big armchair." He handed what looked like a thick book to Barstow. It was bound in smooth black leather and tied with a matching strap. "Some kind of diary, and looks like a lady's handwriting to me."

Barstow turned the book around in her hands, then lifted it to her nose before kneeling down next to one of the boxes on the floor. "No doubt it came from one of these boxes. Has the same musty smell. And look—I bet this is the bag it was wrapped up in. Linen, I think." She held up a mottled, cream-colored bag that resembled a small pillowcase. She held it up to catch the light from a window before reaching inside. "Few loose papers in here, and what's this...oh I see. A few old bits of leather flaked off from the book. This must be the 'diary' that Kane mentioned in that last recording. She showed it to this guy Aaron, they talked about it, and after a while he left."

"And then later decided that he wanted to get his hands on it, and came back," Saxby said. "Or... he told someone else about it, and maybe it meant more to that person, and they came looking for it. I can't help but get a kind of 'treasure map' vibe from all of this."

Barstow undid the leather strap from around the book, carefully opening it to the first page. "Yeah, it's a diary. Says so right here. 'The Personal Diary of Mary Kane'. The first entry is dated July of 1932, and let's see..." She leafed to the back of the book, finding blank pages, then went backwards to the most recent entry. "Last entry is from 1936. So, this was Jolene Kane's Aunt Mary, or great aunt, more likely, based on the timeframe."

"Clearly she didn't write all the time," Connor said, "for that one book to cover four years."

"How many blank pages are at the back there, Vic?"

Saxby said. "Twenty or thirty? That would appear to indicate that it was her last entry, don't you think? That's a lot of pages to leave blank if you were planning to keep writing in another book.

"Good point Chief," Barstow said. "I sure hope to know more once I've read through it, along with this other stuff. And we need to pin down the Kane family tree too. I'll add that to the list of things to ask her brothers about. Hopefully then we'll know more about your treasure map."

She wrapped the linen bag around the book along with the loose papers and set the package back into the box. "Seems like a good night for Chinese take-out and reading through a pile of dusty old stuff back at the station. You busy tonight Three?"

"How did I know you were going to ask me that Vic," Connor said, with a chuckle. "No, I've got nothing special going on. I'm in."

"I'm going to let the two of you handle that," Saxby said, "and I know it's in good hands. If you order in some food, put it on my tab." He turned his attention to Dunnigan and Lathrop. "That goes for the two of you also, if you want to do some O.T. to work on those prints. Oh, and check out the window farthest from the fireplace in the sitting room over there. It was open yesterday morning so that could be how the intruder got in. I'm headed back to the station for an hour at the most. Call me if you need me after that. Good work today, all of you. We have a mystery but we are off to a decent start."

7

W hen Chief Saxby walked into the Ugly Mug Tavern at six o'clock that evening, he was surprised by how busy it was. He took a minute to look around the room, deciding that the out-of-town visitors outnumbered the locals he recognized. He walked over to the bar, where Cody, the long-time bartender, was arranging wine glasses up on a high shelf.

"Hey Cody, how are you?" Saxby said. "Oddly busy here for a Wednesday night in November, isn't it?"

"Evening Chief," Cody said. "Just fine, thanks, and yes, it is. The lobster special is my theory. That, and also, we have live music tonight, in about an hour."

"A band tonight? That's great," Saxby said. "Angela must have told me that and I forgot. Who is it?"

"You'll be surprised," Cody said. "She was finally able to get Bluebone in here. You know them, right Chief? Awesome trio."

"Oh yeah, I know them," Saxby said. "Amazing the

sound they put out for three guys. I saw them one day last summer out in back of Mayer's, and they were just wailing away."

"That guy from WCFA Radio is here too," Cody said. "He has a table in the other room with a friend of his."

"Oh yeah, Mark Allen," Saxby said. "I thought I saw his golf cart outside when I came in. Not surprised to see him here; he's Bluebone's biggest fan. I'll check in with him before I go. But first, is my favorite restaurant manager around?"

"She sure is Chief," Cody said. "Up in the office. Go ahead on up unless you want me to get her for you."

Before Saxby could answer, a door across the room to one side of the kitchen opened and his girlfriend of several years, Angela Andrews came out. She had a small pile of dishes in her hands as though she had just bussed a table after the diners had left. Seeing him across the bar, her face lit up and broke into a broad smile. She set the dishes down onto a tray next to the kitchen door and started around towards him. She was wearing one of her favorite uniforms of faded jeans, leather riding boots, and a thin sweater over a white oxford button-down. Her dirty-blonde hair was shorter than usual in a shoulder-length blunt cut. *She must have just had that done*, he thought to himself, making a mental note to try to remember to compliment her on the new style.

"There's my handsome hero," Angela said. She grabbed him in a hug, tight and long, before releasing him with a kiss on the cheek. "I hope that wasn't too much PDA for you, Chief Saxby."

"Oh dear me, I think you just made the Chief of Police blush," Cody said. "Can I get either of you a drink? Or maybe a fire extinguisher?"

"Oh you shush up," Angela said, wagging a finger at Cody before turning back to Saxby. "I was thinking of grabbing something to eat here. Can you have a drink and hang for a while? Or are you still on duty?"

"Well, as the Chief of Police," Saxby said. "I guess I'm always on duty, but right now it's my duty to have a drink. Maybe even a burger. Can we get a table?"

They gave a drink order to Cody and settled into one of the booths along the wall. A few minutes later Cody brought their drinks over and one of the young waitresses took a dinner order. It had been a slow process, but Saxby had gradually gotten more comfortable with eating and drinking as a customer at his favorite tavern, after unexpectedly inheriting the business from his older cousin Earl Parrish the year before. Tragically, Parrish, along with his son Buddy, had been part of the collateral damage from the serial killer case that Saxby and his team had worked on between the snowstorms of that frozen winter when the Cape May bridge had been closed for several months of repairs. As the only surviving relative of Earl Parrish, Saxby had taken control of the bulk of a large business empire, including several successful restaurants, a fishing fleet, and a real estate portfolio that included two local hotels. Fortunately for Saxby, Parrish had hired good people and the businesses ran smoothly, without him having to get deeply involved with the nuts and bolts. Angela had continued in her role as manager of the Ugly Mug, and had added co-management of the other restaurants to her duties. She was invaluable to Saxby in helping him to avoid letting the massive inheritance change his life very much so he could focus on his position as Cape May Police Chief.

"I heard there was a lot going on up on Kearney Avenue this afternoon," Angela said. "Was that you?"

"You know I can't talk about that," Saxby said. "It's top secret."

"No, it is not top secret," Angela said, "and anyway, you work for me, I'm a taxpayer."

"Hmmm, I guess that's true, but it's also true, come to think of it, that you work for me. How 'bout that?" He took a sip of his drink and looked around before continuing in a lower voice. "For your ears only—your grapevine information is correct. We spent a few hours going through the house, you know, the one I told you about yesterday. Looks like what happened the other night was a break-in. Just why is something we don't know yet."

Angela did a sharp intake of breath and her eyes went wide as she also looked around to see who might be within earshot. "Oh God, you mean another mur...that...you know? The M word?"

"It looks like it," Saxby said, "but it's very early days. We think she may have surprised an intruder." He made a tamping-down gesture with his hands as he saw the waitress approaching. "Let's talk about something more pleasant while we eat, shall we? I'll fill you in later."

"Oh I can't wait," Angela said, reaching for the salt and pepper.

When they had finished, and the table had been cleared

and they had ordered a third round of drinks, Saxby noticed that the band members had started to set up their equipment on the small corner stage. He looked at his watch.

"You know what Ang, I wanted to go over and say hi to Mark Allen, and I think I'd better do it before the band starts so we don't have to yell at each other."

"Let's move over to the bar then, and free up this table so Bonnie can get another party," Angela said, waving a hand to indicate a row of empty seats at the bar. "You have some cash, boss?"

"Oh yeah, right," Saxby said. He pulled a money clip out of a hip pocket and peeled off a twenty, dropping it on the table. "Back in a few."

He walked past the row of booths and into the other dining room. With a quick scan around the room, he spotted Mark Allen seated with another man at a table near the small stage.

"Well, if it isn't Chief Tate Saxby," Allen said, taking Saxby's outstretched hand as he arrived at the table. "Can you join us Chief? Take a seat."

"Only for a minute, thanks," Saxby said. Allen's companion stood briefly to shake hands. "Tate Saxby, nice to meet you. Just wanted to say hi before the band starts."

"Well, I'm glad you came over Tate," Allen said. "This is an old friend of mine from, oh geez, too long ago now, Johnny Fantasio. Johnny's working on a book about all the shipwrecks along the Jersey coast. We've been talking New Jersey history all week. I had no idea about how much I didn't know."

"Really? That's fascinating," Saxby said. "Isn't it the

Jersey coast that people mean when they talk about 'the graveyard of the Atlantic'?"

"No, that term mostly refers to North Carolina, off the Outer Banks," Fantasio said. "But it would fit for Jersey too, on a smaller scale. There's been a hell of a lot of shipwrecks out there. Some not far from Cape May. I'm afraid it's gonna be a long book."

"Johnny's gonna be on my show this week," Allen said. "Tune in if you can, Friday at 1:00. I know the life of a crimefighter is a busy one, but it should be a good show."

"I'll try to catch it if I can," Saxby said. "Sounds really interesting. I can't imagine the work that goes into writing a whole book, but good luck with it. Say Johnny, your name sounds a little familiar. Is it possible we've met, early eighties maybe? Weren't you in a band?"

"Your memory's good Tate," Fantasio said. "Yes, I was. It was my band actually. I went by Johnny Farghin back then. Got together with the Bastich brothers, Cliff and Zeke."

"That's right," Saxby said, "I thought you seemed familiar. Amazing how time has passed. Did you keep up with it for long?"

"Nah, not really," Fantasio said. "We played the clubs up and down the shore towns for a few years as 'The Farghin Bastiches', but that life wears you down fast. Too much booze and too many late nights. Wouldn't trade the memories for anything though. Now I research shipwrecks and try not to worry about my prostate."

Saxby laughed and started to stand up.

"Hang out for a while Tate," Allen said. "Let me buy you another drink."

"Thanks Mark, I appreciate the offer," Saxby said, "but I'm close to flagged already and I've got a hot date waiting for me over at the bar. I can't keep Angela waiting much longer." He held up a hand in a wave as the guitar player started a sound check. As he started to turn away, he had a thought and instead leaned back into the table.

"All this talk of shipwrecks and New Jersey history made me think of something I've been wondering about lately. This may sound silly, but, is there much talk, or lore —whatever, about treasure in South Jersey? Like, I don't know, a shipwreck close to shore, or even anything in the marsh or the back bays? That mean anything to either of you?"

"Hmmm, not that jumps to mind," Fantasio said. "I mean, as far as ships, I haven't heard about any big load of gold coins or anything like that. No missing Spanish Galleons. But there could always be valuable cargo lost when a ship goes down."

"Okay, thanks," Saxby said. "And the land, no big rumor of missing loot or any great unsolved mystery of New Jersey. Nothing like the Oak Island treasure pit around here?"

Both of the other men thought for a few seconds before shaking their heads.

"What's going on Tate?" Allen said. "You working on a missing treasure case or something?"

Tate shook his head and let out a small laugh. "Nah, just

old background on something I read about. Just trying to fill in a few blanks. Forget about it."

"You know who you should talk to," Allen said, "if it's something you want to dig into. The number one expert on New Jersey history is right down the road in Cape May Point. He's a crusty curmudgeon and an egotistical son of a bitch, but nobody knows more than he does."

"Easton Sinclair?" Saxby said.

"That's him," Allen said. "The one and only. If you can stand him, he might be the one to answer your questions."

"Hmmm, okay, maybe I'll give him a call," Saxby said. "My father knew him, and I think Earl did too, so that might count for something. I met him once, years ago, at some event or other, but I don't recall that we talked very much. Hopefully the legend is inflated. Anyway, thanks for the idea, and here comes the band. Good meeting you Johnny."

As Bluebone started their set with a cover of a Tom Petty hit, he gave a last wave to the other two men and left them to enjoy the music.

"How is Mr. Allen this evening?" Angela said, as he joined her at the bar.

"He's just fine," Saxby said. "It was good to chat for a minute. He's got a friend with him, Johnny Fantasio. I met him at least once years ago. He's working on a book about New Jersey shipwrecks. Say, you don't know Easton Sinclair, do you?"

"I know of him, but never met him. Sort of an eccentric local character as far as I know, and very rich. Lives in one of those huge houses just off the dunes in the Point. Why? Is he a suspect?"

"Oh no, just looking for some background on something that Mark thought he might know about. Whether he wants to help or not is a question."

"I guess you can always shine a light on him and yell at him. Hit him with a rubber hose or something like that. Isn't that what you guys do when you want answers?"

"Sometimes I wish we could Ang. Sometimes I really wish we could. What do you think, one more here, or make it an early night?"

"Let's settle up and get out of here," Angela said. "If you give me a ride home in your fancy police car, I might be inclined to invite you in."

"Oh, interesting," Saxby said. "You might be inclined to invite me in, huh?"

"Okay, it's quite likely."

8

W hen Saxby arrived at the police station early the next morning, he found Sergeant Barstow looking over paperwork in the conference room, her open laptop off to one side.

"Morning Vic," Saxby said. "Please tell me you haven't been here all night."

"Good morning to you Chief," Barstow said. "And no, don't worry, Three and I didn't have to work too late, and I actually just got back in about twenty minutes ago. We're expecting Detective Dooley at nine. Is that a good time for you?"

"That's fine, but we could have offered to meet him up in Courthouse," Saxby said.

"Actually, I did offer to go up there," Barstow said. "But he wanted to come to us. Said he had something to do in North Wildwood anyway."

"Okay, good for us then," Saxby said. "How did it go with the Kane lady's papers? Find anything interesting?"

"Interesting, yes, very much so," Barstow said, "and I think we may have a start on figuring out a motive. Do you want to hear about it now, or wait for Dooley?"

"I'm anxious to hear it Vic, but I don't want you to have to go through it all twice," Saxby said, glancing at his watch. "I'll do the rounds and check in with the rest of the crew and then I'll be at my desk. Plenty to do there. Give me a yell when he gets here."

———

It was a little over an hour later when Saxby heard a familiar voice out in the front reception area. He went out and found County Detective Tom Dooley signing in at Doreen's desk.

"Well, hello there, Detective Dooley," Saxby said, holding out his hand. "Thanks for coming down, but you know we would have come up your way."

"Yeah, I know," Dooley said, "but I still like to get out of the office when I can. Anyway, I need to get over to North Wildwood after this to see your counterpart over there. You know Marty, right? Marty Banks?"

"Sure do, Marty and I go way back. We try to meet for lunch or a beer now and then, but you know how it goes," Saxby said. "What's he got going on over there?"

"Another body. They just found it this morning, what I know so far," Dooley said. "Somebody got beat up too bad to shake off is what it sounded like. I don't know what you guys got going on down here at the shore, but it's looking like a bloody week."

"Sheesh, you aren't even kidding," Saxby said. "I'll give Marty a call later to see what's what with that. Anyway, we're glad you're here Tom. Vic's waiting for us in the conference room."

After a quick stop in the small department kitchen for coffee, the two men joined Sergeant Barstow at the conference room table. After greetings and introductions, she took thirty minutes to summarize the particulars of the case.

"And the couple of partials we found upstairs and on the sitting room window aren't giving us a match in the system," Barstow said, "though they do appear to be from the same person. At least we know they don't match the reference prints we got from the brothers."

"Okay well, that's something anyway," Dooley said. He took a few seconds to add some words to the neat lines of notes on the legal pad in front of him. "We know that somebody else was there in the recent past. A person who has a clean record but appears to be the intruder."

"And who we think goes by the name of Aaron," Saxby said. "Vic, any help from those recent calls in her phone?"

"Not much there Chief," Barstow said. "Doesn't look like she used her phone much at all. In the past three weeks there were just four calls that didn't match anything in her contacts. There were two calls to a restaurant in North Cape May, one to some investment company in Wildwood that isn't even in business anymore as far as I can tell, and one to the L.L. Bean store up in Marlton. No luck on her email either. Just tons of spam mostly, for a few weeks back. I don't think she paid much attention to that at all."

"A mystery man," Dooley said. "We'll find him somehow. What we need to know more about now is motive. Tell us about the boxes you found when you executed the search warrant yesterday."

"Right, yes. I think we may be getting somewhere with that," Barstow said. "Three and I, sorry, that's Deputy Connor—we went through it all last night, and spent some time on an ancestry site, and I think we were able to draw a fair picture." She shifted papers around until she found several pages filled with notes. Arrows pointed here and there on what looked like a small version of a family tree. She handed Saxby and Dooley each a copy of the family tree page.

"We think those boxes belonged to Jolene Kane's late father," Barstow continued. "That would be Wendel Kane, who died in 2003. The contents are mostly from his father, Anders Kane Jr., who died in 1944. I figure Wendel Kane cleared out his father's house, or office, or both, and this is what's left. It's mostly business related, ledgers, asset lists, that sort of thing. Nothing unusual jumps out, but Three plans to spend more time going over it today. Other than that, there was a personal diary from Wendel Kane's sister, Mary Kane, who died young, at age 36, from some illness that isn't mentioned. Also, there was some correspondence between her and her father while she was staying with a family friend out on Long Island. That's the part that, I hope, will help with motive. We don't have specifics, but it's clear that the gist of what they were talking about is some agreement that Anders Kane Sr.—Jolene Kane's great-grandfather—and his partner, a man named Morgenstern, made with the federal government. What I make out is that Kane Sr. and Morgenstern, as partners, agreed to sell some land along the Jersey coast to the government very cheaply for some purpose or other."

"Interesting," Saxby said. "But so far that sounds to me like an ordinary business deal. I imagine there was a lot of that going on in the aftermath of the Civil War."

"Right Chief," Barstow said, "but there's more. One of the exchanges between Mary Kane and her father makes a vague reference to the possibility of Kane and his partner cashing in big on the deal if certain conditions were met in the future. I don't see anything about exactly what those conditions are or what the payoff might be. Here, take a minute and read this letter from Anders Kane to his daughter." She passed sheets of paper across the table to Saxby and Dooley.

Transcript of a letter from Anders Kane Jr. to Mary Kane, dated June 20, 1934

My Dear Mary,

I hope this missive finds you well and in a full and hearty recovery. A traveling friend has told me that the weather is quite pleasant out there at this time of year. I hope that the cool water and sea air suit you.

Yesterday, something reminded me of the conversation you and I had the last time we were together. I refer to my father's agreement with his partner and the government regarding the land along the New Jersey coast. My firm belief on that matter is that it is all what the English of the last century might have referred to as a "pipe dream", but I have certainly been wrong before. I believe you would agree with me on both of those points. Nevertheless, as the specter of my own mortality looms ever more near, I have been looking to get my affairs nearer to a state of order so as to avoid causing trouble for you and your brother at my passing. (A day, dear daughter, that I hope to be far in the future.)

I want to assure you that, when your brother Wendel is old enough, I will fully brief him on that old agreement. As you know, the terms apply only to the male line, so I will also endeavor to impress upon him my strongest wish that he will share any related gains with you equally, in the unlikely event that there ever are any gains to speak of.

And now, my dear Mary, Mrs. Hudson is calling me to dinner. I will write again soon, as I sincerely hope you will write to me when you have the time.

Your loving father

———

"This is good stuff Sergeant," Dooley said, as he finished reading and put down the paper. "Good work finding this. Any more about it in the back and forth?"

"Yes, a little more," Barstow said. "There's a letter from Mary Kane to her father dated a few days later. I didn't copy it out for you because almost all of it is her telling her father about a trip to some county fair, and a clambake on the beach at a friend's house—that sort of thing. But in a post-script at the end, she asks him to refresh her memory about the duration of the agreement. Four days after that, he writes back, and I did copy that out for you. Actually, this is an edited version, because more than half of his letter was reminiscing about family trips into the city and something about a favorite pudding that his housekeeper used to make, something called 'Victoria Sponge'." She handed each of the men another sheet of paper.

Transcript (partial) of letter from Anders Kane Jr. to Mary Kane, dated June 29, 1934

...I have almost forgotten to answer your question about the New Jersey land sale. Specifically, you asked about the duration of the agreement, and yes, there is a definite expiration date, or, more accurately, there are two. Allow me to explain. When I first told you about all of this, you may recall that I expressed my profound regret regarding my father's actions on that point. As he explained it to me when I was close to the age that you are today, the terms that were discussed and agreed upon included a time limit of 80 years from the date of signing, meaning that it will expire in November of 1951. But then there is the detail that strains what good memories I have of my father. There were three copies of the document signed. One for the government records, and one each for my father and Mr. Morgenstern. Somehow, I gather through some subterfuge, or trickery, my father came away with a document specifying a duration of 150 years, giving it an expiration date at the end of November 13th in the year 2021. The other copies, of

course, had the 80-year term. I was never able to determine how he managed it, because the several times I tried to speak with him about it he would fall into a rage and I would end up in tears. I soon learned to not broach the matter. As to why he caused this to be, I can only surmise. Based upon a conversation I once overheard between him and one of his attorneys, my guess has generally been that it was a spiteful maneuver in retaliation for an instance where Mr. Morgenstern, in my father's perception anyway, had managed to get the better of an earlier land deal somewhere up around Buffalo. In any case, the document I have in my possession represents a contract that expires in 2021. The land in question remains undeveloped, and I am told that there are no known plans to change that, so the point is likely moot.

I will be placing this document, along with many other papers relating to my business and legal matters into a strongbox that will be kept at the house in Cape May. You may recall the box as the one that sat in my office for some years. Shiny black lacquer with brass corners, and with the three large red lotus flowers on the top. I can recall you sitting on that box while you sketched in your book as I worked at my desk.

Until next time Mary,
Your devoted father

———

"Well, I'll be a monkey's uncle," Dooley said. He leaned back in his chair with both hands clasped behind his head, looking at the ceiling for a moment. "That is fascinating stuff. Sounds like there may be a contract floating around out there somewhere that's still valid. But a contract for what? All this and yet we still don't know that piece, do we?"

"No, we don't. Yet," Saxby said. "Seems like the more we find out, the thicker the fog. Vic, you mentioned Mary Kane's diary. Anything there that adds to all this?"

Barstow looked at her notes briefly before shaking her head. "Not materially Chief. It mostly just reinforces what we've already covered. Looks like whenever she wrote to her father, she would say a bit about it in her next entry. She wrote some about her brother also, but no mention of this mystery deal. To me that shows that she kept her father's wish that he be the one to tell the son about the whole thing at some point. She died about two years after these letters, in 1936. I've spent some time going through Jolene Kane's desktop computer also, but I haven't found anything that looks like it's about Aunt Mary. My take is that she was more of a 'pad and paper' person.

"We did find a bundle of about a dozen letters from Anders Kane to his son Wendel, when he was serving in England in WWII. They were sent to two different APO addresses. Mostly just 'be safe', and 'come home safe' kind of stuff. He does mention to his son how he can't wait to tell him all about the family affairs when he gets home. But then Anders Kane died in 1944, so assuming that son Wendel didn't get home until sometime in 1945 or later, then it looks like he never got that briefing after all."

"We may very well be looking at a motive here,"

Dooley said. "This land deal could be the 'why', but we need more details before we know the 'who'. What about mining? Were there ever gold and diamond mines in New Jersey?"

"Hmmm, I know there's a long history of mining in New Jersey," Saxby said, "but I don't think gold or gems had much to do with it. Iron is big, along with copper and zinc, but that's way up north for the most part. The markings on the map in her office didn't say much, but it seemed more like she was interested in the southern half of the state."

"Okay, so that probably isn't it. Hey, I really need to catch up with Chief Banks in North Wildwood," Dooley said, after checking his watch. "Gotta keep up with this crime spree you folks have going on. What do you think your next steps are?"

"I ran into a guy last night," Saxby said, "who I've known for some years—Vic, you must know Mark Allen, right? Anyway, we chatted for a few minutes, and he introduced me to a friend of his who's in the area working on a book about the shipwrecks off New Jersey. Mark's always been a big history buff too, so I asked them if they knew of any old treasures of New Jersey, like, are there any legends of buried pirate loot or anything like that. I just said I remembered reading about some old rumors of this or that and it made me curious. Neither of them came up with anything, but Mark reminded me about another local character who he thought would know whatever there was to know about things like that. Easton Sinclair. He knew my father years ago and I think he was friendly with my late uncle, Earl Parrish, also. I was thinking I might bounce all of this off him to see what he thinks."

"Name doesn't mean anything to me," Dooley said, as he stood up and started gathering his things, "but it sounds like a good next step. Good work so far Sergeant, keep doing what you're doing. How about putting together a quick summary at the end of each day, something I can cut and paste into my own report if I need to. That work for you?"

"Sure Detective, I can do that," Barstow said. "Thanks for coming down here for us."

After walking Detective Dooley out, Saxby came back into the conference room where Barstow was gathering up her materials and talking quietly to herself.

"Am I interrupting anything interesting?" Saxby said.

"Oh, sorry Chief. No, you're not interrupting. I'm just rehashing all this in my head. I need to get back to my desk and clean it all up. Are you going to contact this person, Easton Sinclair?"

"Yes, that's my priority. I'm hoping he's in the area and I can get in to see him as soon as possible. I'll let you know what happens and maybe you'll be able to come with."

———

Saxby was catching up on paperwork at his desk a few hours later when Doreen put through a call from Detective Dooley. He looked at his watch and punched a button to take the call.

"Hey Tom, I wasn't expecting to hear from you so soon. Don't tell me you've found yet another body."

"Now Tate," Dooley said. "You know it's in bad taste to joke like that. Funny though. No, nothing new, just the one I mentioned to you earlier. I'm up here with Chief Banks in North Wildwood, and they've got an interesting situation. But let me ask you something first. Were you able to get hold of that Sinclair person yet? The one you thought might know all about the area?"

"Actually, I was," Saxby said, "and he's expecting me at his house at 4:00 this afternoon. Vic is up to her ears so I'll be going over alone."

"Okay, great then," Dooley said. "If you have no objection, I'm going to suggest that Chief Banks go with you. I think you'll have a common interest."

"Sure Tom, if you think that's the right way to go," Saxby said. "But what's the common interest?"

"A local man out for an early run saw a neighbor's door open and found this guy. There must have been a hell of a fight, with some back and forth, looks like. Our man here ended up beaten to a pulp and with a kitchen knife in his chest. Early talk is that it was probably late last night, midnight or thereabouts. Maybe two or three. Anyway, here's the interesting thing: he's got a map of New Jersey taped to the back of his bedroom door. It's folded to show the southern part of the state, and somebody's drawn lines on it with a highlighter, like outlining different spots on either side of the Parkway. Question marks in a few places, and a few notes I can't make out."

"You weren't kidding about 'interesting situation' were

you?" Saxby said. "Do you have a name for the dead guy yet?"

"Yeah, I think so," Dooley said. "The neighbor knew his first name and there's a wallet here with ID that matches. His name is Starr. Aaron Starr."

9

S axby was just coming out of the station house when North Wildwood Police Chief Martin Banks pulled up and parked.

"Great to see you as always Marty. Sorry for the occasion," Saxby said. "Okay if we ride over in my car? We're just going out to the Point."

"Likewise, and likewise again Tate," Banks said. "Bad times at the beach. Good thing it's off-season. That's the last thing we need right now—all those crowds never help."

"Yeah, you're right about that Marty," Saxby said. "Easier to move around now, without the crowds everywhere. That's something." They settled into the car and Saxby drove out of the lot. "I know you had an early start and a busy day. Did you have time for Tom to fill you in on our case and what we've found so far?"

"He did go over it, yes," Banks said. "And I know there's a lot we don't know yet. Seems to all revolve around some mystery about an old land deal, with at least a few people thinking there could be money to be had. Be a double shame if all this was about some hoax, or fake treasure map or something silly like that. You've got the Kane lady, who might have been on to something, meets with Mister X who gets interested and probably comes back later and kills her. Then she's got two brothers who you think may know more than they're saying. Then this morning a guy named Aaron—who may be your Mister X—turns up dead in my town. I'm finding it hard to not be thinking of those two brothers right now. How about you?"

"I'm with you so far Marty," Saxby said. "I only had about ten minutes with the Kane brothers, but at the moment I'm liking one or both of them for beating up your Aaron Starr. Sometimes the obvious thing really is what works."

"So, what do you know about this guy we're going out to see?" Banks said. "Dooley didn't know much about him, except he sounds like some kind of historian."

"And I'm afraid I don't know a whole lot more," Saxby said. "Some kind of historian—yes, reclusive, very rich—all of that. He knew my father and uncle at least a little, so maybe that'll count for something. Everyone seems to be afraid of him, so I don't know what to expect. Let's go in easy and not try to throw any weight around. I'd really like to get his help to put some of these question marks to bed. I put together a quick summary of our cases and what little we know so far and Doreen faxed it over to him a couple hours ago."

They kicked ideas and theories around during the short drive out to the town of Cape May Point at the tip of the peninsula. As was his long-time habit when heading out that way, Saxby made the left onto the quiet and lovely Seagrove Avenue to follow it up to the dead end at Lake Lilly. Following the lakeside road around the small park, he turned into the compact residential grid of the small town that most of the local people would have referred to as "The Point".

"I've driven by this house before," Saxby said, as he turned onto the last street before the dunes. "But I've never been inside it. It's big for a big family, but immense for one man. One man and a servant or two. I'm pretty sure he has a live-in cook and a housekeeper. Or maybe one person who does everything. We'll see."

"Do you know how he made all his money?" Banks asked.

"Far as I know it was something in the book binding business," Saxby said. "His father built up a company that printed the books, or glued them all together, something like that. He ran it for a while after he took over himself, and then eventually sold out to one of the big New York publishing houses for some huge amount."

The road came to a dead-end at a steep pathway up through the dunes and the beach beyond. Saxby made a right turn to drive past a series of million-dollar houses on the right, with the dunes now to the left, punctuated with the occasional set of wooden stairs leading up and over to the beach. The timeless seashore smell of bayberries and dune grass filled the crisp air as the sky began to darken with the first hints of evening.

"Are you kidding me? Is that it?" Banks said, as they entered a small cul-de-sac, from which the only other exit was up a hundred-foot driveway. The drive was lined with well-trimmed boxwood hedges and was barred completely by a center-opening gate of black cast iron in a gothic style. The two swinging doors were each mounted to square stone columns of at least eight feet in height. Beyond the gate, and partially obscured by staggered rows of mature cedar trees, they could see parts of the upper floor of a huge structure. A pair of white stone chimneys rose up above the slope of a slate roof in a dark blue-grey.

"Yep, that's it," Saxby said. "I don't know much about architecture, but that sure looks like a French Chateau, doesn't it? I think he bought up three other houses just to tear them down and build this. Kind of medieval, isn't it?"

Saxby pulled the car up to the gate and stopped. They watched as a camera mounted on the top of one of the square columns panned over towards them, and twenty seconds later, the gates slowly opened inwards. They drove on through, entering a wide circular driveway as the gate closed behind them. Saxby stopped the cruiser near the front entrance to the house, and they stepped out onto the gravel, admiring the scene. The façade of the house was dominated by an arched entryway made of huge blocks of roughly-cut grey stone. The stone arch surrounded an oak door trimmed in thick iron bars. Forty feet to the right of the door, a covered walkway connected the corner of the house to a separate two-story building whose bottom level was a three-story garage. One of the garage doors was open, and they could see a workman polishing the grille of a classic Rolls-Royce.

"What do you think," Saxby said, as they got out of the

car. "A 1960s Silver Cloud?"

Just then the front door swung open and an impeccably groomed fiftyish man in a double-breasted suit stepped out.

"Good afternoon gentlemen," the man said. "Mr. Sinclair is expecting you. Please come in."

———————

"I had no idea there was a small castle hidden out here in the dunes," Banks said, as they were led through an entrance hall, richly paneled in red-brown oak. A gleaming collection of a hundred or more swords, maces, flails, and other antique weapons adorned the walls on either side. Pairs of ten-foot spears and pikes bracketed the several doorways that led off to other rooms.

The servant gestured to an open door near the end of the hall. "Please make yourselves comfortable in the library gentlemen. Mr. Sinclair will join you momentarily. My name is Bramford. May I offer you coffee or tea?"

"Thank you, Mr. Bramford," Saxby said. "I would appreciate some coffee if it isn't any trouble." He looked at Banks, who nodded to Bramford, who then excused himself and left them alone.

The room they found themselves in was a classic example of the library of a wealthy man at his country estate. Most of the wall space was lined with shelves that stopped short of the fourteen-foot ceiling, with hidden lighting mounted above and ringing the room. The bookcases, like the paneling between them, were of more dark hardwood, highly polished and free of dust. A massive oak desk dominated the center of one end of the rectangular room, with a tufted leather sofa and matching set of armchairs balancing it near the other end. The thousands of books that filled the shelves were of all colors, shapes, and sizes, but were neatly arranged. A fire crackled away in a black marble fireplace.

"There's a huge collection of law books here," Saxby said, perusing a stretch of volumes that appeared to make up a set. "He must have studied to be an attorney at some point."

Across the room, Banks was looking over a particularly colorful array of books, and as he leaned in for a closer look, he saw that the case was filled with a varied selection of thrillers and mysteries from the recent twenty or thirty years, many in paperback.

They both turned towards a corner of the room behind the desk as a door-sized portion of paneling opened and a tall, elegant man stepped through. He wore a deep red smoking jacket over a cream-colored silk shirt and black slacks that ended at black velvet slip-on shoes adorned with a gold coat-of-arms design. He had a full head of hair that was closely cropped, and ran somewhat closer to the salt than the pepper. His beard was trimmed short and was of the same color. His clear, deep blue eyes shone with an alertness and energy that seemed younger than the rest of his body, though he must have been seventy. When he spoke, his voice had a natural resonance that was firm and commanding without being loud. He was clearly American, and spoke with a softened MidAtlantic accent that was less theatrical than the 1940s Hollywood version.

"Chief Saxby and Chief Banks. How nice to see you. I am Easton Sinclair. Welcome to my home."

"It's a pleasure to meet you Mr. Sinclair," Saxby said, stepping forward with an outstretched hand. *The most interesting man in the world*, he thought to himself. *Don't rush it.* "I'm Chief Tate Saxby of Cape May, and this is Chief Martin Banks, from North Wildwood."

"Good to meet you Mr. Sinclair," Banks said, "and thank you for taking the time to meet with us on such short notice."

Just then, Bramford came in from the hall with a large silver tray, setting it down on a table near the sofa and chairs. He poured steaming coffee into cups and gestured to the creamer and sugar bowl. "There is a brandy also gentlemen, on the side table, if you would like that with your coffee. Will there be anything else for the moment sir?"

"That will be all for now Bramford, thank you," Sinclair said. "I will ring if we need anything else.

"I understand that you're on duty gentlemen," he continued, "but let's visit for a few minutes before we jump to the business at hand. I rarely have company and your respective positions interest me. Oh, and please do consider Bramford's offer of the brandy. It's a very fine twenty-five-year Armagnac from a small village in Gascony. With some difficulty and great expense, I was able to acquire several cases from a 1968 bottling."

"I was four years old," Banks said, "but I don't understand. That's a lot more than twenty-five years ago."

"Ah, my apologies," Sinclair said. "I shouldn't expect everyone to know the fine points of liquor production. The brandy was twenty-five years old when it was bottled, and, unlike wine, bottling brandy suspends the aging process. Therefore, despite being put into glass over seventy years ago, in essence it is still twenty-five years old. Many liquors are that way, such as bourbon whiskey, which I understand to be a favorite of Chief Saxby."

"You have done your research," Saxby said. "And that is accurate. Do you investigate everyone before meeting with them?"

Sinclair laughed. "Not everyone, no, but I do like to know a little something about anyone who comes to see me, rare though those visitors may be. A few phone calls here and there. Aside from being an excellent Man Friday and estate manager, Bramford appears to be able to find out anything, either known or not yet known. Which reminds me—Chief Banks, I am sorry to hear that your wife twisted her ankle on your basement stairs. Is her recovery going well?"

"Oh yes, Mr. Sinclair, she's fine," Banks said, somewhat surprised. "We're glad that nothing was broken. That's nice of you to ask."

"Rumors of my being anti-social and irascible are highly exaggerated," Sinclair said. "In reality, there are numerous people I can tolerate. Bramford has a list somewhere. No doubt you are both greatly relieved. So, you were looking at my 'thriller shelf' when I came in, Chief Banks. I have read many of the great works of literature in this room, but I will confess an occasional desire for a simple and contemporary thriller or mystery. Are you a reader?"

"Mostly just on vacation or sometimes late at night

when I can't sleep. I like a good beach read," Banks said. He turned and pointed to the bookcase. "In fact, you have two that I've read, on the top shelf there. '*The Privilege of The Dead*' was quite a blast from a few years ago, and also, I really enjoyed '*Murder at Wrigley Field*', though I wouldn't have taken you for a sports fan."

"Oh, good heavens," Sinclair said, "I would never spend a moment on such pedestrian matters. Sports—no. Murder —yes. If I skim over the sports nonsense, that book is a fair murder mystery. I've always been fascinated with murder and what drives people to the act. There are few deeds more ancient and primal than to kill another person. It is fascinating, isn't it? Obviously, your profession causes you to see the nuts and bolts of it in a way that most never do. That must be trying."

"That is true," Saxby said, "It is both horrifying and fascinating at the same time. The urge to kill. Unfortunately, Marty and I are both familiar with the damage that old urge causes. Which brings us to—if I may sir—in the past few days, we have had two murders. One Monday night in Cape May, and another very early this morning up in North Wildwood. They seem to be connected, but we can't yet tell exactly how, and frankly, if they are, what the whole thing is about."

"You are a direct man, Chief Saxby," Sinclair said. "Which is a quality I admire in a person. Your late father and Mr. Parrish were also direct men. I remember appreciating that about them as well, in the brief course of our several interactions. So, yes, let's do talk about your case now." He got up from his chair and walked over to the table against the wall, where he poured some of the brandy from a heavy cut crystal decanter into a matching snifter. He brought the glass to his nose and inhaled thoughtfully, with eyes closed, before taking a sip. He swayed his head back and forth a few times, as though savoring the memory of a favorite movement of a Beethoven symphony, before returning to his chair. "I read through the synopsis that your Deputy Watson sent me. Very interesting indeed. I know something about this. I think I may be able to shed some light."

"That would be great, Mr. Sinclair," Saxby said. "Certainly, you know that, with murder, it usually comes down to motive. If you know the thing of value that people are fighting over, it's easier to figure out who the 'fighters' might be. That's our weakness here. What the heck is the thing of value here?"

"Yes, I understand," Sinclair said, deep in thought. "That is the crux of the matter, isn't it? What is 'The Thing' that makes people kill? So here we are, the three of us. I've read through your notes, and spent an hour or so looking things up and refreshing various memories. I made a few notes of my own." He stood and went to the desk, bringing back a thick manila folder. He opened the folder and skimmed briefly over a paper inside. "Hullo, here we are. This woman you found in Cape May early Tuesday morning—Kane was her name. As you have already ascertained, her grandfather was a man named Anders Kane, but he was a junior. His father, Anders Kane Sr., was a successful businessman, who, along with partner Paul Morgenstern, had vast real estate holdings across New

York, New Jersey, and Pennsylvania in the latter part of the nineteenth century.

"Kane and Morgenstern were either very patriotic, or very greedy and attracted to the idea of 'the long shot', or— more likely I suppose—some combination of the two. In any case, they somehow heard about an idea going around the halls in Washington, to build a stretch of train tracks, that would connect other lines already in place across North Jersey and the New York City area, with the southernmost point of the state, at Cape May. The line was intended to be for military or other government use."

"Ah, so that's it then," Banks said. "It was all about train tracks. But that line was built a long time ago, right? When I was a kid, I heard about people taking the train up to the city."

"I took that train several times as a teenager," Saxby said. "The station was right off Lafayette Street, across from the Acme, but "the city" you heard about was Philadelphia. Actually, the train only went as far as Lindenwold. Then you had to switch to something else to get into Philly."

"You are both on the right track," Sinclair said, "if you'll pardon the dreadful pun. There was a train line from the Philadelphia area to Cape May that was built during the Civil War. It shut down and opened up again a few times until it finally went out of service once and for all about ten years ago. The tracks are still there, but they don't sit on the land we're talking about today. The land that Kane and Morgenstern sold to the government. No, that land never had a train line built.

"Here is where luck smiles upon you today, because it

was some fifteen or so years ago that I first learned about all this in the course of research I was doing on the history of the United States road system, or rather, lack of an organized road system, in the early part of the last century. It really was quite a mess. I never did publish anything on the topic, but I always found it interesting, and happily for us today, have retained my original notes. The sale of the land was made, and the deal signed, in 1871. Back then, and after, it was openly discussed. It wasn't a secret. Well, no, that isn't entirely correct. There was one aspect to it that was kept secret, and you may know it already but may not know that you know it. Bear with me on that point—I will elaborate in due course." He took two sheets of paper from the folder and handed one to each of the two other men. "This is an excerpt from a 1905 article in The Atlantic City Daily Press, which we now know as The Press of Atlantic City. They were doing a series on train travel along the east coast, and one of the writers somehow came upon this story and found it worthy of inclusion. Now, in 1905, The partnership had been long dissolved, and Anders Kane had been underground for a full nine years, but the article includes parts of an interview with his partner of many years—Paul Morgenstern, who himself would pass away less than a year later. This interview, along with other materials I have dusted off, and complimented by the information you provided earlier today, gives us a good general picture.

"It is quite an interesting story, and it begins one hundred and fifty years ago…"

10

I t was an unseasonably cold November in Washington DC, and an icy wind blew in off the Potomac and whistled through the city streets. Small groups of people, bundled against the cold, hurried along, anxious to get home, or to the warmth of the theater or the restaurant where they were meeting friends. It was a clear night, and a full moon ruled the sky.

In a large high-ceilinged room inside a house not far from the river, four men were seated around a small but sturdy and intricately worked wooden table, playing cards. The room was lit with globed gas sconces on the red-painted walls, along with a chandelier that hung over the card game. A fire blazed away in a huge fireplace of Vermont Marble that occupied a third of one of the walls. A uniformed attendant came in from time to time to tend the fire, poking the embers or adding a log from an adjacent pile. Each time he came in, he would empty ashtrays and check the men's snifters, adding splashes of amber liquid from a crystal carafe that stood on a nearby side table, before leaving and shutting the door behind him.

"Five Card Stud, deuces wild," said the man with the pipe stuck in the corner of his mouth as he gave the first face-down card to the man on his left, before lowering the deck to rest on the table. "Who didn't ante? The pot is lacking."

"Me again George—I am sorry," said the fourth man, with a raspy and tired-sounding voice. The host of the gathering, he sat at the dealer's right. "It seems that the long day and an abundance of cares has whittled me down." He dropped a coin into the small pile near the center of the table. "You know how I feel about wild cards though—they are an unnecessary complication." He lifted a hand to scratch at his beard, which was dark, full, and neatly trimmed. His voice was stern, though his failure to contain a small chuckle betrayed the humor behind his comment.

"Yes Sam, I know," said the dealer, "as you have told me. And this is your house, but we all did agree that the dealer calls the game. If there are no objections, we'll make this the last hand." He continued the deal until all four men had one card face down and one card face up. The highest of the up cards was the king of clubs in front of the man directly across from him "Looks like the bet is to you, Columbus."

The man considered briefly before dropping a few coins into the pot. He looked to their host. "How did you ever acquire the nickname of 'Sam' anyway? I don't believe I've heard that story." The dealer continued with the next round of cards and the next and then the last, always with the player showing the highest hand initiating the bet. The men talked back and forth, occasionally dropping coins into the pot.

"You know what Columbus, I really don't know where that came from, but it seems to have stuck. They call me worse in the press sometimes, so I suppose I won't complain. In any case it has a better ring to it than that blasted 'Unconditional Surrender' rubbish. I never did care for that one bit." He turned his attention back to the table, thinking for a moment before dropping a quarter into the pot. "Well then, let's flip 'em over gentlemen. See if you can beat my pair of jacks."

"I'm rightly sorry Sam," said the man called Columbus, turning over his hole card to reveal the king of hearts, "but I think my pair of kings will do the trick."

"Well, I'm glad we only play for a few coins then," said the host, standing and stretching. The other three men joined him in a laugh. "What with me merely a poor civil servant." He drew a silver watch from a vest pocket and consulted it. "We have ended our game in time for the last meeting of the day, and I hope it does not go late into the night. Gentlemen, are we ready to meet with our friends from New Jersey and conclude this train track business?" Each of the other three men nodded their assent. At that moment the attendant appeared through a side door. "Ah, Stevens, have the gentlemen for my last meeting arrived?"

"Yes Sir, Mr. President," the attendant said. "I have made them comfortable in the Green Room, and I took the liberty of laying out coffee, sherry, and cigars for six."

"Thank you, Stevens," the president said, "We'll see

them now, and you may take the rest of the evening off. Wake me at the usual time in the morning."

The attendant nodded deeply to the president and went out. With the president in the lead, the four poker players left through an opposite door, crossing through a larger oval-shaped room with blue walls, to enter the room beyond that, which mirrored the red room they had just left in size and shape, but with walls painted a rich green. There were two tall, well-dressed men standing together near the fireplace. They came forward to meet the other four men. One of them held out his hand to the president.

"Mr. President, it is an honor, and thank you for seeing us at this late hour. My name is Paul Morgenstern, and this is Mr. Patrick Jordan. Mr. Jordan is personal attorney to my partner, Anders Kane."

Jordan reached out his hand to the president. "It is an honor for me as well, Mr. President. Please accept my apology for this small surprise. Mr. Kane has taken to his bed with a fever. There is no doubt that he will overcome the malady, but he thought it prudent to quarantine himself rather than risk passing his illness to you or these other gentlemen. I am fully empowered to discuss the deal at hand and to sign in his stead."

"Ah, I understand then," the president said. "That will be fine, and please send my best wishes to your client for a speedy recovery. Welcome to The White House, both of you." He gestured to the other three men, and hands were shaken all around as he made introductions. "Allow me to introduce Attorney General George Williams; and this is our secretary of the interior, Columbus Delano; and I believe

Mr. Morgenstern, that you already know our secretary of state, Mr. Hamilton Fish."

"Yes Mr. President, Mr. Fish and I have known each other for some years now," Morgenstern said, "and I've also met Mr. Delano once or twice at some event or other in my travels."

"In fact, Mr. President," Hamilton Fish said, "Columbus was at the dinner at my house in New York last July, as was Mr. Morgenstern. I recall it was later in the evening when our conversation came around to the idea of this train line down through New Jersey. We talked it out back and forth. Paul sent word to me in the morning, suggesting that he and Mr. Kane might be able to help."

"And here we all are today," the president said, waving his arms to take in the group of men. "I thank you for your help, and the country thanks you. Let's sit and get to it, shall we? The French Ambassador has been nice enough to send over a case of very fine sherry. Will you do the honor of pouring, Columbus? Help yourself to coffee and cigars as you please gentlemen. George, I believe you have the documents, is that correct?"

"That's right Mr. President," Williams said. "My office received them yesterday and I have studied them carefully. Let me just get my legal case from the other room."

He left the room as the other men seated themselves around an expansive round table that was covered in a thick leather matching the color of the walls. The president worked at lighting a cigar while Columbus Delano poured sherry into crystal glasses and Secretary Fish chatted with the two visitors. When the attorney general came back into the room, he set a leather satchel on a chair and drew from it three bundles of papers, folded into thirds, and each bound with a wide linen ribbon.

"Now, I have here three copies of the agreement. It's quite straightforward really, just two pages and the signature page. There are also three copies of a map and the relevant surveyor's notes, making six pages in all." He brought the documents over to the table, offering a copy to the president, who waved it away.

"I trust you to tell me what it says, George," the president said. "Sum it all up for us please."

"Yes Mr. President," Williams said. He set two copies of the agreement on the table, retaining one in his hand. "And the rest of you have all read this—is that correct?" He looked in turn at everyone around the room, noting a nod or verbal assent from each man. "I'll give a brief background to ensure that we are all in agreement." He gathered his thoughts for a moment before speaking.

"As we all know, the country has recently been through a great conflagration. We have lost much, much has been destroyed, and we are still rebuilding. We have also learned much. One thing we have learned, from a military perspective, is the utmost importance of being able to move men and material around the country efficiently. To be able to bolster our capabilities in that area, we are looking at a host of ideas concerning improvements to our infrastructure. Several of our top military leaders, including our own President Grant, here at this table, have suggested the idea of extending a rail line from the industrial centers in the New York area, southward all the way to the southern tip of New

Jersey. It would terminate in or near the city of Cape May in Cape May County. That could allow authorities, for example, to have an easier task of defending the mouth of the Delaware Bay. Or potentially, to improve the efficient movement of goods across the mouth of the bay to Delaware. The idea is that such a line would run near to the coast, say, no more than five to ten miles inland, to ease the possible future addition of short spurs eastward out to various small ports or other points on the barrier islands that make up most of the New Jersey coast." He paused for a sip of sherry.

"Very good so far George," the president said. "Let me just add that this whole scheme—and I do believe it is a good idea that could be of great utility to our military—will probably never make it through the Congress. It may and it may not, but regardless of that, I believe it to be an idea worth pursuing. And more so in light of the generous offer we gather here to discuss tonight. Please continue, George."

"Excuse me, before you continue," Secretary Delano interjected, "if I may, I'd like to add to the president's comments. I give this rail line a fairer shot at being completed, perhaps a twenty or thirty percent likelihood, but probably decades away. In any case though, I concur with the president in thinking the idea to be well deserving of some reasonable preparation. That's all I wanted to add, thank you."

"Thank you both for your comments," Williams continued. "That which I have now laid out, is the gist of the idea. As our friend Secretary Fish here described earlier, Mr. Morgenstern came forward to him after hearing of the plan, with an offer to sell to the government a series of contiguous land parcels along the New Jersey coast that, when added to existing government lands and rights-of-way, would make up some ninety percent of the property needed for the project. Roughly speaking, the parcels in question extend from just outside the town of Tom's River, all the way to the Delaware Bay at a point west of the city of Cape May."

"If I may say so," the president said, "your firm is asking for an oddly low sum for this land. That is not a complaint, but I find it interesting."

"You are correct, Mr. President," Morgenstern said, after several of the men around the table had indulged in a brief laugh. "It is true that our price is low, relative to other recent real estate transactions within the state, and there are several reasons. One is that, frankly, the land in question is not rich farmland, nor is it land on which a lode of valuable ore has just been discovered. Some of it is marsh, which is not very useful to us, and which means that pilings will be needed to support any future rail line. Put plainly, the strip of land in question is more valuable to the idea of this rail line, than it is to any profitable operations of our company. Another reason, and a powerful one for Mr. Kane and me, is that our being in a position to transfer this land to the government for a minimal consideration gives us a chance to contribute to the security and well-being of the country that has given so much to us."

The president sat forward and cleared his throat as he reached for his glass. "Mmmm-mmm. I must remember to ask for your oratorical assistance before I next have a need to debate my political opponents. But well said Mr. Morgenstern, and I thank you again."

"We are glad to be in a position to help, Sir," Morgenstern said. "But as long as we are on the topic of compensation, it is fair to mention the reference in our agreement to potential future income. Mr. Williams, as I am not an attorney, would you care to continue your summary in regard to those particulars?"

"Certainly Mr. Morgenstern," Williams said. "As I stated earlier, the overall agreement is straightforward. Morgenstern Investments will transfer ownership of the land parcels in question to the government for the sum stated here. That is the core matter of the agreement. However, there is an additional paragraph outlining the possibility of further payment in certain situations. I will spare you the legal jargon and summarize that part for you plainly.

"This section of the document concerns the possibility that any part of this land is developed in future as a revenue generating enterprise, such as for one of the various types of roads where the traveling public pays a fee, or a toll, to use. In that event, Morgenstern Investments will be entitled to a twenty percent share of any income thereby generated. This would apply as well in the case that the government does in fact build a rail line for military use, but later decides to convert the line to passenger rail. Further, in the event that the government decides at some future time to sell off the land to a third party, then the Morgenstern company would be entitled to fifty percent of any income from such a sale. If the government either never uses the land, or eventually uses it for any purpose that does not generate income from the public, then there is no further effect."

"As someone sprung from simple country stock," Secretary Delano said, "and who is not trained as an attorney, allow me to test my understanding. Mr. Morgenstern and Mr. Kane agree to sell this land to the government for a very low fee as long as it is used for the purpose for which it was originally sought. If the circumstances are such that the land instead becomes a public business venture, then their company will be entitled to twenty percent. Mr. Jordan— you are also an attorney—do I have that about right?"

"Yes Sir, Mr. Delano," Jordan said. "You have distilled that correctly. The only modification to the basic terms will be in the event that the land is ever used 'to make money', if I may put it so coarsely."

"Tell me Columbus," the president said, "what do you think the chances are that something like that might happen in the future?"

"Well, it's hard to say, Mr. President," Delano said. "Future administrations will undoubtedly have their own ideas. The State of New Jersey may petition the Federal Government for a change of terms. Anything is possible, but, as I stated earlier, I believe that this rail line will be built as the generals have requested."

"I have to agree with Delano gentlemen," Secretary Fish said. "A snowball will fly through hell without dripping before that strip of marshland will ever take money from the public."

"Well good then," the president said. "I don't see any reason for that part of the agreement to be of concern. Oh—

mustn't there be some point of expiration for this? Is there more George?"

"There is Sir, and specifically to your question," Williams said. "The terms of this part of the agreement will be in effect for eighty years from the date of the signing of this document, and will apply to Mr. Morgenstern and Mr. Kane as well as to any of their direct descendants down the male line, who are able to produce a copy of this document. Any provision for revenue apart from the original sale price will expire in eighty years, at midnight on November 13th of the year 1951."

"Oh, hells bells," the president said. "God only knows what travel will be like then. Probably some sort of flying contraptions bouncing about through the air. I see no problem with any of this. Are we ready to sign?"

"I believe so, Mr. President," Williams said, "unless there are any other questions or concerns?" He allowed a moment as he looked around the table, but no comments were made. "Well then, Columbus, would you be so kind as to bring the blotter and the pen set over?" Several of the men stood and started to move ashtrays and glasses out of the way to make room on the table. As the president reached to pick up a coffee cup, it slipped from his hand, splashing the dregs out onto the table. Mr. Jordan reacted quickly, snatching the three folded documents up in time to save them from getting wet, and stepping back from the table.

"Blast, I am clumsy in my golden years," the president said. "Forgive me gentlemen."

"It is nothing Mr. President," Secretary Delano said. "It is late and we all grow tired." He used a thick napkin from the coffee service to wipe away the small spill before setting down the blotter pad. Mr. Jordan returned the document pile to the table and Delano added the pen and ink set.

Attorney General Williams unfolded the three documents in turn, turning them to the signature page. "Now then, as previously agreed to, we will have three signers for the government on the left and then both principles of Morgenstern Investments on the right. Mr. Jordan will sign for Mr. Kane in his absence. On the government side, I will sign as attorney general, Mr. Delano will sign as secretary of the interior, and of course President Grant will sign at the top. Secretary Fish, if you would please, sign in the open space at the bottom as a witness." He motioned to the president, who reached for the pen.

As signing progressed, Williams passed the finished documents over to Mr. Jordan, who pressed them with a sheet of blotting paper. When all three were finished, he gathered them up, looking at Williams. "May I have the honor sir?" Williams signaled his assent with a wave of a hand. Jordan handed one to Williams, and a second to Mr. Morgenstern. He held the third in air before folding it back into thirds and tucking it into an inside pocket of his coat. "And I will carry Mr. Kane's copy to him tomorrow."

"Good work tonight gentlemen," the president said. "Now please join me in a toast in celebration of this agreement, and then I shall take my leave, as the calls of my bed grow louder by the minute."

A bright morning sun teased the promise of a warmer day as Mr. Anders Kane was finishing breakfast in the sunroom at the rear of his townhouse in Georgetown. As he pushed his plate to one side and refilled his coffee cup, there was a soft knock, and he looked up to see his valet in the doorway.

"Excuse me, sir, but there is a Mr. Jordan to see you. He says that you are expecting him. Shall I show him in?"

"Oh yes Benson, that will be fine," Kane said. "You may show him in, and you can clear all this away save the coffee. Oh, and bring a cup for my visitor please."

The valet gathered up dishes and went out, returning a minute later to show Kane's guest into the room. Kane stood to greet the man.

As the men exchanged pleasantries, the valet poured coffee and left the room.

"I trust you have good news for me," Kane said, when they were alone.

"Of course you are anxious to know that," Jordan said. "And you may be at ease. All went well and I have something for you." He took a bound sheaf of folded papers from inside his coat and handed it to Kane, who opened the document eagerly and read quickly through the pages.

"Excellent. Excellent. Simply wonderful," Kane said, as he reached the end of the document. "One hundred and fifty years. And these signatures, oh my word. I see that President Grant himself has signed."

"Yes sir, he was in fact the first to sign," Jordan said, "and also, as you see, the secretary of the interior and Attorney General George Williams."

"And the other two copies?" Kane said. "Eighty years?"

"Absolutely. Both of the other copies specify the expected duration of eighty years," Jordan said.

"You have done well then. I could not have asked for better," Kane said. "And I see that our famous secretary of state has signed as a witness. Well, Mr. Jordan, if such a document as this wouldn't carry weight, I can't begin to imagine what would. Tell me, if I may, how did you accomplish this feat? Certainly, you were not in a room full of dullards."

"Oh, nothing more than a simple sleight of hand," Jordan said. "I learned much during my time at university, but last night was likely the first time that my years as head of the Harvard Magic Club have proven their value. It was President Grant himself who upset a coffee cup. That caused a small commotion that I was able to take advantage of."

"Well, remind me to keep a hand firmly on my notecase when in your company then," Kane said. The two men shared a hearty laugh. "Oh, and speaking of that, I have something for you." He took a thin envelope from an inside coat pocket and handed it to Jordan. "The remuneration that we discussed. The deed itself, sixty acres along the river, signed over to you and notarized."

"Thank you, good sir," Jordan said. "My aging parents will be thrilled no end to have the old farm restored to the family. It will be a beautiful summer in Bucks County for them."

"Mr. Kane," Jordan continued, with a slight hesitation in his voice, "you asked me *how* I did it. Only to satisfy my curiosity, may I ask you *why* I did it?"

Kane nodded at the question but lost himself in thought

before answering. "Years ago, my partnership with Paul began with the two of us as good friends. I miss that time, Mr. Jordan, but it is truly passed. Over time, our friendship fell victim to the rigors of pursuing profits in the business world. A missed communication here, a petty offense there. A minor disagreement over the terms of a contract—that sort of thing. We still have much to attend to, but now we act strictly as business partners. Several years ago, our firm handled a series of real estate transactions in a growing part of Buffalo. Paul handled most of the details as I was busy at the time with other affairs in New York. The details aren't important, and I'll spare you a long story, but in any event, I later satisfied myself that I had gotten, as they say, the shorter end of the stick. So, this government deal that you have, ah, assisted with, has given us a small profit, and I doubt that anything further will ever come of it. No matter. Business is good and I am already a wealthy man. I will make new friends. This contract trickery is as much for my personal amusement and for some small sense of justice, as it is for any thought of great profit. And, well, if that profit ever comes—so much the better. I am sorry Mr. Jordan; I have failed in my intent to spare you a long story."

"I have enjoyed your story, Mr. Kane," Jordan said, "and you have in fact helped me make peace with my recent, ahem, ethical lapse. I thank you for that."

"Believe me when I tell you that I understand fully," Kane said. "We will both need to make peace with our ethical lapses. Either that or live with them."

11

E   aston Sinclair went to the side table to pour
        himself another brandy, as Saxby and Banks sat in
        silence for a minute, processing the story. A
grandfather clock chimed the hour.

"I am most pleased that you brought this mystery to me," Sinclair said. "Quite fascinating. I'm going to have Bramford cancel my next appointment." He picked up a phone on his desk, waited a moment, then spoke a few sentences into it.

"I'm sorry Mr. Sinclair," Saxby said, "is there another guest you need to meet with?"

"Oh no, don't be silly," Sinclair said. "All my other appointments for today are with myself. That helps me to avoid being distracted by other people, who, with rare exception, are not worthy of my company. I find the two of you more than acceptable, and your case interests me. It is shaping up to be a well-crafted murder mystery indeed. What are you thinking so far?"

"One thing I'm thinking," Banks said, looking at his watch, "is that it's after five and I'd better try a bit of that brandy. I don't want you to remember me as a rude guest. Just a taste of course. Tate?"

Saxby gave a slight shrug and Banks went over to the side table to pour brandy into two glasses. He handed one to his friend and sat down again.

"So, they made this deal, and drew up a document," Saxby said, "and everybody agreed that it was for a duration of eighty years, including the president and the attorney general. But then somehow, Anders Kane Sr. pulled a fast one and ended up with the same document except for a hundred and fifty years. Expiration in 2021 as opposed to 1951."

"I don't imagine that we'll ever know why he did it," Sinclair said. "Remember the letter that your deputy found, from his son Anders Kane Jr. He describes his regret that his father had, as you say, 'pulled a fast one'. And the reasons behind it remained a mystery to him. Kane Sr. must have had some bitterness towards his partner, Morgenstern."

"Or maybe he was just a crook," Banks said. "You're a fan of mysteries, Mr. Sinclair, you must know that sometimes the simplest answer is the right one."

"You are absolutely right," Sinclair said. "That could be the simple answer, but I find it unlikely that we'll ever know with any certitude. We now know the 'when' and the 'where', but we'll never know the 'why' or the 'how'. We also know the 'who', at least in terms of the major players."

"That still leaves one of the 'w's," Saxby said. He had been leaning against a bookcase, deep in thought and savoring the brandy. "The 'what'. For one reason or other, Kane managed to give himself a seventy-year advantage over his partner for the possibility of some future windfall. And again, in Kane Jr.'s letter to his daughter in 1934, he talks about that possibility very dismissively. It seems as though nobody who knew about it thought it would amount to anything."

"But yet, here we are in 2021," Banks said, "and it sure seems like two people have been killed over this thing. What I keep coming back to is, that train was never built. Other lines, sure, but you say not on the lands in question. What the hell else is there?"

"Forgive me for reducing myself to a sports metaphor, Chief Banks," Sinclair said, "but you have been a good sport. I will put you out of your misery. Do you remember the date that Anders Kane Jr. mentioned to his daughter as being the end of the contract term?"

"As a matter of fact, I do," Banks said. "I remember it because it was so close to today. The last day of the contract is November 13th."

"Precisely correct," Sinclair said. "Midnight on the 13th. And Chief Saxby, if you please, what is today's date?"

"Today is November 11th," Saxby said. "The whole thing is invalid in a little more than two days."

"And gentlemen," Sinclair said, "what is the longest highway in the state?"

"What? Ah…longest highway," Banks said, "that's gotta be Route 9, right?"

"No, I think Route 9 is the second longest," Saxby said.

"The longest highway in the state is the Parkway. It's about ten miles longer."

"Correct again," Sinclair said. "The Garden State Parkway is the longest highway in the state, at one hundred seventy-two miles. And aside from that, the Parkway is something else as well, isn't it?"

"Oh my god. I mean holy shit." Banks said. "Damn right it's something else—it's a toll road. Are you telling me…"

"That's right Chief Banks," Sinclair said. "If my calculations are correct, something more than half of the Parkway was built on the land that Kane and Morgenstern sold to the government, and it's a toll road. The Garden State Parkway is the busiest toll road in the United States."

12

T he ticking of the Grandfather Clock was the loudest thing in the room for a full minute. Sinclair shuffled through the papers in his file, stopping every now and then to read. Saxby poured more coffee into his cup. Banks paced back and forth along the row of bookshelves on one side of the room.

"My first thought is to knock myself on the head," Banks said. "It seems so simple now."

"I'm with you Marty," Saxby said. "I don't know how I didn't think of that. It was right there, running down the map along the coast. The Parkway."

"Don't be so hard on yourselves gentlemen," Sinclair said. "You've only just now learned about the clause in the contract that would give them the additional revenue. The 'twenty percent clause', if you will. I knew about because I was familiar with Morgenstern's 1905 newspaper interview. Remember, at the time he gave that interview, it had already been thirty-four years since the deal was made, and there were no plans to build anything at all. Almost thirty years after that, Kane Jr. still had no expectations, and he wrote as much to his daughter. It wasn't something that people were planning on or excitedly waiting for."

"Anders Kane Jr. died in November of 1944," Saxby said. "That was about ten years after he had told his daughter Mary that he planned to bring her younger brother up to speed on the family business as soon as he was old enough. Seems more and more likely to me that Kane never did tell the son about this deal. Think about it—if he did tell his son, it must have been in the early forties. They started building the Parkway in the late forties, so why didn't the son raise this whole thing with the government then? Whatever would have come of it would have been big news in all the papers. I mean, people would know about it. Right?"

"What do we know about this son that Kane Jr. referred to?" Sinclair said. "If he wasn't old enough in 1934, how old was he? Let's look at that for a moment. How young is 'too young' to learn about the family business? Ten? Twelve? Early Teens? If he was ten when Kane Jr. wrote that, then he was seventeen in 1941. That's about the right age, and like many thousands of American boys, he joined the service and went off to war. Millions of lives were interrupted in the forties. And Anders Kane died before his son was able to get home and learn about the business."

"I would say that you're right about that," Saxby said. "And we have several old letters that his father sent overseas that bear it out. In any case, it all suggests that the son didn't know."

"And his sister did know," Banks said, "but she didn't tell him either, because she died not long after those letters."

"If we're on the right track then," Sinclair said, "meaning, that the son who was too young never found out, it would appear that the whole thing went dormant in the Kane family until resurfacing very recently."

"Hmmm, yes," Saxby said. "Resurfacing when Jolene Kane decided to go through a couple of old boxes full of her father's office stuff. If we're right that he never knew about the deal, then that tells me that he was saving some things from his father and sister—like the letters and the diary—that he never bothered to read through."

"I'll buy that," Banks said. "I have piles of old family stuff that I've never completely gone through. There could be a map to Blackbeard's Treasure in there somewhere for all I know."

"But what about the Morgenstern family?" Saxby said. "That's another family tree that I need to get my people working on. You said earlier that Paul Morgenstern died not long after that interview, so let's just say 1906. He could have had a son who lived to see the Parkway being built, or maybe a grandson is more likely."

"Sure, sure, that would make sense," Banks said, "and, if you were that son or grandson, and if your family communicated better than the Kane family did, you would know about the deal, and you would be jumping up and down when you found out that they were starting to build the Parkway. Wouldn't they have come forward with their copy of the document?"

"Good thinking all," Sinclair said, "but let's keep a few

things in mind. If, as you say Chief Banks, Morgenstern had male descendants who were aware of this deal, yes, they might have been interested in the start of construction on the Parkway in 1947, and they might initiate inquiries. But ultimately, they would learn that there were no plans for the new road to collect tolls."

"You know, that's right," Saxby said. "I read that somewhere. It wasn't originally supposed to be a toll road, was it?"

"No, it wasn't planned that way," Sinclair said. "A few sections of roadway were built, mostly north of New York City, but then the whole project ran out of money in 1950. It wasn't until 1952 that the effort was reborn as a self-supporting toll road from Cape May up to the border of New York State. It was completed about four years later."

"Yikes. 1952. A year or maybe just a few months after the Morgenstern document expired," Banks said. "Glad I wasn't in the room with them when they heard about that."

"Oh man, you're telling me. What a story this is," Saxby said. "The Parkway starts taking in revenue the year after Morgenstern's copy becomes worthless. Kane's copy could be worth a mint, but he doesn't know about it. I'd better have another splash of that brandy."

"Excellent idea. Please help yourself," Sinclair said. He was up and walking, circling the group of chairs. "Let's put ourselves in 1952 for a moment. The Morgenstern family, if there is such an entity, tears up their now-worthless document, or frames it for posterity. In any case, the matter is now closed for them. As for the government document, well, who knows. That would be quite the interesting relic if it was still intact somewhere. It's hard to imagine that anyone at that point would have cared about it or even known about it. Thousands of documents were destroyed in the 1929 fire in the White House attic. Our document could have been one of them. No, nobody had a reason to come forward with a copy of that document other than a male member of the Kane family."

"I agree with that assessment," Saxby said. "Then Jolene Kane reads about the switcheroo her great-grandfather pulled, and starts trying to look into it, and tells her brothers about it. The thing is, as near as I can tell, they don't know all of it. They know there's some deal that expires soon and could be worth money, but they've never actually read the document, so they don't know the details. Remember that voice memo we found, from Jolene Kane? I don't think the Kanes knew about the Parkway toll angle until Aaron Starr came over and told her about that part. He learns that a valid copy of the document could still exist, and she learns what the whole thing is about. But neither of them has any idea where it is. And then she never gets a chance to tell her brothers. That's all a theory anyway."

"And the hornet's nest has been kicked," Sinclair said. "Aaron Starr goes home and thinks about it, confers with person X perhaps, and then decides to go back to the Kane woman's house to get the diary. If that is what he did, it doesn't seem very well thought out. Who and what is he, and why did she contact him? Or who was he, I should say."

"Right. That is the big question now, isn't it?" Banks said. "What did Aaron Starr have to do with it? Could he be a descendent of the other partner? Or just someone who thinks he might be able to finagle his way in somehow."

"Right. And by the way," Saxby said, "where is the Kane family's copy of the document? If Jolene Kane read the letters and the diary entries, she must have started to look for it. Her grandfather had written about how he was storing it in a black strongbox, but we searched her house from stem to stern and didn't find anything like that. He also said it would be in 'the Cape May house', so we need to find out where that was. That predates the Jolene Kane house on Kearney."

"Let me work on that if you don't mind, Chief Saxby," Sinclair said. "I'll find out where he lived and when. I'll also see what I can learn about the Morgenstern family."

"That would be great Mr. Sinclair," Saxby said. "We're grateful to you for your help with this. I'll speak with my team and see if they've found anything more of interest in those old boxes."

"There's one thing in all of this that I can't shake," Banks said. "Tell me what you think Mr. Sinclair. If one of Jolene Kane's brothers got his hands on this document, and came forward to the government in the next few days, saying, I don't know, 'hey government, the Parkway's been making a lot of money, please pay me my share…', I mean, wouldn't he just be laughed out of the room? Could this thing really work?"

"That is a fair question indeed, Chief Banks," Sinclair said. "I studied law for several years as a younger man, so I do have some thoughts on the matter. I imagine they would have to start by bringing it to their local courthouse, or to one of their elected representatives, and I don't see why it wouldn't get a fair hearing. The state government would undoubtedly do anything it could to get the idea tossed out as some ancient folly. On the other hand, it does supposedly bear the signature of the President of The United States, as well as those of the attorney general and the secretaries of interior and state. If authenticated, that would carry a lot of weight. Any number of high-profile law firms would take up the case, given the potential money involved. Even if the twenty percent was somehow got around, some sort of settlement could be possible."

"But wouldn't the whole thing take a year or more?" Banks said. "I mean the investigation, the legal paperwork, etc. If there's only a few days left, even if someone ran into the courthouse this afternoon, that can't possibly leave enough time."

"Another good point, Chief Banks," Sinclair said. "But I think the original document may address that. In the newspaper interview of 1905, Mr. Morgenstern is clear in his belief that someone—a male heir—simply needs to 'show up' with the document, and present it to any officer of a New Jersey court, and that would be a tolling event. In layman's terms, it would stop the clock ticking. That is my understanding."

"Well, I am skeptical, but I've been that way before and been wrong," Saxby said. "I think we need to go forward with the idea that this all might just be possible. What kind of money are we talking about? What kind of revenue does the Parkway bring in?"

"I imagine that would be public information if we

wanted to know exactly," Sinclair said, "but I can say that it's something over four hundred million dollars per year. Having not read the actual document, I don't know the fine print as to how any compensation would be determined. For example, does it call for a yearly income, or some sort of lump sum? In any case, even if there was only a settlement, you could be looking at numbers in the hundred million range."

"Whoo-weeee," Banks said. "That is what I call big bucks. Very big bucks."

"Yep, you got that right Marty," Saxby said. "Very big bucks is right. I don't think we need to wonder about motive anymore. And I think we can assume that we have a person or persons out there somewhere looking for this document that may or may not still exist. We've got some work to do. Mr. Sinclair, I think we've taken up enough of your time for one day. This afternoon has been very helpful."

The three men talked for a few minutes more as Sinclair walked Saxby and Banks to the door. They agreed on a loose plan to pursue certain avenues of investigation and to share what information they managed to uncover. Saxby and Banks thanked Easton Sinclair profusely, and went outside to the car.

"A hundred million bucks," Banks said, as Saxby clicked his seatbelt and started the car. "You know what kind of money that is, don't you Tate?"

"Yeah Marty, I sure do," Saxby said, stepping on the gas. "The killin' kind."

13

S axby and Banks agreed to get together in the Cape May station to catch up and get everyone on the same page before Banks had to leave town.

"Give me fifteen or twenty to check in with my guys," Banks said. "And I'll give Dooley a call to fill him in and see if he's got anything to add."

"Okay, good. You can use the spare office for your calls and I'll do the same with my team," Saxby said. "I'll round up Vic and Three if I can find them and we'll meet in the conference room. I'll put on a fresh pot of coffee."

Half an hour later, Banks joined Saxby and Barstow in the conference room.

"Deputy Connor was out on patrol but I've asked him to join us," Saxby said. "He should be less than ten minutes but we don't need to wait. We can catch him up. How are things with Dooley?"

"All good," Banks said. "But I could tell he was rushing me off the phone. Apparently, there's been a series of arsons over in Town Bank and The Villas with at least one fatality, and he's had to get into that up to his eyeballs. He said he knows this thing is in good hands with us, and to not hesitate to call if he can help with anything. Aside from that, he didn't have much to add."

"All right then, that's fine," Saxby said. "As long as we can call if we need him. I guess they're as short staffed up there as everywhere else. You want to go first Marty? What are your folks telling you about the late Mr. Starr?"

"Yeah sure," Banks said. "So, what we know so far. Aaron Starr is his name, fifty-nine years old, found dead in a first-floor apartment on 8th Avenue, just off Surf, a few blocks in from the beach. My people got hold of the landlady, who's owned the place since her parents left it to her thirty years ago. She said Starr's lived there for six or seven years and was never any trouble. She didn't think he held a regular job. She had the idea that he had some kind of trust fund or something like that. Preliminary from the medical examiner is that he died between about 4:00 and 6:00 a.m. this morning. Cause of death looks like blunt force trauma to the head and torso; with one big kick to the head in particular. He had a paring knife sticking out of him too, but that seems almost like an afterthought. Basically, someone beat him up. Whether they meant to kill him or just got caught up in it is a question. A few cuts on his hands suggest the attacker may have taken a few punches too. Aside from the neighbor who saw his door open, we haven't found anyone in the area who says they saw or heard anything. Still working on next of kin."

"Chief Banks, I realize you just had a short call to catch

up with your team," Barstow said, "but I spoke earlier with your Sergeant Hopkins. He told me pretty much what you just recapped, but he also mentioned that he thought the man's laptop was missing. Starr, I mean. He said there was a charger cord for an HP laptop under the table, but no laptop. There was also a note pad and some office-type items on the table, like he used that for his desk sometimes."

"Okay, good. That makes sense," Banks said. "So, let's assume for the moment that whoever killed him took a quick look around and grabbed the laptop. Far as I recall from when I was at the scene this morning, other obvious valuables had not been taken. His wallet, some cash—the things someone would grab quickly if robbery was their motive."

"So, if the laptop was taken," Saxby said, "it was for the information on it, and possibly not because it's a valuable thing."

"That's what I was thinking Chief," Barstow said. "Which is all in keeping with this whole weird treasure map thing going on. Somebody's after something and we don't know what it is."

"Well, actually, I think we've made some progress on that," Saxby said, after exchanging a look with Banks. "Our meeting with Easton Sinclair answered some big questions. Not all the questions, but at least I think we know what the motive is now. The 'treasure map', as you say, Vic."

Just then Deputy Connor came into the conference room and took a seat to join them at the table. "Sorry Chief, I hope I didn't hold things up too much."

"No problem Three," Saxby said. He introduced Chief

Banks. "You're just in time to hear what we learned in our meeting with Easton Sinclair this afternoon."

Barstow and Connor listened carefully as Saxby and Banks related the details of their time with Easton Sinclair. The two police chiefs switched back and forth several times, each telling different parts of the story and commenting on the other's additions. Barstow and Connor interrupted with questions at numerous points, adding to the lively, fifteen-minute discussion.

"So, I think our motive is clear," Saxby said, after a long pause, during which everyone either made notes or sipped coffee. "And surprise, surprise, like most murders, it comes down to money. A lot of money."

"I gotta say Chief," Connor said, "I'm having a hard time thinking that this whole thing isn't just plain nutty, but if you think there's a real possibility that this claim to big Parkway money could have merit, I guess we need to take it seriously."

"I'm with you Three," Saxby said, "on both points. Yes, it all sounds crazy, but Sinclair gave some good reasons why he doesn't think it should be so easily dismissed, and anyway, it does look like we have some people out there trying to kill each other over it. And that right there is our problem. To be clear, whether someone comes forward with this document or not, and whether it's worth a hill of beans or not, isn't our concern. What is our concern, is finding out who killed who and trying to stop any more of that kind of thing from happening."

"I understand Chief," Connor said. "We need to take it very seriously, because other people sure are. But now that we think we have a motive, can we talk about who? If I've got it straight, we're looking at direct descendants of either of the original partners. So, that would include Jason and Erik Kane."

"You've got it right Three," Saxby said. "Just male descendants though. Keep that in mind. And yes, we believe that Jason and Erik Kane are the great-grandsons of Anders Kane Sr., so they qualify. It's an assumption, but it appears that they do not have the document. Or maybe they have it but don't know they have it. When was the last time we spoke with them?"

"I spoke with them late yesterday," Connor said, "and again at about ten this morning. Both times I called Jason Kane first, and it turned out his brother was there and they put me on speaker. Last night, I told them that we had executed a search warrant and that we would try to turn the house over to them as soon as possible. I definitely got the impression that they were anxious to get into the house, because they both asked about it, but didn't push too hard. I called again this morning just to clarify something about their addresses. That was a short call."

"That's interesting," Saxby said. "If you talked to them at ten, then that was after Aaron Starr was killed but before any of us here in Cape May knew about it. How did they sound to you?"

"Well, again, it was a short call," Connor said. "I asked them a few background questions and they asked if I knew anything else about the house or their sister. I told them no, I didn't, but would get back to them as soon as I could.

There wasn't a lot of conversation to go on, but I didn't get a sense that anything was wrong."

"Right, well, maybe they have nothing to do with Starr," Saxby said, "or, they're just cool characters. Anyway, it's high time we had another talk with them. Where do they live?"

"Jason Kane has a condo in the Crest, near Wildwood," Connor said, "and Erik rents an apartment up in the northern end of Sea Isle City."

"Do you think the two of you can get up there to check in with them before you call it a day?" Saxby said. He looked at Banks. "Maybe Chief Banks would want to have one of his crew with you? You'll need to check in with The Crest and Sea Isle too."

"I can grease the wheels with that last part," Banks said. "I know those folks well."

"Sure Chief, I'm up for that," Barstow said. Connor nodded his agreement as well. "We'll head out as soon as we're done here. Be interesting to see if either of them has bruised knuckles or a black eye."

"Good, thanks—and call me after, whatever the time. Now, we talked about the Kane family so far," Saxby said, "but let's not forget about the other partner, this Morgenstern. Have we gotten anywhere yet with a family tree, or do we have any indication that Aaron Starr could be related?"

"Found out a little Chief," Barstow said, "but no solid answers yet. Records going back that far are sketchy at best, and sometimes just aren't there. Children born at home and sent to private schools, that sort of thing. With that in mind, it looks like Morgenstern had at least one son, Daniel, born in 1870, but then it stops there. Coming from the other end, I'm waiting for a call back on Aaron Starr, and Chief Banks' guy —Hopkins—said he would let me know when they found anything. He was born in Princeton in 1962. No marriage on file, or at least not in New Jersey. There were no pictures, cards, or bric-a-brac in his apartment to indicate that he had any children, or siblings for that matter. I have a friend who works a night shift up at the Atlantic City Press, and she told me she'd try to dig up anything she could find and would let me know, so I'm keeping an eye out for that. For my two cents, Starr was probably related to Morgenstern, or somehow had a plan to pose as somebody else who was."

"I agree that it makes sense to go with that idea for the moment," Saxby said. "And hopefully we'll know more soon. Somewhere out there are one or more people hot to get their hands on this Kane document, and they must know they're running out of time. Anything else Marty?"

"No, I think we've covered it" Banks said. "And I should be heading back. Make a stop in the station then home for some dinner." He jotted something down on a slip of paper and pushed it across the table to Barstow. "That's my cell and the main dispatch number. I'll check in with the Crest and Sea Isle for you. Call the dispatch when you're headed over and they'll send someone to meet up with you. Probably be Hopkins if he's available. Whoever it is will update me afterwards."

The group chatted for a few minutes longer before breaking up. Saxby walked Chief Banks out to his car while

Barstow and Connor went back to their desks to prepare for meeting with the Kane brothers.

————

It was a few minutes after nine that evening when Saxby's cell phone rang, catching him in the midst of cleaning up after dinner at Angela's apartment. The display told him it was Barstow calling.

"Hey Vic, saved by the bell. I was just about to start doing dishes. You just getting back?"

"About ten minutes ago Chief," Barstow said. "Three needed a few minutes at his desk so I volunteered to give you the update. We were able to catch up with one of the Kane brothers but not the other."

"And did you have someone from North Wildwood join you?"

"Yeah, good guy too, Sergeant Hopkins. He met us at Jason Kane's place, and then followed us up to Sea Isle."

"Okay, good. Lay it on me then," Saxby said. "Tell me how it went."

"We found Jason Kane at home," Barstow said, "and he let us in to talk, the three of us. We told him about how Aaron Starr was found, and how a voice memo from his sister had referenced meeting with an 'Aaron' hours before she was killed. We told him how it looked like Starr had been doing research similar to what his sister had been doing, though we didn't know specifics. He said he didn't know any Aaron Starr and wasn't aware of either his sister or brother having known him. He had a visible reaction when we hinted that Starr had been beaten, and Three and I agreed after we left that it was a strange reaction for finding out about someone he claimed to not know. He said he had been in bed at home this morning until about seven, and his brother Erik had come over around nine. They were both there when Three had called at ten, and then he thought it was almost noon when Erik left to go back up to Sea Isle."

"Okay, so he still denies knowing Starr," Saxby said. "What was the sense that you got from him? Nervous? Lying?"

"Well, he did answer all our questions," Barstow said, "so if I told you he was evasive, it would only be because that's the vibe I got from him. Pretty sure Three would agree with me on that. When we were leaving, we mentioned that we were going up to see his brother, and it seemed like that jarred him a little. He did confirm the address for us, and also, he said he had tried to call the brother a few times this afternoon and early evening but the call had gone to message. If I had to wrap it all up for you Chief, my guess is that he did know Aaron Starr, or at least knew of him, and also, he knows more than he's letting on about this Parkway document situation, just based on when we told him about the research angle. I strongly doubt that he had anything to do with Starr's death, but I got the feeling that he thinks his brother might. Maybe that's too far Chief, but I'm giving you my take on it."

"No, it's all good Vic," Saxby said. "It's important to pay attention to your gut with these things, and I want to hear that from you. So, then you went to see Erik Kane in Sea Isle. What happened there?"

"Nothing to report on that, because he wasn't home. It was a ground level apartment in a complex of eight or ten units, looked like a pretty nice place. There was no answer and the lights were out, blinds were closed. We saw a neighbor walking a dog who thought she had seen him leaving sometime in the early afternoon—she wasn't sure but probably about two is what she thought. We called back to Jason Kane to ask if he had any ideas about where his brother might be but he didn't add anything."

"Okay then, well, good work to both of you," Saxby said. "We'll need to track down Erik Kane tomorrow, and keep a close eye on both of them. How about if we get an early start tomorrow and I'll buy you breakfast at George's. That sound okay?"

"Sounds good Chief," Barstow said. "I'll stop in at the office first to check a few things, and I'll meet you there at seven thirty."

Saxby hung up and set down the phone as Angela came back into the room.

"Was that Vic? She's sure working late," she said.

"Yeah, her and Three had to go up to Sea Isle City to talk to a couple people," Saxby said. "This treasure hunt mess. I'll be meeting her for breakfast tomorrow."

"Well, if the Police Chief finishes the dishes," she said, "I'll fix us a drink and we can watch a little TV and make it an early night. I could use an early start tomorrow too."

With that, Saxby turned back to the sink and set to work on pots and pans, while his mind wandered to images of dusty old documents, toll booths, and chalk outlines of dead bodies.

14

———

Saxby was looking through the latest Star and Wave over a cup of coffee when Barstow came in. The bell on the inside of the door announced her arrival, and she stopped to say hello to the waitress before scanning the room. He raised a hand in a wave and she smiled and started towards his booth. As she took her seat across from him, he could tell she was excited about something. She set a well-scuffed leather portfolio down on the table next to her.

"Good morning Vic. Your face has a touch more than the usual glow about it. Did you get some early news?"

"Sure did Chief, and I think it's some good stuff. I heard back from my friend up at The Press, you know, about Starr."

She paused and sat back as the waitress arrived with a cup of coffee and a menu for her.

"Thanks Lexi. I don't think I need to look at the menu.

I'll have a western omelet with whole wheat toast. Glass of water too please. Oh, sorry Chief. Are you ready to order?"

"You want your usual Chief?" the waitress said. "Or are you gonna really live it up today and try one of the specials?"

"I have no doubt that all the specials are fantastic gourmet creations, Lexi," Saxby said, "but I think today calls for the usual. Scrambled dry please, and burn the bacon."

The waitress gave him an exaggerated wink, topped off his coffee, and walked away to talk to the cook and greet a young couple who'd just come in. He tore the top off a creamer and poured the contents into his coffee as Barstow did the same with hers.

"Okay, so you heard from your friend at the paper already this morning?" Saxby said. "Overnight shift?"

"That's right, my friend Shayna," Barstow said. "She's mostly a researcher but she does other jobs there too. I thought of her yesterday and she said she'd try to look into it when she could. When I got up this morning, I saw I had an email from her, and I stopped at the station to print some of it out. Some big project had been cancelled at the last minute, so she had a lot of free time and started digging."

"Well, whatever it is she found," Saxby said, "be sure to pass on a big thank you from me."

"Will do Chief," Barstow said. "So, she started searching on the name 'Starr', and look at this." She took a sheet of matte photo paper from the portfolio and slid it over to Saxby. "This is from a Sunday edition in 1980. It was a special section featuring new businesses in the shore towns."

The page was half filled with a grainy black and white photo of three people standing in front of a brick building. Saxby studied the picture closely. A tall, slim man in a double-breasted business suit was standing between two younger men, with a hand on their shoulders. The younger men were also wearing suits. There was a caption under the picture, which read: "Mr. Peter Starr, CPA, is proud to announce the opening of his new firm, *New Morning Investments*. Mr. Starr is shown here with his two sons, Phillip and Aaron, 21 and 18 respectively, in front of the new offices at 629 Pacific Avenue in Wildwood. The proud father hopes his sons will one day join the firm". The door to the building was behind them, and to the right side of the door was a large oval sign dominated by a stylized graphic that Saxby didn't recognize, along with some lines of text.

"The sign is a little hard to make out," Barstow said, "but it's just the name of the company, New Morning Investments, with the address below that. The picture in the middle, something of a logo I guess, looks like a rising sun. I got a better look at it on my screen before I printed it out."

Saxby and Barstow both sat back as the waitress brought their food and topped off their coffee.

Saxby studied the picture again while taking a few bites of scrambled egg. "The kid on the left looks younger. So, if that's Aaron Starr at age 18, that would put him at about fifty-eight or fifty-nine today. Does that fit with our dead guy?"

"Yep, it does. According to Aaron Starr's driver's license, he was born in '62, so that works. And now we know he has a brother—Phillip—older by a few years."

"That's really big news," Saxby said. "And we'll need to have a talk with the guy soon. Do you know if our friends up in North Wildwood know about him yet?"

"At the moment I'm assuming they do not," Barstow said, "but I'll call them as soon as I get back to the station and give them everything I have on him." She set another paper down next to his plate. "Ta-da! As soon as I had his name, it only took me five minutes to look him up in the system. New Jersey license in the name of Phillip Starr, and look at the address. 629 Pacific Avenue."

"Would you look at that—good work Vic," Saxby said. "He must have inherited his father's old business, or building anyway. Maybe he lives there, or just uses it as an address."

"And one more thing on that note," Barstow said. "Remember when I told you I went through Jolene Kane's phone, and checked out those few recent numbers that she didn't have a contact record for?"

"Yeah, I remember," Saxby said. "You thought that was a dead end at the time. Something new come up?"

"Well, you may remember there was this one number I had tried," Barstow said, "and all I got was a message for some financial company. I had looked up that company and found it wasn't in business, and apparently hadn't been for years. Now it all adds up. That number was for Starr's old company, New Morning Investments."

"Well, well, well, the plot thickens, doesn't it?" Saxby

said. "Wow. So, the company is defunct, but Starr, or both brothers it looks like, still use it like some kind of office. If Aaron Starr called Jolene Kane to talk about getting together, he called from there. But why? He must have had a cell phone, or maybe even a land line at his place. I think I may have to order you to take your friend Shayna out for a nice dinner. I don't want to push my luck, but is that it? Did she find anything else on the Starr family?"

"One more thing Chief, that's…I don't know, interesting at least," Barstow said. "Once she found that family picture, which gave her the father's name—Peter Starr, she looked up property transactions in the county. You know all that stuff is public information. She found the records for the building he bought at 629 Pacific Avenue, in the picture there. But she also found a record of a man named Peter Starr having sold another property—a single family home, on Atlantic Avenue about ten blocks from the office building. That was back in 1973. The weird thing is that there's no record of that same man ever buying the house. Like he just appeared there, lived for a while, got married presumably, had two sons, then sold the place. Anyway, Shayna's having fun with this and she's going to try to track that down for me. She said she'd call me when she figures it out."

"I see, well good then," Saxby said. "We need to learn anything we can about this Starr family. You okay Vic?"

He had noticed that Barstow seemed to be entranced by something on the wall across the room. He turned to see the chalkboard hanging there, where the staff wrote the daily specials, usually adorned with some colorful drawing or smiley face.

"Yeah. Yeah, sorry Chief, I'm fine." Barstow said. "It's just the names of the breakfast specials there. They have a 'New Day' omelet, and something called 'Morning Riser' pancakes. I don't know, it just struck me as funny right after we were talking about the New Morning company. Morning this, new that, early this, and morning again. Maybe I didn't get enough sleep. And then there's this Morgenstern business."

The waitress had come back to the table and was gathering up dishes. "Morning Star," she said, to nobody in particular.

"What's that Lexi?" Saxby said. "You said 'morning' something?"

"Oh, I'm sorry Chief," Lexi said. "I didn't mean to butt in. My grandmother's been drilling me on German for most of my life. My name is actually Neubacher, which is Austrian, but Austrians speak German. Anyway, when I heard you say that, I guess I thought you might be trying to learn. I should keep my mouth shut more."

"You're fine Lexi, don't worry about it," Saxby said. "But what do you mean? You heard us say what?"

"Oh, well, when I came up just now," Lexi said, "I heard Vic say something about 'morgenstern', and I just kind of unconsciously translated it. Morgenstern is German for morning star. I'll get your check."

She walked away with the armload of dishes, leaving Saxby and Barstow looking at each other in wide-eyed silence.

"Why is it so hard sometimes, to see things that are right in front of you?" Barstow said.

"If you find the answer to that one," Saxby said, "let me know right away. I think this puts a bow on our working idea that the Starr brothers are descended from Paul Morgenstern. You agree?"

Barstow nodded up and down, slowly. "Yeah, agree on that. That's got to be it. Must be it. And if we're right, that gives them a big motive to be looking for this document. Or I should say, him—Phillip."

There was a buzzing sound and Barstow reached for a coat pocket, pulling out a phone. "Oh, I think it's Shayna, let me take this outside. Be right back." She tapped the screen to take the call as she walked quickly to the door. Saxby could see her through the side windows as she paced back and forth a few times, engrossed in some animated conversation. It was only a few minutes before she came back in, and Saxby thought she looked as excited as she had when she'd first arrived. He watched her as she sat down again, silent, but with questions all over his face.

"That was her, Shayna. I told you she was having fun with it," Barstow said. "And she said she couldn't sleep. So, this Peter Starr who sold the Wildwood house in 1973, but didn't appear to have actually bought it, right? Working backwards, it looks like the only other transaction for that house on Atlantic Avenue, was when another man bought it as new construction in 1947. That buyer is listed as Deiter Morgenstern."

"He changed his name, didn't he?" Saxby said, after a long moment of silence on both sides of the table. "Deiter

Morgenstern bought the house and Peter Starr sold it. Did we look at name change records?"

"I have not, because we haven't had any reason to," Barstow said. "As of yet anyway. Shayna told me that she thought of that just this morning and did a check but didn't find anything. I'll dig into it myself."

"Good. See if you can track down anything on that," Saxby said. "I'm thinking that it must have been common back then, say during or after the war, for people with German names to change them. You know, Americanize them. Morgenstern to Starr, Deiter to Peter. A lot of people must have done that to avoid being hassled—or worse. If that's why he did it, I wouldn't be surprised if he slipped the clerk a few bills to make sure the ledger entry was accidentally erased. Stranger things have happened."

Saxby paid the check and they walked outside, taking a minute on the way out to thank Lexi and the other staff.

The sky, which earlier had shown the promise of another sunny day, had darkened substantially while they had been inside the restaurant. Saxby could feel a pressure drop in the air, and had to grab his hat as they crossed Beach Avenue to their cars, as a strong gust blew down the street, parallel to the beach.

"When I was getting it together this morning," Barstow said, raising her voice to compete with the sudden winds, "the weather guy said we might be in for a nor'easter. Something about whether or not that Canadian high comes far enough south."

Saxby heard the buzz of his cell phone and reached for it

to answer, not recognizing the number on the screen. "This is Chief Saxby, who is calling please?"

"Good morning, Chief Saxby," came a man's voice that sounded vaguely familiar to Saxby. "I hope I'm not catching you at a bad time. This is Bramford Oakes, calling for Mr. Sinclair. We met briefly yesterday afternoon, when you were here with the gentleman from North Wildwood, Mr. Banks."

"Oh yes, of course Bramford, er, Mr. Oakes," Saxby said, "I would probably have called myself later, I've found some further information that I'd like to discuss with Mr. Sinclair."

"That's perfect then Chief Saxby," Bramford said. "I believe it to be the case that Mr. Sinclair has also come upon new information that he would like to discuss with you. Would one o'clock this afternoon suit you?"

"That would be fine," Saxby said. "I will be there at one. Oh—Bramford, I'll probably have one of my officers with me, if that isn't a problem. Someone who's working closely on this case."

"Certainly, Chief Saxby," Bramford said. "I will tell Mr. Sinclair to expect you and Sergeant Barstow at one. Good morning to you."

Saxby hung up and shoved his phone back into a pocket. He and Barstow huddled beside her car, against the wind. "Well, if that wasn't Easton Sinclair, or rather, his valet, Bramford. Sinclair must have found something out because he wants to see me again, and I told him I'm bringing you. I hope you don't mind. It'll be an adventure. We're due there at one, out at the Point, so don't get caught up in anything that could make us late."

"Sounds good Chief, that'll give me time to start calling Jolene Kane's friends. The 'Mahjong Ladies', as her brother put it. But I heard the tail end of your call—how did he know my name?"

"Oh, he's an interesting character Vic. You ain't seen nothin' yet."

15

"What's this guy like Chief? Is he as hard to take as people say?"

"Nah, I didn't get that impression yesterday at all Vic. He's a character, sure. Very egotistical, obviously, but I think he's one of those people who just operates on a different level from most. I wouldn't like to be an idiot in his presence. Since neither of us are idiots, I think we'll be fine. Feel free to make conversation when you meet him. He seems to prefer that over jumping right to business."

For the second time in as many days, Saxby was winding his way out to Sunset Boulevard on the way to see Easton Sinclair. A light rain was falling, though the weather people were warning of a storm on the way and the likelihood of a heavy downpour coming with it. The sky was completely dark aside from a thin band near the horizon, where, to the west and south, a strange glow spilled through, a gauzy layer of yellow-orange holding up the massive darkness above it. A half-dozen thick drops splashed across the windshield, and Saxby moved the switch to adjust the intermittent wipers.

"Oh my God," Barstow said, as they pulled up to the great iron gates. "I had no idea. This guy must have money out the wazoo. How much are we telling him? I mean, he's a civilian, what does he know already?"

"My instinct is that it's okay to tell him all of it," Saxby said. "I think we can consider him a reliable confidential resource, though I do plan to remind him about the need for all this to be on the QT at this point. I know it's irregular, but we're a small department and getting info from people who want to help is a good thing. If we can trust them, of course. In this case I believe we can."

The light shower had almost stopped as Saxby parked the cruiser and they stepped out onto the drive. Barstow did a slow circle, taking in the whole picture of the great house and expansive lawn, all set in a clearing in the middle of a small but dense forest of mature trees. The smell of the ocean, not more than two or three hundred feet away but completely hidden by the ring of cedars and a wall of dunes beyond that, was thick in the air.

A low-slung and portly dog came out from under a manicured bush next to the house and ambled over to them, sampling the air. Barstow knelt down to allow her hand to be sniffed, and gave the creature a few pets before he wandered unhurriedly off into the trees.

They turned back to the house and were approaching the stone steps leading up to the door, when it swung open wide and Bramford stepped out.

"Good afternoon Chief Saxby and Sergeant Barstow, and thank you for being punctual. Mr. Sinclair is expecting you. Please come in."

This time, when Bramford showed them into the library, Easton Sinclair was already there, appearing to be in deep concentration over a pile of papers spread across the desk. Several thick volumes were open on either side. His outfit was similar to the one he'd been wearing the day before, except that this time the velour smoking jacket was in a rich purple instead of red. His shirt, of thick silk in a rich cream color, was accented by a loosely-knotted ascot tie in light grey silk with small purple dots that matched his coat. There was a smell of pipe smoke in the air. He looked up only after Bramford announced the visitors.

"Ah yes, Chief Saxby," he said, coming around the desk to greet them and shake hands. "How good of you to come again. I enjoyed our meeting yesterday very much. And Sergeant Barstow—it is a pleasure to meet you. It is good to finally meet some of the law enforcement community."

"It's good to meet you as well, Mr. Sinclair," Barstow said. "The Chief tells me that you've already been of some help to our investigation. We appreciate that."

"Yes, we do appreciate your help sir," Saxby said. "And I hope we aren't catching you at a bad time. It looks like we might be interrupting something."

"Oh this, don't worry about this at all," Sinclair said. "I was just catching up on something I've worked on now and again for some time. I've been studying the history of glue. Really quite a fascinating subject. We take it so much for granted today, don't we? One can go to any hardware store and choose from dozens of sophisticated adhesives for any imaginable application. Did you know that primitive glues, made from tree sap, were in use some 200,000 years ago? I was taken aback when I first learned that."

"That is amazing, Mr. Sinclair," Barstow said. "I knew glue went way back, but I had no idea it was anything like that far. When I think of something like that, I can't help but remember something I read once—that there are lots of people who think the earth itself is only something like six thousand years old. What do you say to someone like that?"

"I wouldn't say anything to someone like that," Sinclair said. "They are not worthy of interaction. And that is my advice to you as well, Sergeant. But are you familiar with epoxy? My word, one could write volumes about epoxy. Incredible stuff. One of the truly great inventions."

"We saw a dog outside when we drove up just now," Saxby said. He had raised a hand to his mouth in an attempt to stifle a laugh. "Is that yours? He seemed to be coming from the house."

"Ah yes, that would be my neighbor's Bassett Hound," Sinclair said. "Just down the street on the left. Professor van Wyck."

"Oh, Professor van Wyck," Barstow said. "That sounds vaguely familiar. Does your neighbor teach at one of the state colleges?"

"What? College? Oh—good heavens no," Sinclair said. "She has a small chain of gift shops along the coast. Mrs. Manderly, I think her name is. Nice lady, acceptable in the main. No, Professor van Wyck is the Bassett Hound. Wonderful creature. He wanders by now and then, perhaps every other day, and I find that I look forward to his visits and enjoy his company. He is quiet, intelligent, and utterly without the instinct to deceive. Bramford makes up special treats for him, which I believe are largely based on diced Chanterelle mushrooms, along with something called 'turkey jerky'."

"That is fascinating, Mr. Sinclair," Saxby said, "but I was hoping we...."

"Ah yes of course, Chief Saxby, the conversation wrangler," Sinclair said. "Alas, I must admit it to be true that one of my very few flaws is that I can occasionally go off on a tangent. Guilty as charged. In fact, that reminds me of one summer many years ago in Tuscany. It was hot that year, unusually so. There was a rented cottage, and the young lady's name was Antoinette... Ha! Don't worry, I was just having a bit of fun with you there. Please pardon my indulging myself. Now, let's get down to business, shall we? Bramford should be here momentarily with coffee, or there's brandy if you prefer."

"Coffee will be fine, thank you," Saxby said. "We have made some progress on our investigation, and I had decided early this morning that I would call you to see if we could meet again, when Bramford called me first. Have you been able to learn anything about where Anders Kane Jr. may have lived in this area? He mentioned the 'Cape May house' in one of the letters to his daughter Mary, but we haven't yet been able to find anything more on that."

They were briefly interrupted when Bramford came in to set a large coffee service tray down on a side table.

Sinclair spoke again after the officers had helped themselves.

"Yes, in fact I was able to find some information on that," Sinclair said, "but if you don't mind, would you first give me a general update on the case so far?"

"I'll be happy to do that," Saxby said. "But I must ask you to bear in mind that this is an ongoing investigation, so all of this must be in strict confidence for the time being."

"Now, Chief Saxby, if I were a lesser person, I might be offended at your feeling the need to say that, but I accept your terms with no offense. I realize that you are probably bending a few rules with this case, and I am grateful to be 'part of the team', as it were. Bramford helps me with my research now and then, but apart from that, you have my word that neither I nor Bramford will discuss the case with anyone else. Will that suffice? Now, where do we stand?"

"Thank you, Mr. Sinclair," Saxby said. He stood up to walk over to the wall of bookcases, gathering his thoughts before speaking. "Okay then, where do we stand. With your help, we've learned that the core of the matter is this deal that Jolene Kane's great-grandfather and his partner made with the government back in 1871. It appears to be conceivable that any of the direct male descendants of those two men who manage to produce a copy of the original agreement before a certain date could be entitled to a huge financial windfall. As far as that date, though we'll never know how or why, one of the original signers—Kane—managed to end up with a copy that expires at the end of November 13th of this year." Saxby glanced at his watch. "Which happens to be tomorrow."

"Very interesting. Tomorrow is the 13th and is a Saturday," Sinclair said. He appeared lost in thought for a moment as he looked down at the floor and lightly scratched his chin. The other two strained to hear. "Easter was April 4th this year…hmmm…the last blue moon was October of last year…ah, that's it then, the meeting at the White House in 1871 was on a Monday, quite obviously. Pardon the interruption, Chief Saxby, please continue."

"Yes, well, a Monday then, good to know, thank you," Saxby said. "So, the other partner was a man named Morgenstern, and his copy, along with the government's, expired back in 1951. It was just this morning that Sergeant Barstow here figured out that we have a pair of brothers in the area who we think are Morgenstern's great-grandsons. Actually, I should say one brother living in the area, because the other one is the guy Chief Bank's people found beaten to death up in North Wildwood yesterday morning. It appears that their father had changed his name from Deiter Morgenstern to Peter Starr at some point in the 1940s. Well before the boys were born."

"I do recall your telling me yesterday that man's name was Starr," Sinclair said, "who you also think is the man who may have killed the Kane woman. Upon reflection, I now recall that 'star' is 'stern' in German. Star, stern, Morgenstern. No doubt he made the change to insulate himself from the anti-German sentiment that was the zeitgeist of the times during and after the war. Very clever, and good work on your part Sergeant."

"Thank you, Mr. Sinclair," Barstow said. "It's mostly

circumstantial at the moment, but that's about what we have so far on the Morgenstern-Starr family."

"But you've uncovered some good information," Sinclair said. "If these Starr brothers and their father had a copy of the document, or at least knew about it, they surely would have understood that it was worthless after 1951."

"That's the way we're looking at it, yes," Saxby said. "But I consider it likely that they recently found out—from Jolene Kane probably—that another copy could exist that isn't expired yet. And I say 'could' with a capital 'C'."

"Yes, yes. I understand. And, am I correct in thinking that the Kane brothers haven't been acting as though they have this document?" Sinclair said.

"That's correct," Saxby said, "based on our assumption that, if they did have it, they would be running up the court-house steps as fast as they could. We've spoken with them a few times. Vic?"

"Yes, we met with Jason Kane last evening," Barstow said, "mostly to question him about Aaron Starr. He seemed nervous, and probably scared by all this, but I don't think he killed Starr. We tried to meet with this brother Erik also, but he wasn't at home. We'll be working on that today. Like the Chief said, it was just this morning that we learned about the other Starr brother, Phillip, who has an address in Wild-wood, so we'll also try to meet with him today. It's quite possible that he may not know about his brother's death yet."

"Is all that a reasonable summary of where the case stands at this point?" Sinclair said. "Or is there anything else to add?" He looked from Saxby to Barstow.

"That's about where we stand," Saxby said. "The key points anyway. A person or persons, probably named either Starr or Kane, are trying to find the last copy of this document, and they have until midnight tomorrow to do it. Oh, and it also seems that one or more of them are willing to kill to prevent the other side from getting to it first."

"Well then, where is this document?" Sinclair said. "If it still exists. When you were here with Chief Banks yesterday, we talked about the correspondence between Anders Kane Jr. and his daughter. Kane mentioned in one of those letters that he was keeping his important papers in a lacquered wooden chest that would be in his 'Cape May house'. As we broke up our meeting, I said that I would try to look into that, and I have had some success. Bramford was a big help. Frequently it seems that he can find out anything—even things that nobody knows. Well, in the early part of the last century, at least in the twenties and thirties, there was a local grocer in Philadelphia by the name of Vincenzo Abbandonzo. At some point, he opened an outpost in Atlantic City, which was enjoying its heyday at that time, and a few years later, a third location in Wildwood. His niche was providing imported luxury items to the wealthy shore visitors who he knew were accustomed to greater quality and variety than could typically be found anywhere around here, and he was very successful until he had to leave the country for one reason or other in the late thirties. My father, as a young boy, remembered that my grandfather used to order various hard-to-find items, such as caviar and foie gras, which would then be delivered by a small white truck. When Abbandonzo closed up shop rather quickly, he sold the rough contents of his Wildwood store to a local man at some fire-sale price. That man, Charles Dickson, had apparently planned to continue the business by another name, but didn't get far with the idea. Fear not, officers, there is a point to all this and the moment approaches. I came upon Mr. Dickson because, back in 1978, he, along with his basement full of Abbandonzo paraphernalia was mentioned prominently in a Philadelphia Inquirer feature on the great old Italian markets." Sinclair paused to walk over to the long side table to pour himself a glass of brandy.

"I don't want you to think I'm trying to rush you Mr. Sinclair," Saxby said, "but what made you think to look into this Italian market in the first place?"

"That is an excellent question Chief Saxby," Sinclair said, "and I have an equally excellent answer. Anders Kane wrote that letter in 1934, when he had a house around here somewhere. At that time, the Abbandonzo market in Wildwood was the chief purveyor of exotic luxury foodstuffs in the area. My point being, if you were a wealthy, tasteful man from the New York City area, and living in Cape May County in the thirties, you were quite likely to have been an Abbandonzo customer. A large part of Abbandonzo's business was deliveries, and he kept detailed records. Dickson passed on in 1982, leaving whatever was left of the old Abbandonzo records to his daughter, Sylvia. Like her father, Sylvia Dickson had long nurtured the dream of resurrecting the old Abbandonzo market, but had eventually settled for running a small Italian restaurant, which is doing quite well today. The important thing to know about Sylvia Dickson, is that, until just a few hours ago, she still owned four of the old Abbandonzo delivery books."

"Until a few hours ago—damn. But what does that mean?" Saxby said. "Those books might have given us an address for the Kane house."

"Be at ease, Chief Saxby," Sinclair said. He walked over to his desk to pick up a faded, cloth-bound book of about an inch in thickness. "The only reason she doesn't own them anymore is that I bought them from her this morning. My theory has been proven correct, naturally, in that Mr. Kane did have a taste for fine foods and wine, and took regular deliveries. At least once a month, and frequently two or three, over several years, and all to the same address. Here, I've marked a page for you." He handed the open book to Saxby. Barstow came close to look over his shoulder at the faded writing.

"Let's see here, what am I looking at," Saxby said. "March fifteen of 1937, okay. Delivery to Anders Kane… about ten or so items. French Champagne, imported ham, Italian breadsticks…looks like expensive goods for back then."

"The list continues on the next page there," Sinclair said, "and the delivery address is halfway down the page. You see that?"

"Yes, I see it. A little faded," Saxby said. "Corner of Mt. Vernon and … oh that is just too much."

"It is, isn't it Chief Saxby," Sinclair said. "How do you read the address?"

"It's right here, plain as day," Saxby said. "Blue house,

white shutters, corner of Mt. Vernon and 8th Avenue, Cape May."

"But Chief," Barstow said, her face a mask of confusion, "8th and Mt. Vernon? I've lived in Cape May all my life, and you know as well as I do…there's no such place."

16

"You are absolutely correct, Sergeant Barstow," Sinclair said. "There is no such address as 8th Avenue and Mt. Vernon. There is no such house or junction. As a matter of fact, there is no such neighborhood. But in the 1930s, there certainly was."

"I'm sorry Vic," Saxby said, "I didn't realize you weren't familiar with South Cape May. Most people aren't, so don't worry about it. Beach Avenue and Mt. Vernon used to extend a lot farther, like almost to where the bunker and the lighthouse are. I think there were at least a few dozen houses there before they were all washed away."

"Ah, so South Cape Beach we're talking about then," Barstow said. "Where the water cuts way in. That's all marshland and bird sanctuary now. When was this?"

"The area was first settled in the mid-1800s by a very few people," Sinclair said. "When that land was all part of Lower Township. Speculators bought up as much acreage as they could, with dreams of a grand hotel and a vibrant town.

It was incorporated as a borough of Cape May County for about fifty years, until it ceded back to Lower Township in 1945. As soon as they started building houses there, it was an ongoing battle with mother nature, and then came the hurricane of 1944. What wasn't completely washed away was heavily damaged. Within a few years after that, and another storm or two, the last people still there finally threw up their hands and moved. A large part of the area is now underwater. The Atlantis of New Jersey."

"That storm of 1944 took a big bite out of the shoreline," Saxby said, "including most of what would have been Mt. Vernon past 2nd Avenue. The corner where Mr. Kane's house stood would have to be underwater now. Talk about an underwater mortgage. Do we know anything about what might have been saved as the storm approached? Or did people have any warning at all?"

"Hurricane tracking in the 1940s wasn't what it is today," Sinclair said, "but people knew the storm was coming. In the materials I've read about South Cape May, there have been several mentions of families scrambling to prepare for the storm. There was a great effort to get children and pets, even furniture and other valuables away to less vulnerable locations, but I don't know the details." He picked up a slim volume from his desk and handed it to Barstow. "There you go, '*The Town That Vanished, A History of South Cape May and The Hurricane of 1944*', by *Florence Thompson.* You may keep that copy, Sergeant. It covers the story well, and can be read in an evening."

"I'll read it tonight, thank you," Barstow said. "Is the author a local person?"

"She is, yes," Sinclair said, "and it has occurred to me Sergeant, and Chief Saxby, that the author, Florence Thompson, would be a good person for you to speak with regarding preparation efforts as the storm approached. I imagine she might also know something about salvage and recovery in the aftermath. If anyone would know about the Anders Kane house or his personal effects and where they went, she is a good candidate. I had a brief but enchanting conversation with her at a charity event last year, and found her to be a very interesting lady. And sharp as a tack."

"That's a good idea Mr. Sinclair," Saxby said, "and I think that needs to be one of our next steps."

17

D uring the ride back into Cape May, Saxby and Barstow went over what they had learned about the Anders Kane house in South Cape May, and where their next focus should be.

"That was all very interesting," Barstow said, "but we don't know much more that really matters, do we? We know Kane's house was destroyed in 1944, but we don't know if his important papers were saved or recovered, or if he was even in the area at the time, right?"

"Yeah, you're right Vic," Saxby said. "But it looks like we may have a good lead with this Florence Thompson lady. If she knows the area as well as Sinclair thinks she does, hopefully we can get a better picture."

"Remind me Chief, why is it we've got ourselves involved in looking for this document?"

"That's a fair question, and the answer is that we're only looking for it peripherally. Our job is to find out who killed those two people, and to try to keep other people from being killed. But I think if we're able to get our hands on that old document, maybe we could put a stop to any further hostilities. I could be wrong, but I think it's worth a try."

"If we manage to find it before anyone else does, what would we do with it?"

"Another good question, and I'm not sure. Get it up to a county judge I suppose. The city solicitor would probably have an opinion."

Barstow's phone rang and she tapped the screen to take a call from Deputy Connor.

"Hey Three, what's up?" Barstow said. "The Chief and I are just on our way back from the meeting with Sinclair. That was an experience."

Saxby could hear bits and pieces of the conversation as she listened to her phone for a minute. "Hang on a sec," she said, "I'm putting you on speaker. Run through that again so the Chief can hear please." She tapped the screen and adjusted the volume so they could both hear Connor's voice.

"Afternoon Chief. I was just telling Vic that Hopkins and I went back up to Sea Isle to see if we could catch up with Erik Kane, but again, he wasn't home. We talked to a neighbor who couldn't recall seeing or hearing anyone since early yesterday. But then, just when I got back to the station, a half hour ago, I got a call from Jason Kane. He said he remembered that his brother had a girlfriend with a place not far from his, and he sometimes stays over there. Lady by the name of Jackie Dillane."

"And I'm assuming that Erik Kane still isn't answering his phone," Saxby said. "That correct?"

"Correct, yes. I've tried quite a few times," Connor said.

"And left messages. Another thing is that I definitely got the sense that Jason was worried about Erik. He told me he had been calling and leaving messages, and that it wasn't like his brother to not get back to him pretty quickly."

"Hmmm, yeah, I don't like the sound of that," Saxby said. "Are you at the station right now?"

"Yes Chief," Connor said. "After I got the call with the girlfriend's address, I figured since I was already back here, I'd check to see if Vic or both of you wanted to head back up there with me. I've already called Hopkins, and he's available too."

"We're going to pull in the driveway in about two minutes," Saxby said. "We'll do a quick pit stop and then we can head on up to Sea Isle."

———

Back at the station, Connor made a call to Sergeant Hopkins of North Wildwood, and another to the Sea Isle City officer, Sergeant Hanna, arranging for all of them to meet in the parking lot of a restaurant a few blocks from their destination. Ten minutes later, he and Barstow were driving north up the Parkway, with Saxby following in a second car. Barstow briefed Connor on the meeting with Easton Sinclair.

"I know it's only been a few hours," Barstow said, "but were you able to find out anything on Phillip Starr?"

"Not much yet, but a little," Connor said. "Dishonorable discharge from the Army back in '82, when he must have been twenty-two or three. He was most of the way through

Ranger training at Ft. Benning when he got into a scrap at a local bar and punched out some officer. Apparently, that wasn't his first offence and I guess they'd had enough of him. I didn't have time to read the whole report, but I did see that he was sniper qualified and had an armorer rating, you know, a weapons specialist. I didn't find any record of a marriage or children. That's as far as I got."

"Sounds like he could be a tough dude to tangle with," Barstow said. "Hopefully nothing like that will happen."

Connor took the left-hand ramp to enter the Parkway rest area, looping through it to join the south-bound traffic and immediately moving right to catch the exit for Sea Isle Boulevard. He could see in the mirror that Saxby's car was still behind him, going through the same process. "You know, if this isn't the dumbest thing in the world, it is on the list. Why in hell haven't they ever built a north-bound exit? It's almost like, you can't get there from here."

Barstow laughed out loud, shaking her head. "I don't know Three, but you're right, it's up there on the list. I guess it was too wet and marshy where they would have had to build the ramp, but then that doesn't make a whole lotta sense, does it? It's marsh everywhere around here, so who knows. It's always something."

There wasn't much traffic on the long causeway across the wetlands and out to the bridge over to Sea Isle City. Barstow bent low to look up at the sky through the windshield. "That is a pretty ominous sky up there. The weather report says the storm could hit anytime, or at least by overnight, and it could hang out for a couple days. I'm glad I'm not out there on a boat."

A few minutes later Connor pulled into the parking lot of a local seafood restaurant that showed all signs of being closed for the season. Saxby pulled in behind. The two police cruisers from North Wildwood and Sea Isle City were already there. Everybody got out of their cars and hellos were said all around.

Saxby addressed Sergeant Hopkins and Sergeant Hanna. "Thanks for making time to meet with us. The Cape May Police Department appreciates your help, and please give my regards to Chief Banks and Chief Hawkins. So where is Erik Kane's apartment from here?"

"We're at 35th and Landis right now Chief," Sergeant Hannah said, "so his place is seven or eight blocks away, over on 38th near the bay. Right before we came here, Sergeant Hopkins and I went by and knocked on the door again and got no response. He drives a dark grey Explorer, 2016, and we didn't see that either."

"Okay, good idea to check that again," Saxby said. "And this girlfriend of his, where is she and what do we know about her?"

"Dillane is her name," Connor said. "Jackie Dillane. The DMV says she's fifty-two and drives a 2017 Camry in dark blue. Don't know much else about her at the moment Chief. Her address is 223 31st Street. Apartment 2A."

"That's just a few blocks up, between Landis and Central," Hanna said. "I did a quick drive by earlier, just to get a visual. Two-story apartment building with ten or twelve units. There's a small parking lot, plus cars on the street. I'm pretty sure I saw a blue Camry, but can't say about the Explorer without a closer look. I did see an

"OFFICE" sign on the left side ground floor wall, so maybe there's a landlord or manager we can talk to. I didn't stop."

"Good work, and that's good info," Saxby said. "Well, let's do it then guys. No sirens. Let's just pull up quietly and try not to freak out the neighborhood. If Erik Kane is there, we want to speak with him to see if he knows anything about Aaron Starr. And depending where the conversation goes, we may also want to confront him with all this document business. We don't have any basis to arrest him yet, but he is certainly a person of interest. Let's keep guns in holsters but stay on your toes. It's possible that he is a person who recently beat someone to death. Let me go up first and see if I can find that landlord. I'll get Sergeant Barstow on the radio when I want the rest of you to join me."

The four police cruisers made the short trip to Jackie Dillane's apartment building and parked in a row on an adjacent side street. The houses on the block all looked empty, buttoned up until spring and the start of the next rental season. Saxby got out of his car and motioned for the others to stay put. He walked around the corner to approach the apartment building from the office side. Although it wasn't quite five o'clock as he approached the building, it was dark enough that he could see where some windows showed lights on inside while others didn't. He saw the "OFFICE" sign Sergeant Hanna had mentioned, and followed an arrow to the closest door, over which was a smaller, matching sign. His knock was answered by a slim woman in jeans and a heavy wool sweater. Her eyes were bright blue and friendly, and seemed to Saxby to be the bright spots in a face that had a lifetime of stories written across it. He guessed her to be about fifty-five. She looked him over and smiled warmly as she stepped outside to talk.

"Hello officer," she said, "what can I do for you?"

"Sorry to bother you ma'am," Saxby said. "Chief Tate Saxby, over from Cape May. I was hoping to speak with someone who we think might be staying here. Do you have a tenant by the name of Jackie Dillane?"

"Sure do, Jackie's been here for, oh, I guess it's more than three years now. But you're going to be disappointed, because she's away. She's doing one of those European river cruises with a girlfriend of hers. Viking, I think, or one of those companies. I happened to be getting out of my car when the friend came to pick her up for the Philly airport. Sunday, I think that was. I think she's away for about two weeks."

"Well, that's really okay, Mrs…"

"I'm sorry Mr. Saxby. My name's Betty. Betty Grable actually. Yes, it's true, my parents were film buffs with a sense of humor. Conversation starter anyway. And it's 'Miss', for now. Or just Betty will do. There was a mister for a while, a ways back, but he's just a bad memory at this point."

"Oh, I didn't know Miss Dillane was away, but actually, I was looking for a man named Erik Kane, who we think may have been in a relationship with her. Is that someone you know of?"

"Yes, or I think so anyway. I've seen her with a guy named Erik. He helped me carry groceries in once last summer. About your age, maybe a few more years, but not as nice to look at. Decent enough guy it seemed to me, the few times I saw him. Is he in trouble for something?"

"No, not at the moment. But he is a person of interest in a case we're working on and we'd really like to speak with him. I suppose it's less likely that he'd be here, with her away in Europe, but as long as we're here I'd like to check. Could you point me towards her unit?"

"Sure, it's 2A, just to the right up the stairs on this side. Number's on the door. You know, now that you mention it, there's been a dark colored Ford Explorer here since yesterday sometime, maybe dinner time. It's down there next to that white van." She pointed out to the parking lot. "I think that might be his. If it is, it wouldn't be the first time he's ever spent the night, but maybe the first time that she wasn't here with him. He might have a key, which I don't mind. Her checks don't bounce."

"Okay then Miss Grable, I'll call the other officers and we'll go up and see if anyone's home. Please just stay here and I'll check in with you before we leave."

Miss Grable stepped back inside and closed the door. Saxby used his radio to call Barstow.

"We're here Chief, how's it going over there?"

"I've been speaking with the landlord, who tells me Jackie Dillane is away in Europe. She thinks Kane could be here though, and it looks like we could have his car in the little lot here. Also, I see a blue Camry. That would make sense, since we think a friend picked her up and took her to the airport. I want you and the others to come up now and meet me at the corner of the building by the office. The apartment's on the second floor."

The apartment building was U-shaped, with the main part parallel to the street and twice as long as each of the equal wings on either end. Each of the two inside corners had a wide staircase of cement steps in a white-painted steel frame going up to the second floor. It all looked like a small version of a typical roadside motel, except that there was no pool in the middle, the small parking lot taking up most of the open space. The officers started up the stairs on the left side, in a close single file, with Saxby in the lead, with his two officers behind him. When Saxby reached the second floor, he could see that the door just off to the right was clearly marked '2A'. There was a pair of double-pane windows on each side of the door, with any possible view of the interior hidden behind cream-colored blinds that were drawn all the way down. He paused for a moment to reach to his hip and push the holster safety strap forward and away from his pistol, leaving the pistol holstered, but now more readily accessible. The other officers saw him and did the same. They all exchanged looks telling each other that they were ready. Saxby walked to the door and knocked.

He waited thirty seconds with no answer before knocking again, a bit louder. Still no answer. When he knocked a third time, he thought he felt the door give a little. He ran his fingers down the edge, all the way to the bottom.

"I think this door might have been forced, see those scrapes along there?" Barstow stepped closer to look, nodding. Saxby tried the knob and found it locked. "Three, go back down to the office and get a key from the landlady.

Miss Grable is her name. If she asks about probable cause, you can tell her about the door."

Connor went quickly back down the stairs. While they waited for him to return, Barstow tried to look through one of the windows where there was a small opening between the blind and the frame. "Dark in there. I can't be sure, but I think there's someone on the floor."

Connor arrived with the key and Saxby motioned to him to go ahead and unlock the door. He did so and pushed the door partly open, calling out to the inside. "This is the police, if anyone's here, show yourselves immediately." He knocked loudly on the open door and repeated the call before pushing it all the way open and stepping inside, with a hand ready on the butt of his pistol. "Man down inside," he yelled to the others behind him, as he drew the gun. Saxby and the others piled in quickly, guns drawn. They all looked down on the body of a man who was stretched out face up on the floor of a hallway that went straight towards the rear of the apartment, his feet about eight feet in from the door. Immediately, Saxby motioned for the others to check the rest of the apartment while he knelt down next to the body.

"Nobody else here Chief," Connor said, coming back to the entryway a moment later, holstering his gun.

"Okay, that's good. First things first," Saxby said. "Hanna – this is your territory. You need to call this in and get your people out here, including whoever does your crime scene work. This man is as dead as it gets, and he's down to about room temperature. Vic, Three, you spent more time with the guy than I did, would you agree that we've just found Erik Kane?"

"Yeah, that's him Chief," Connor said. "He's a twin, but I remember his hair was much longer than his brother's."

"I remember the hair too," Barstow said, "it's him. Only thing is, the last time I saw him, he didn't have those bullet holes in the center of his chest."

18

While they waited for the Sea Isle City crime scene team to arrive, Saxby pulled on a pair of disposable gloves and found a wallet in the dead man's pocket. He looked through it briefly before setting it down beside the body.

"Yep, that's him, Erik Kane. Killed late last night is my guess, but we'll see what the ME says. I don't see any signs of a struggle. Looks more like a short conversation followed by a shorter execution. What do you think Three?"

"Have to agree with your initial there Chief. His hands are all banged up and scabbed up, like he was in a fight a day or two ago, but it sure doesn't look like there was any fight in here. Unless it was really short and they tap-danced around the furniture. No robbery either, from the looks of it. Laptop on the coffee table over there is a recent iMac. That's a thousand-dollar item right there. My guess is, he came up to the door when he heard, or saw, someone trying to break in, there was a confrontation, and the guy shot him.

Hey—is that a shell casing over there?" Connor knelt down next to where the carpet met the wall along the side of the room. He took a pen out of his pocket and used it to skewer a shiny metal object. "Sure is, and look, there's another one there. Forty-five auto, Winchester. Smells like it could've been recently fired."

Saxby stood with his back to the door, looking down at Erik Kane's body. "I bet that's just what happened. If someone came in, and stood about here with his back to the door, and fired an automatic in that direction, the ejected shells would have flown over that way. Seems like about the right distance. And a forty-five too. That would explain the size of the holes he's got in him. Thing is, an apartment like this, with tile floors and hardwood cabinets, you fire a gun like that in here, that's going to be a hell of a boom. Three times, three booms."

Barstow had just come back in from outside and was nodding her head. "I was just outside talking to the neighbor in 2B, right next door. She's a grad student who said she was at home yesterday, from around two in the afternoon and all night. She said she was up late studying for an exam and didn't hear anything unusual. She thought she might have heard someone watching TV for a while, but doesn't seem really sure."

"Well, we need to get a time of death for Mr. Kane," Saxby said, "but if this neighbor was home all night and says she didn't hear gunshots, what does that tell us? Makes me think of the dog that didn't bark in the night."

"He used a suppressor, Chief?" Barstow said. "Could that be it?"

"There's no other way a person could have fired a forty-five in here without someone right next door hearing it," Connor said.

"You could shoot through a pillow or something like that," Saxby said, "but I don't see any feathers or little bits of cloth laying around on the floor. You could hold the gun right against someone, but then there would be substantial powder burns all over his shirt, so that isn't it."

"But last time I checked, this is still New Jersey, not Texas," Barstow said. "I mean, who the hell has a suppressor?"

"Good question Vic," Saxby said. "A serious gun nut, ex-military maybe, some kind of gangster. They aren't that hard to make if you know what you're doing. Probably someone breaking the law in any case. Then of course, if you're going to murder someone, the fact that your weapon is against the law probably isn't high on your list of concerns."

A group of Sea Isle City officers had arrived and Saxby waved to Connor and Barstow to follow him outside and get out of the way. He took a minute to speak with the commanding officer, who agreed to send him a copy of the crime scene report as soon as it was available. He motioned for Sergeant Hopkins to join the three of them at the bottom of the stairs, where they could have some privacy.

"Let's get out of here and let these folks do their work," Saxby said. "Seeing as how our suspects keep turning up dead, here's my thought process at the moment. Let's connect the dots. We think someone by the name of Aaron met with Jolene Kane and may have killed her. Three and I both had the feeling the Kane brothers knew more than they were telling us. Next day, Aaron Starr turns up beaten to death. Within another day, Erik Kane turns up dead, and his hands look like they might have been punching someone recently. Who do you think would have wanted to kill him?"

"Someone who thinks that Kane killed his brother," Barstow said. "Remember the Golden Rule—family first."

"Right Vic, always look at the family first," Saxby said. He looked at Sergeant Hopkins. "Have you, or someone from your department, met with Aaron Starr's brother Phillip yet?"

"Yes. About an hour after Barstow called me this morning," Hopkins said. "Chief Banks and I went to his office on Pacific Avenue to tell him that his brother had been killed. That was right about noon. Not one to let emotions show by any stretch, but I'm sure he was upset about it."

"Do you know if Chief Banks is in the office now?" Saxby said.

"Yeah, he is," Hopkins said. "I spoke with him a few minutes ago when you were still inside. Want me to call him again?"

"No, that's okay," Saxby said. "Let's head down to your station, and I'll call him from the car to give him a heads-up that I'm coming in. I want to hear all about this meeting you had with Starr. Vic and Three, you can head on back to Cape May and start shutting down your day. You have a lot to tell Dooley, but try not to make it too late a night. Nothing to Jason Kane yet about his brother. Let me think about that. I might drop in on him on my way back to Cape May. Good work today, both of you."

Twenty minutes later, Saxby was munching on a power bar washed down with burnt coffee in Chief Martin Banks office at the North Wildwood police station. Banks had been catching him up on the gist of the noon meeting with Phillip Starr.

"So yes, he was upset about his brother," Banks said, "but he kept it mostly bottled up. I think he's just that kind of man. You know, keeps his cards close to the chest. If it was him who offed Erik Kane last night, man, I don't know Tate, that's one ice cold bastard."

"Yeah, I agree Marty, but he could be just that. And when you asked him if he knew Jolene Kane or her brothers, what was your read on his reaction to that?"

"Well, he said he didn't know them, except that he had read about Jolene in the paper. I didn't see that he was bothered by the question. He asked why I was asking about them, and I told him we believe Jolene Kane had recently been in contact with someone named 'Aaron', and were looking at a possible connection to his brother or anyone else we come across by that name. He seemed to take that in stride."

They were interrupted by an officer knocking on the open door. "Sorry to disturb Chief, and Hello Chief Saxby, good to see you. Officer Parks just called in. He wanted me to tell you that he just saw Starr entering his building. He said the windows are covered with blinds or curtains, but lights are on in the front room and he could see shadows moving around. The second thing is, you asked me to call

Sea Isle to see what they know about time of death for Erik Kane. It's preliminary, but they're thinking between nine and eleven last night."

"Okay, thanks Jim," Banks said. "Tell Parks to stay where he is for now, and not to be surprised if he sees me show up soon."

"Will do Chief, I'll call him right now."

"Well Tate, what do you think," Banks said, after the officer had left. "Since you're here in town and we know Starr's at his place, whatta ya say we drop in on him?"

"I think that's what we need to do Marty. We'll tell him about Erik Kane and find out where he was last night. Also, I think it's time we brought this old document thing out into the open, see what he says about that."

———

It was almost seven, and had already been a long day when Saxby and Banks got out of their respective cruisers on Pacific Avenue in Wildwood. On the short drive down from the North Wildwood police station, Banks had called in to his counterpart in the city of Wildwood, Chief McGarry. She thanked him for the heads-up and said she would be sending a car over to observe and to be available in the event that any backup was needed.

"It's just up there in the middle of the next block," Banks said. "The door that looks like a storefront, number 629." They saw the Wildwood and the North Wildwood patrol cars parked together on a cross street, and Banks waved to them and motioned for the officers to stay put in their cars.

The building looked exactly like it had in the old photo that Saxby and Barstow had looked at earlier. There was a large plate glass window with a center divider, like a typical store display window, but with a pair of blinds pulled all the way down inside. To the right of that was a heavy door with a decorative geometric design etched into a single sheet of frosted glass. Between the window and the door was an oval sign proclaiming "New Morning Investments", above a painted version of a rising sun. The sign had clearly been bright and colorful at a point in the distant past, but was now well-faded, with the paint peeling at several spots around the edges. There was a doorbell button, which Saxby pushed, twice.

At the side of the window nearest the door, a hand pulled the blind back enough for a man's face to look out. The blind fell back into place before they heard the sound of a deadbolt lock turning and the door opened wide. The man had a sturdy but athletic build, and stood an inch or two over six feet tall. His medium brown hair was going grey at the temples and had been recently cut in a short, almost military style. Saxby's first impression was that the man must be about sixty, and still quite fit. He was neatly dressed in pressed khakis and a blue oxford shirt. His brown leather belt and watch strap matched his shoes. *Very together*, Saxby thought.

"Good evening officers," the man said. "You were here earlier today—Chief Banks, isn't that it? To what do I owe the pleasure?"

"Good evening Mr. Starr," Banks said, "and yes, Chief Banks is right, from North Wildwood. We spoke earlier. This is my counterpart from Cape May, Chief Tate Saxby. We're sorry to disturb you again so soon, but we have a number of things we'd like to speak with you about. May we come in?"

"Of course, please do," Starr said. "This is a simple office, but there's a small sitting area where we can talk." He stood aside to let them come in, and gestured to a quartet of chairs positioned around a low table, like the waiting room of a small medical practice. "Good to meet you Chief Saxby. I gather you already know that I am Phillip Starr."

"Yes Mr. Starr," Saxby said. "And firstly, please accept my sympathies on the passing of your brother Aaron yesterday. I realize you only found out about that earlier today, but I hope you don't mind answering some questions."

"Thank you, Chief Saxby, I appreciate that," Starr said. "I don't think it's really kicked in yet, you know, that he's gone. We hadn't been close for years, and well, I guess it's my nature to keep things inside. Anyway, no, I don't mind. I'll do my best to answer your questions. I have one question for you though. Here I am with the Chiefs of Police of both North Wildwood and Cape May, yet we're in Wildwood right now. Why isn't there someone here from Wildwood?"

"That's a reasonable question Mr. Starr," Banks said. "But it's really quite common for our departments to work together. I spoke with Chief McGarry of Wildwood earlier and we are here with her blessing. Also, there's a Wildwood patrol car parked across the street, as a, well, an observer from a distance."

"Ah I see then," Starr said. "Thank you for explaining that. I hope you didn't think I was going to give you any trouble."

"Are you going to give us any trouble, Mr. Starr?" Saxby said.

"Oh no, no sir. No trouble from me," Starr said. "I really was just asking out of curiosity. So then, what questions do you have for me?"

"A few hours ago," Saxby said, "I, along with some other officers, went up to Sea Isle City, hoping to speak with a man by the name of Erik Kane regarding several matters. As a matter of fact, Mr. Starr, we considered it possible that he might know something about the death of your brother Aaron."

"That's good," Starr said. "Sounds like you're getting leads already. I'm glad to hear that. How did it go—what did he say?"

"Well, he didn't say anything," Saxby said, "because he was dead when we got there. It looks like somebody killed him late yesterday evening. Executed, basically. So, you see how we couldn't help but be concerned Mr. Starr. Somebody violently attacks and kills your brother, and within less than twenty-four hours a person of interest in that case turns up dead. Can you account for your time last night? Say from about eight to midnight?"

"Oh, well, let's see," Starr said. "I had a meeting—a Zoom call—that started at 7:30, and went a full hour to 8:30. That was with two friends up in Moorestown. We've been kicking around some investment ideas off and on. I first thought I'd cancel it, you know, after finding out about Aaron, but then decided it would be a good distraction for me. Anyway, after that, I took a walk up to the boardwalk, just to think. I was probably out for about an hour. And then I was here."

"You say you were here," Banks said. "Do you actually live here?"

"Yes, I do. There's this office, and a small kitchen and bathroom in back, but upstairs there are four apartments. I live in one and the other three are year-round rentals. The rental business is the main reason I maintain this office. It's a big tax advantage. My brother and I own the building. Or, I guess that's just me now. I'm sure my friends would confirm the Zoom call, but I suppose I can't prove anything after that."

"Do you own a gun, Mr. Starr?" Saxby asked.

"I do own several guns, yes," Starr said. "I have four handguns—revolvers, and two rifles. I'm an occasional target shooter, but way out of practice. There's just one here, upstairs, and the others are in a locker in the basement of a friend's house up in Montgomery County, Pennsylvania. I get together with him now and then for a trip to the range. Everything was legally bought."

"And the one you have upstairs here," Saxby said, "what is that?"

"It's an old Colt Python," Starr said. "In .357 magnum. Would you like to see it?"

"No, I don't think we need to bother with that at this point," Saxby said. "So, no 'old slab-sides' for you then?"

"I used to have one, years ago," Starr said. "But it wasn't a favorite and I eventually sold it to a dealer. That must have been twenty, twenty-five years ago. I was in the Army a long time ago, so naturally I handled plenty of forty-fives back then. I prefer revolvers for target shooting."

"Mr. Starr, when I was here earlier," Banks said, "we spoke briefly about the Kane family—Jolene Kane and her two brothers, Erik and Jason. At that time, you told me that you didn't know them, apart from reading about Jolene in the papers. Is that still your recollection?"

"Actually, Chief Banks," Starr said, 'I did remember something after you left, and it's been on my mental to-do list to call and tell you. I hope you understand that I've had quite a shock today."

"We understand that Mr. Starr," Banks said. "What is it that you remembered?"

"Well, when you asked me about the Kanes," Starr said, "I mean, Jolene and her brothers, as I told you, I had read about the woman in the paper, and I guess I was in sort of a tunnel vision about today, yesterday, and the day before—something like that. But later, I was thinking about family I guess, and something reminded me that my grandfather, no, sorry—my great-grandfather, was in business with a man named Kane. And then I started remembering things."

"So, are you now saying that you have known the Kanes?" Banks said. "Jolene, Erik, or Jason. Any of them?"

"No, I'm not quite saying that," Starr said. "What I am saying is that I remember my father talking about the old family business, and the Kane family came up a few times."

"And your father, Peter Starr," Saxby said, "was born

Deiter Morgenstern. He changed his name in the mid-forties. Do I have that right?"

"You have that right," Starr said, "he did change his name, just like thousands of people with German-sounding names did around that time. I'm interested to hear why you've been researching my family history."

"I'll explain that," Saxby said, "but first, if you would please—you were talking about the old family business and how it related to the Kane family."

"Okay, well, my great-grandfather, Paul Morgenstern, had a business partner by the name of Kane, don't know his first name. I never knew exactly what they did, but it had to do with land speculating, commercial real estate rentals, something like that. They were successful and quite wealthy at the time, back in the late 1800s, but then they had some kind of falling out and eventually went their separate ways. All the property was sold off and split up except for a few buildings or pieces of land that the next generations had to deal with. The last contact between my family and the Kanes, that I'm aware of, must have been when my father met with the guy who I figure was Jolene Kane's father. It was something about the last shares in a property out on Long Island. My father drove Aaron and me into Philly for the meeting, and I have a foggy memory of meeting one or two of his kids while we waited for the meeting to end. There you have it, Chief Saxby. That's about what I know about the Kane family. That is, until I heard about Jolene's death the other day. And now today you come and tell me one of her brothers was killed, and it kinda sounds like you think I'm a suspect."

"A person of interest for now, Mr. Starr. That's all," Saxby said.

"Okay, and I guess I can understand that from your point of view," Starr said. "But what does any of this have to do with my great-grandfather and his partner? That was over a hundred years ago."

"Okay Mr. Starr, fair is fair," Saxby said. "Something has come up in our investigations, that we believe could be related to the deaths of Miss Kane, your brother Aaron, and most recently Erik Kane. Or I should say, any or all of those deaths. Are you aware of a deal that your great-grandfather's company made with the government back in 1871, where the Federal Government got possession of certain tracts of land along the New Jersey Coast?"

"You mean the land that was intended for the Army to build the train line?" Starr said. "Yes, I know about that, and I'm sure Aaron must have too. My father told us about it when we were little. I still have that document somewhere. Probably in my safe deposit box. It's actually signed by President Grant and some other bigwigs."

"Are you aware of anything else about the deal?" Saxby said.

"Well, yeah, I'm familiar with it," Starr said. "The basic deal was simple, but you're asking about the part that said if the land was ever used in some way that made money, the company would get a part of that. But it was only good for eighty years, which ended in 1951. Before the Parkway started collecting tolls. After that it was just an interesting piece of paper. I'm sure it took my father some years to get over how close it came, but all that was years before Aaron and I were born."

"All right then, you seem to know all about it," Saxby said. "And you say your brother Aaron would have known about it also?"

"I'm sure he did," Starr said. "I mean, it wasn't a secret. They made lots of deals back then, land sales or whatever. That was just another one. I guess my grandfather and my father kept an eye on things, hoping for the big payoff, but like I said, the expiration was 1951, and that was that. It was never anything that mattered much to me. Or to Aaron."

"What if I were to tell you, Mr. Starr," Saxby said, "that it has come to light that there may be another copy of the document out there somewhere with a different date on it? In other words, a copy that hasn't expired yet. Is that something you've ever heard of?"

"What? No, I've never heard anything like that," Starr said. "And that seems like an important detail that my father would have told me about. I find the idea very hard to believe, frankly. Who told you that?"

"We can't say right now," Saxby said, "and by the way, I share your skepticism, but the main thing is that we have reason to believe that somebody—maybe more than one somebody—appears to believe that a copy still exists that could be worth a lot of money. If you're telling me that you have the Morgenstern family copy, and presumably the government in Washington may still have their copy, then we seem to be talking about the Kane family copy. So, I'll ask you again, are you sure you're not aware of any of this?"

"No. If there's any truth to this at all," Starr said, "you telling me about it right now is the first I've ever heard about it. This document, if it exists, which I doubt—are you willing to tell me what the date on it is? The expiration?"

"The historical information we've found," Saxby said, "refers to a time span of a hundred and fifty years, rather than eighty. As you say—if it exists."

"Whoa, okay," Starr said, after a quick whistle. "If memory serves, our family's copy expired an even eighty years from the day it was signed, which was November 13th. A hundred and fifty years would be this year, so, wow, I guess that's tomorrow."

"That's right," Banks said. "Midnight tomorrow as far as we can tell. So, you can see our concern then. Whether this is real or not, we don't want anyone else killed over it."

"I understand that," Starr said. "I assure you that I have no plans to kill anyone, nor have I killed anyone."

"That's good to know Mr. Starr," Saxby said, after exchanging a look with Banks and standing up. He handed Starr a card. "Please let us know if you think of anything else, or if anyone contacts you about this document. Also, let us know if you have any plans to leave Cape May County."

19

"He's either legit or a hell of an actor," Banks said. They stood under the eaves of a combined beach-wear and souvenir shop that was shuttered for the season, across from their two cars. As they walked back from Phillip Starr's office, they had waved at the two patrol cars on the cross street, dismissing them. A light rain was falling, becoming bursts of sideways spray now and then as strong gusts of wind whipped by. Banks pulled the zipper of his coat up as high as it would go. "He sure didn't seem like a guy who mowed somebody down last night. But then, maybe he really is a hell of an actor."

"I'm with you on all points Marty," Saxby said. "Between you and me, I went in there thinking he was probably the guy. Maybe seventy, eighty percent, but now, I don't know. I might be down to fifty or sixty. Let's not drop our guard with him though."

"What was that with the 'old slab-sides' question?" Banks said.

"Oh, it's probably nothing," Saxby said. "Common nickname for a forty-five automatic. I was just trying to get a feel for how much of a gun-guy he was. If Kane's killer really did use a suppressor, that's some serious stuff right there. Course, if he was in the military in the eighties, he couldn't help but know his way around a forty-five. Like I said, probably nothing. Anyway, I know it's been a long day, but can you stand taking care of one more thing?"

"Jason Kane?" Banks said. "Yeah, sure. We really shouldn't wait on that. Let's keep it as brief as we can, just tell him about his brother, clearly homicide, but can't give out any details yet."

"Agree on that," Saxby said. "Give him the basics, give him our sympathies, and then let him think on it overnight. He seems nervous and scared, is what I heard from Deputy Connor. Give him some time to stew and maybe he'll feel more like talking to us. Do you have his address in the Crest?"

"Let's start heading south, and I'll call in for it," Banks said. "Follow me and let's get this done. After that, I'm going to be in need of some dinner and a few beers. My stomach is starting to drown out the sound of all this wind."

"Sounds like a good plan," Saxby said. "I think a hot dinner and a cold drink in a warm place is calling my name too."

———

Two hours later, Saxby finished the last of his dinner in The Ugly Mug, and pushed his plate to the edge of the table. At eight thirty on a Friday evening, he was surprised at how quiet it was, knowing that weekends in Cape May can be very busy in the fall.

"The weather report probably convinced some people to stay home," Angela said, as she slipped into the booth across from him. The waitress cleared away the last of the dinner things and Angela motioned for a round of drinks. "I think we're going to start getting hit with some heavy rain during the night. Last report I saw was that it's somewhere near Cape Cod and moving our way slowly. We might even get some hail."

"Yeah, I can't blame people for wanting to stay home this weekend," Saxby said. "Probably not going to be a good time to stroll around and look at the pretty houses. Do you have to stay late tonight or can Cody close up?"

"No, I'm free to go just about any time," Angela said. "Nothing more I need to do that can't wait for morning. Except, uh-oh, here comes trouble."

Saxby turned to see Sergeant Barstow coming around the bar towards them. As she approached, she reached to the back of her head and fiddled for a few seconds, unleashing a thick cascade of dirty blond hair with a few quick tosses.

"I hope it's okay if I let down my hair," Barstow said. "I've been needing to do that for the last hour. You know what I mean, Ang, right?"

"Oh, you better believe it," Angela said. "I can make it for so many hours and then it just has to break out. Are you meeting somebody, or can you join us?"

"I'll join you if you're sure it's okay," Barstow said. "If you're on your way out I can slam one at the bar."

"Join us please Vic," Saxby said. "Can't have my hard-working deputies slamming drinks alone at the bar. Especially now that they've let their hair down."

Just then the waitress came back to the table with the drinks Angela had ordered. She looked at Barstow. "Having something Vic?" she asked.

"Yes please. What have you got there Chief?" Barstow said. "That looks tasty. I feel like something strong tonight."

"Bourbon on the rocks," Saxby said. "One of my favorites. Want to try it? Pretty sure I don't have cooties."

Barstow picked up his drink and took a cautious sip. She made her face into a comical grimace and her eyes opened wide. "Oh yeah, that's strong stuff, but good. That'll do nicely." She looked at the waitress and pointed to Saxby's glass.

"Double Maker's Mark it is then," the waitress said. "Coming right up."

"Hell of a day Chief," Barstow said. "Did you and Chief Banks get to meet with Phillip Starr?"

"We did, and it was very interesting," Saxby said. "It was a few hours after he found out his brother was killed and he didn't seem very affected. I don't know, that may or may not mean anything. People handle things in their own way."

"Now listen you two," Angela said, as the waitress dropped off Barstow's drink, "I know you want to talk shop, so you can have ten minutes. After that, the drinks triple in price."

"Ten minutes? Come on Ang," Saxby said, "we've got bodies popping up all over the place this week. And I am the Chief of Police, by the way."

"I know, but you aren't going to be any good to the town if you don't relax and take it easy every once in a while," Angela said. "That goes for you too, Vic. Tomorrow is another day and it'll be here soon enough. Fifteen minutes, that's my final offer." She made a show of carefully checking her watch.

"Fifteen minutes, fair enough," Barstow said "and, sorry to say this, but is it okay to…"

"Talk about all this in front of Ang?" Saxby said. "Yes, she's a good civilian sounding board."

"Not to mention that I hear what he says in his sleep anyway," Angela said, poking Saxby in the side and almost making him spill his drink.

"Okay now, the clock is ticking," Saxby said. "So, we met with Phillip Starr for about a half hour. He denied knowing anything about Erik Kane, and I gotta say, either he was genuinely surprised to hear about that, or he's a damn good fake. Marty and I agreed on that. He had an alibi for earlier, but not for a chunk of time where he could have zipped up to Sea Isle. Said he was walking up on the boardwalk."

"Three or I can check with the DMV and E-ZPass in the morning," Barstow said. "Might tell us if he drove up to Sea Isle last night."

"Good idea," Saxby said. "And see if you can find out about any cameras up on the boardwalk that might have caught him out strolling. I think almost everything up there is closed now, but it's worth a shot."

"Did you talk to him about the land deal thing?" Barstow said. She looked over at Angela. "Do you know about that?"

"Yeah, Tate told me all about it," Angela said. "That's a crazy story. Like out of a movie."

"It is all of that, isn't it?" Saxby said, with a laugh. "Yeah, we asked him about it, and he freely admitted that he had known about it since he was a kid. He said it was never any secret, just something his father had some regrets about, since it expired before the family got anything out of it. He denied ever having heard about the possibility of a version that isn't expired yet. He seemed skeptical about the idea, but you know, that's what he would want us to think if he was in this thing up to his neck."

"Hmmm, that's right," Barstow said. "He wouldn't want us to know that he knew about that. And after that, did you decide to stop in on Jason Kane?"

"We did, Marty and I. Chief Banks I mean," Saxby said. "We decided we had no reason to wait on that. It was very brief, he made it clear that he needed some time. My take is that he was very hurt, but not completely surprised. I think he'll be worth talking to again soon, and I'm interested to hear what he has to say. He did just lose his sister and brother in the past four or five days. Your turn Vic, we're running out of time and we don't want the drink prices to triple."

"Okay, right. No, we don't want that," Barstow said. "When I got back to the station I called that Florence

Thompson—the author of the South Cape May book Sinclair told us about. She's expecting me to come by tomorrow morning. Sounded very happy to talk about it. Also, I called that list of Jolene Kane's friends, the ladies she played mahjong with. Nothing big there. Two of them had been over Kane's house within a week before she died, but that sounded like a normal friends visit. They didn't seem to know about her researching anything."

"I'm not surprised about that," Saxby said. "But calling them was the right thing to do. We need to cover the bases. Anything else?"

"The only other thing I can think of is that I finished going through the papers from the boxes we found in her house, along with the stuff on her desk and in her trash can. Nothing new and exciting as far as I can see. I think I'll give Jason Kane a call first thing to see if I can get over there to see him. That about covers it Chief."

"And you've been keeping Dooley up to date, right?" Saxby said.

"Yes, absolutely," Barstow said. "Matter of fact, I actually spoke with him today. He called me not long after I got back to the station today. He had a few minutes free and wanted to check in. All up to speed."

"Good Vic, good work then," Saxby said. He glanced at his watch. "Well, I guess we finished the lightning round then. Let me buy us another and then I'm flagged. I'd be happy to be wrong, but I've got a feeling tomorrow's going to be an eventful day."

20

Sergeant Vicki Barstow was in the middle of a pleasant dream when she was suddenly awakened by the distinctive sound of her cat coughing up a hairball at the foot of the bed. Coming quickly to a state of half-wakefulness as the guilty cat ran out of the room and down the hall, she took a moment to gauge the severity of her headache. *One aspirin should do it, but let's remember to stick with wine next time*, she thought to herself. *Leave the whiskey to the boss.*

She had tossed and turned through much of the night as huge rain drops pelted the building, interspersed with the occasional sharper sound of sleet or hail. The storm seemed to be on pause as a few rays of early sun leaked through the blinds, throwing a faint pattern of stripes across the bed and floor. A glance at the clock on the nightstand told her it was just past seven. Good. There would be plenty of time for a long hot shower and some breakfast. That and a mug of strong coffee, and she would be back in tune.

Two hours later, and after a half-hour at her desk at the station, she was ready to head out for her first appointment. She had called Jason Kane to make sure he was home and available. On her way out, she found Chief Saxby at his desk, deep into a stack of paperwork.

"I called Jason Kane. He's home and expecting me," Barstow said. "Did you want to come along for that?"

"I'm up to my ears at the moment, Vic," Saxby said. "If you're comfortable going to see him yourself, I'm fine with that."

"No problem going by myself Chief," Barstow said. "I just wanted to give you the invite. I plan to take it easy on him, all things considered, but I want to push him a little bit to tell me anything he knows about the Starr brothers and the land deal situation. He's got to know more than he's owned up to so far."

"I'm sure you're right," Saxby said. "And I'm hoping his brother being gunned down will be the extra push he needs. That and the irresistible force of your powers of persuasion. Catch up with me later and let me know how it goes."

The wind and rain were picking up again as Barstow drove along the Ocean Drive and onward into the northern reaches of Wildwood Crest. Any sun that had managed to poke through earlier had run for cover, and the sky was again a palette of greys. There was no shortage of parking outside the complex. Of the forty or fifty units that made up the three-story building, Barstow figured there weren't more than a dozen or so occupied at this time of year. She pushed the button beside Kane's door and he answered right away, asking her in. The condo was spacious, with a generous living room on the right, and a hallway leading off from there to the rear of the unit. To the left of the entryway was a dining room with wood furniture in a modern Scandinavian style, and then a kitchen behind that. A reach-through counter space of about six feet in length was set into the wall between the dining room and kitchen. Everything Barstow could see appeared very clean and tidy.

"Good morning, Sergeant," Kane said. "I just made coffee, would you like a cup?"

"That would be great Mr. Kane, thank you. Just cream," Barstow said. She stood next to the counter while Kane went into the kitchen. She watched through the cut-out as he fixed mugs of coffee. "You've had quite a shock, twice now this week. I'm finding it hard to imagine what that must be like, but please do accept my condolences. I'm sorry for your loss. I mean, your losses."

Kane came back around from the kitchen with two large mugs of coffee, handing one to Barstow. It was in cobalt blue, with 'Wildwood Welcomes the World' written across it in a bold white script. He gestured to a part of the living room where a pair of armchairs faced each other across a low table. "Please have a seat. And thank you, I appreciate that. It's amazing how things can fall apart so fast, isn't it? I couldn't sleep much last night. Lots of bad dreams. I kept waking up and remembering about Erik—you know, I only found out about him when your chief stopped by last night. It must have been almost dawn when I remembered that

Jolene was gone too, what, four days ago, right? It's a lot to take in all at once."

His voice was controlled and level, but Barstow could tell that it wasn't without effort. The tight lid that Kane kept on his emotions didn't hide the redness in his eyes or the pain that ran across his face.

"That's understandable of course, Mr. Kane. It's going to take you some time to process, and you might consider taking advantage of some of the professional help that's available," Barstow said. Kane nodded silently and they both sipped at their coffee. Barstow was just about to say something more when Kane spoke first.

"You're right Sergeant. This is going to take some time. A lot of it. But I already know things have gone too far with this. Two people are dead, and it's got to stop. Actually, I'm wrong. Shit. It's three people dead. I forgot about Aaron Starr for a minute."

"I agree with you Mr. Kane, and I'm glad to hear you say that. There's been enough damage done to your family already. And the Starr family. Look, I know you've been hit with a lot in the last few days, but I think you know more about what's going on than you've told us so far. I came here this morning hoping you were ready to tell me whatever you know. Are you ready to do that now?"

Kane looked at her for a long moment before nodding slowly. "Yeah, it's time. I don't know if any of it's going to help, but I'll tell you what I know." Barstow waited while he took some time to gather his thoughts. "I guess I was in shock the other morning. Not just me, but Erik too, you know, after finding Jolene. We did know about something she was digging into. I knew we should have told that officer Connor about it, but we didn't, and I'm sorry about that. I wanted to, but we talked about it and Erik convinced me to keep it to ourselves."

"Are you talking about the land deal that your great-grandfather and his partner made with the government?"

"Yeah, that's it. See, we never knew about it until a few weeks ago. Jo was in a mood to go through the house and get rid of stuff. That was our parent's house you know, so there was lots of old junk, and we didn't know what she was going to find. There were boxes of stuff from my father, and even from his father, and she started reading through all of it. Papers, letters, some old diary—that kind of thing. And she found references to the land deal, but some of it was vague, you know? Like she was trying to piece it together and make sense of it."

"So, between the three of you, you didn't have a copy of the original document?"

"No, No. We had no idea. None of us. That is, until Jo found those letters and Aunt Mary's diary. That's how we learned the thing even existed. I don't think my father ever even knew about it. He must not have, because if he had the document, why wouldn't he have brought it up to a lawyer, or a judge or whoever? We thought, well, Erik and I thought anyway, that the whole thing was nuts. But Jo wanted to find out what she could, and we figured it couldn't hurt. Jesus. Guess I was about as wrong as a guy can get on that one."

Barstow nodded, taking it all in. "So far, what you're telling me syncs up with what we've been able to piece together ourselves. Your sister found out about this old deal, but none of you actually had the document. And you said you didn't think your father knew about it at all, which I have to agree seems like the case. When we went through some of the materials in your sister's house, we found evidence to suggest that she had been in touch with someone by the name of 'Aaron', and that he may have visited her at her house earlier on the night of her death, and then left, apparently with her in good health. When we later asked you about that name, you indicated that it didn't mean anything to you. Do I have that right, or can you tell me something different now?"

"I did say that, yes, and that's another thing I wish I hadn't done. When I found my sister, I was in a daze for a minute, and I realized I didn't have my phone. I saw hers laying there on the stairs and I used it to call 9-1-1. And I saw that she'd been texting Aaron, and I deleted it."

"But why? Why did you do that?"

"I'm not so sure anymore," Kane said, after letting out a long sigh that seemed to partially deflate him. "It was dumb, I was in shock and it was spur of the moment. Something connected and I figured it must be Aaron Starr and it was probably related to that crazy land deal. I pressed the buttons, deleted it, and regretted it almost immediately."

"Was it something like, well, my sister's gone, but the police don't need to know about the old deal? Something like that? Or was it more like you were thinking that this

Aaron might have killed her and you wanted to get revenge yourself?"

"No, no, it wasn't like that at all. I mean that last thing you said. I didn't think about hurting anybody. The first thing you said though. I guess I thought, nobody else needs to know about that, and maybe we can salvage a shot at it. You know, finding that document. Now I can't help but think that Starr and my brother might be alive if I hadn't done that."

"That's possible Mr. Kane. It's always best to tell the police what you know and let us work with it, but what's done is done. So, you knew Aaron Starr then. Tell me about that please."

"No, I wouldn't say I knew him, but I knew of him. Our great-grandfathers were in business. That's when they sold that land to the government. I think they broke most of their assets up around the turn of the century. My father had to meet with his father a handful of times when they were settling some final business. I forget what it was. There was a brother, a year or two older. Frank? No, I think it was Phil, or Phillip. Anyway, we only ever met once, when we were all little kids. Haven't been part of each other's lives at all, though I think they both lived in the area. Jo must have looked up Aaron to see if he knew more about the deal. If he went over her house that night, how do you know she was alive when he left?"

"The timing. Your sister had one of those little digital voice recorders, and there was a memo on it from Monday night saying that she had met with Aaron at her house and that he had just left."

"Hmmm, okay," Kane said. "So, he must have come back later hoping to shut my sister up, or maybe get some more information out of her. I saw the stairwell, there were some broken things laying around. She probably surprised him. Isn't that what the police are thinking?"

"I can't say specifics about an ongoing investigation," Barstow said. She considered for a moment before continuing. "But that could certainly be a possibility. Tell me, Mr. Kane, isn't that exactly what your brother Erik thought?"

Kane fiddled with his empty coffee cup for a while before answering. "I think so, yes. In fact, yes. We went to breakfast that morning, you know, after we were all there at her house, and we talked about how we figured that the 'Aaron' must be Aaron Starr. Erik said he planned to find him and have a talk with him. I was a little worried about that, and it occurred to me that he might want to do more than talk. When he came over the other morning, it seemed like he was trying to hide it, but I could see that his hands were banged up like he'd been in a fight. Tell me Sergeant —do you think my brother killed Aaron Starr?"

"Well, remember what I said about ongoing investigations, but we consider that a possibility, sure. Sorry about that. There are other possibilities as well."

"Look, Sergeant, I understand about your not being able to comment and I get it. You're a professional and you're doing your job. I'm not a cop or an attorney, and my sister and brother are both dead. Let me tell you what I think, and I know you won't be able to comment, but maybe you could look at the ceiling, or scratch your nose. Do something with your coffee cup."

Barstow shrugged.

"My sister found out about this old land deal, and was trying to learn more about it. My brother and I weren't much help, so she got hold of Aaron Starr somehow, he came over and they talked about it. He came back later, maybe thinking that she might actually have the document, or other information she hadn't told him about, whatever. In any case she ended up dead. Then Erik gets wound up, tracks down Starr, and they have a big fight, and that's it for Starr. But Starr must have talked to his brother Phillip, because next thing we know, someone kills my brother up there in Sea Isle. Hard to imagine it wasn't Phillip Starr that did that. I suppose the next thing I'm supposed to do is to go find Phillip Starr and do him up. That's the way the story ought to go, right? That way, I'll be the last living descendent, even if I have no idea where this document is. Only, don't worry about any of that Sergeant, because I'm not into violence, and like I said before, enough's enough already with this crap. How am I doing?"

Barstow gave a smaller shrug than before, and sat still, looking down at the table for a bit before she picked up the Wildwood mug, stood up, and walked towards the kitchen. "I guess I'm out of coffee, mind if I get a little fresh?"

"Or, there's another possibility, right?" Kane said. "If Phillip Starr killed my brother, maybe I'm next. I'm thinking I'd better lay low for a while. You know, watch my back."

"Probably not a bad idea, all things considered, at least until we know more," Barstow said. She set the empty mug down on the counter. "You haven't said anything about the money, Mr. Kane. From what I've learned about this land deal situation, it seems like at least a remote possibility that there could be really big money involved. Like tens of millions of dollars, or more even. Have you thought about that?"

"Oh sure, I've thought about it. I think Erik more than me, but we all thought about it. It's a fun fantasy, like winning the Powerball. But see, here's the thing, I'm sixty-one, I have a nice place here, three blocks from the beach. I own two other units that I rent out. I have no debt. All three of us have—had—trust funds from our father and now I guess that'll all come to me. I'm not super-rich, but I have everything I need and plenty more. I could buy a Corvette tomorrow if I wanted it. If you handed me fifty-million dollars, I don't know if I'd change anything. What I'm saying is—I'm not after that money."

"I see what you're saying," Barstow said. "And I see no reason not to believe you, but we consider it a possibility that there could be someone else out there who feels differently about the money."

"You mean Phillip Starr," Kane said.

"I'm not accusing him of anything at the moment," Barstow said. "But it does appear that you and he are the last descendants who could be eligible. I'd like to check in with you daily, for a while, if you don't mind."

As Barstow moved closer to the door, she paused to look at a framed black and white photo on the wall. Two young boys, five or six years old and obviously twins, stood together on a sun-drenched beach, beaming proudly as they displayed enormous ice cream cones for the camera.

"Must be you and your brother," Barstow said. "What a great picture. Is that Cape May?"

"Sure is. That was the beach near the end of Madison Avenue, not far from our house at the time," Kane said. "Pretty sure that was '66. Jo must have been up at the house when that picture was taken, but the three of us were on the beach all the time. Our father would give us some change for a hot dog or an ice cream cone. Or an Italian ice—that was always my favorite. Those were good times. Before we knew anything about the cares of the world. It was our nanny, Casey, who took the picture. She was with us for years, and we really liked her, Erik and Me, but my parents got rid of her while we were away at summer camp. Our father told us she had stolen something but I don't think we ever believed that. I remember there was this one time…"

Barstow moved to zip up her coat and Kane stopped himself with a laugh. "I'm sorry Sergeant, you're busy and I'm wasting your time. You set me off down memory lane and here I am blabbing about my childhood on the beach. Sorry about that."

"No problem, don't give it another thought," Barstow said. "It's nice that you have that picture and such good memories to go with it. Thank you for opening up to me today, Mr. Kane, and once again, I'm sorry for your losses. Please stay safe and call me right away if anything else comes to mind, or if you need our help."

As she walked to the car Barstow thought about the meeting with Jason Kane. She was inclined to think that he'd been telling her the truth. She figured he must be worth at least several million dollars, or soon would be, and his story about how he wasn't money-hungry made good sense to her. *Now, I just hope he was telling the truth about not wanting to go after Phillip Starr. That guy's gotta be the one we're after.* She looked at her watch. Just past ten-thirty. Plenty of time to catch up on notes and update the Chief before her meeting with Florence Thompson, the expert on South Cape May.

21

Florence Thompson's house was a modest but well-maintained rancher near the western end of Grant Street. Barstow knew, in a town like Cape May, that her house was the type developers would be drooling over, hoping for a chance to buy it up along with the one next door, only to clear the lots and build some gaudy McMansion in their place. There was an old unmarked van in the driveway, and it occurred to her that Mrs. Thompson might have a plumber or handyman over fixing something.

Switching off the ignition, Barstow sat in the cruiser for a minute, watching the rain and listening to the wind, concluding that she could make the forty feet from the car to the house without an umbrella if she moved quickly.

Her arrival must have been observed, because the door opened wide before she could knock, and an elegant older lady welcomed her in. Barstow knew Mrs. Thompson was in her nineties, but the tall, silver-haired woman who took her wet coat appeared to be easily ten years younger than that. The house smelled of fresh baked something, and Barstow had the feeling that it was a house that would usually smell of fresh baked something.

"It's so nice to meet you," Mrs. Thompson said, "though I'm sorry you had to come out in this weather. Let's go sit in the den. I have the gas fire going in there, so it's the warmest room in the house right now. I've been baking cookies this morning, and I've waited for you to help me eat some. I don't get many visitors these days, or at least not at this time of year. Would you like some coffee?"

Barstow didn't really need any more coffee, but the promise of fresh-baked cookies inspired her to accept a cup, and a few minutes later they were settled into matching armchairs in the den.

"I noticed the van in your driveway," Barstow said. "Is there someone else here in the house?"

"Oh yes, that's Coleman. A dear old friend for many years now. He came over to fix a few things in the master bath. Some kind of rubber thing in the toilet needed to be replaced, and also a tile fell off the shower wall."

"Ah, probably the flapper. It's good that you have a friend like that to come over and help you. And mmmm, these cookies are delicious Mrs. Thompson, thank you. I appreciate your making time for me today. I grew up in Cape May, but it was only yesterday that someone told me about South Cape May, and gave me a copy of your book. I'm halfway through it already and looking forward to finishing it as soon as I get time. It's fascinating."

"Oh, you're welcome my dear, I'm glad to have the company, and I'm glad you like the book. I must say I was very intrigued by the idea that the police department had some interest in that part of our local history. Is this about some case you're working on?"

"We aren't quite sure yet, but it could be, yes. We're working on a case that may have some historical implications, and I'm hoping to learn more about what might have been moved out of one of those houses before it was destroyed by the storm in 1944."

"I see. Well, I'll certainly try to help you with that if I can," Mrs. Thompson said. "You know, it's funny how people seem to be getting interested in this all of a sudden. I never realized how little was known about South Cape May."

"It's a very interesting topic," Barstow said. "Was someone else asking you about this recently?"

"Yes, just yesterday afternoon in fact," Mrs. Thompson said. "One of the ladies I play bridge with. I forget how it came up, but someone mentioned South Cape May—or maybe it was the storm that came up first—I forget. But in any case, Sandra started asking about it and we talked for a few minutes. I'm always glad when people want to learn the history."

"If you don't mind Mrs. Thompson," Barstow said, "I'm curious, because I spoke with a person by that name just the other day, a 'Sandra Walsh'. Would that be the friend you play bridge with?"

"Why yes, that's her," Mrs. Thompson said. "She's one of our regular bridge group. Very nice lady. I think she also plays in a mahjong group, but not with me, mind you. I never did learn how to play mahjong. Is she involved in a case you're working on?"

"Oh no, I don't think so," Barstow said. "I came across her name as part of some information gathering we were doing—filling in the gaps here and there with a case. I spoke with her briefly and that was all. I imagine when people hear about the book you wrote it must be common for them to start asking questions about South Cape May. You probably get that all the time."

"Not all the time, but occasionally," Mrs. Thompson said. "And it's always nice when it happens. Now then, you mentioned that you're halfway through the book—let me take a few minutes and give you a summary, and then I'll do my best with any questions you may have. Have another cookie dear."

Mrs. Thompson unfolded a stiff old paper map and laid it over a low table. As she took Barstow through a condensed version of her book and the history of South Cape May, she pointed to various points on the map. A few minutes became thirty, and then forty, but Barstow found the story to be riveting and the company to be calming and pleasant.

"Now, the people who were there that September," Barstow said, "they must have known that storm was coming, right?"

"Oh yes, the whole coast was braced for a big storm," Mrs. Thompson said. "There wasn't anything like The Weather Channel back then of course, but news got around. The fisherman and boat captains always knew what was coming before anyone else did. I don't think more than a handful of houses were occupied at that point anyway. It was a quiet place. I know my uncle wasn't there. He had locked his house up the year before and was hoping to sell. You were asking about the Kane house at the corner of 8th and Mt. Vernon. I remember that house. It was one of the biggest in the neighborhood. He wasn't there much in those last few years, but I remember him as being a very nice man when he was in residence. Anders Kane, that was his name. A real gentleman."

"You say that Mr. Kane wasn't in the area at the time," Barstow said. "Would you remember if he hired anyone to board up the house, or take valuables out? Someone like a caretaker maybe?"

"As I recall it, there was a lot of activity in the day or two before the storm. Friends and relatives came to board up windows and tie down anything they could. A few people who could afford it hired people to help. Mr. Kane was a wealthy man, so he may have been one of those. But I know exactly who we need to talk to. There was a young man who I know worked out there the day before. He had a rickety old truck back then, and he was out there picking up boxes and whatnot from one or two houses. Taking them to higher ground or somewhere else safe. He's a few years older than me, but he's still got his senses about him. He's good at fixing toilets too." With a mischievous wink, she got up and left the room, coming back a minute later with a slim, slightly stooped and grey-haired man in tow. He was moving slowly, and had a noticeable limp.

"Well, such a lovely young policewoman," he said. "How excitin', but I'm hopin' I'm not in any trouble."

Barstow stood up to shake hands with the man.

"Coleman, you are as incorrigible now as you were sixty years ago," Mrs. Thompson said. "This 'lovely young woman' as you put it, is Sergeant Barstow of the Cape May Police Department. And this, Sergeant, is Coleman Shanks. We've been friends since, gosh, well, since we were teenagers. Coleman has always tended to say what he thinks."

"That's not so bad, is it?" Shanks said. His wrinkled face lit up with a smile showing a mouthful of surprisingly white teeth. He eased himself carefully into a chair. "Anyways, you know you caint' teach an old dog new tricks."

"Oh, that's no problem," Barstow said. "As a police officer, I like it when people say what they think. Mr. Shanks, I'm sorry to be interrupting your work in the bathroom, but I'd appreciate it if you could join us for a bit and try to answer a few questions."

"Sergeant Barstow is working on a case that has something to do with South Cape May," Mrs. Thompson said, "and what might have been moved out of one of the houses out there before the big September storm in 1944. I mentioned to her that you were one of the people who helped move some things. I know you haven't yet finished my book Sergeant, but when you get time, you'll see Coleman listed in the acknowledgements. He was a big help to me when I was writing it."

"Yeah, sure, Miss… ah officer," Shanks said, "I'll be happy to help, only thing, I don't think I recall remembering much as I used to remember."

"Oh, you stop that now Coleman," Mrs. Thompson said. "You've still got it all up there and you know it."

"Well, if you say so Flo," Shanks said. "I will surely try, 'cept sometimes things get jumbled up on the way from my old bean to my mouth."

"You're doing just fine Mr. Shanks," Barstow said. "I'll try not to take much of your time. As part of a case we're working on, I'm trying to learn everything I can about personal effects that we think were probably stored somewhere in the Anders Kane house at 8th and Mount Vernon. I understand that Mr. Kane was not in residence at the time, but Mrs. Thompson here thought you might have helped to get the house ready for the storm. Is that right?"

"Hmmm, yes, I remember that," Shanks said. "I didn't have no solid job at the time, and I was getting odd work here and there, down the docks mostly. That's where you went, you know, back then, when you needed some work, working with the fish one way or other. Or the boats and nets. Anyways, there was a man I had done some work for once or three times, he came around. The big storm hit on a Thursday, that right Flo? Yeah, it was a Thursday. So, this man, he come around, must have been that Wednesday, looking for me on account of he knew I had a truck. Not much to look at but it started most days and ran well, so yeah, I had this truck, and this man found me and offered me twenty dollars to move a few loads of boxes and other such things out of that house, and to board up as many windows as I could. Now mind you, that was big money for a day's work back then. Sure as heck for me it was. So, course I jumped on the idea and followed him out there. I don't remember that man's name, but he wasn't the owner. I can still picture the house, right on that corner. It was a blue house, the biggest in the area is my picture of it."

"I think I remember that man," Mrs. Thompson said. "The one who hired you. 'Carlton' is what I'm thinking. Yes, that's it. Mr. Carlton. Some sort of agent for the owner, Mr. Kane."

"If you say so Flo, I'm sure that must be the way it was," Shanks said. "Anyways, we went in the house and he showed me what needed to be moved. Also, he told me to go get whatever I needed from the lumberyard to cover up the windows, and he would tell those folks to put it on account. I did work hard that day, I recall, and this man, Carlton—Flo says that was his name—was happy about it. He gave me an extra five dollars, so we were both happy at the end of the day. I had a sore foot and plenty of splinters, but I was surely glad of that money. You know, that was when you could have a dinner for a dollar and still get some change back."

"I'm very interested in where you took the boxes and the other things, Mr. Shanks," Barstow said. "Do you remember that?"

"Oh, I should have warned you about how I can run on sometimes, sure I remember. I took everything over to the basement at Saint Mary's. Some of the other people took their things there too."

"You mean the big nun's retreat in Cape May Point?" Barstow said. "Saint Mary by The Sea?"

"Yes ma'am, that's the place," Shanks said. "They called it a 'retreat'. Well, I guess nuns need a vacation now and then, like all of us. When they're not doing their nun work.

Anyways, they put out the word that the South Cape people could use some of the basement space for storage. They sure did have plenty of it to go around. That was a huge maze of rooms under that building. I remember that. It was like a fun house at the carnival. I took a few wrong turns down there that day."

"At the time Sergeant," Mrs. Thompson said, "there was almost a hundred feet of lawn between the building and the beach, with high dunes. People thought it would be safe from flooding."

"That's right. People thought it a good place to put things for a while," Shanks said. "I tell you, must be twenty-five, thirty years since I was in that building. My old friend Billy, that's right, Billy Tatters it was. Seems to me his real name was Smith or something regular like that, 'cept everyone called him Tatters due to him always wearing shirts with the sleeves torn off. I guess he got hot easier than most. So, Billy, he asked me over on account of he wanted my thoughts on some repair work he was doing inside there. I thought he was doing just fine and I gave him a thought on this and that, but the thing is that I took a minute and went down into the basement. I was surprised that a lot of that old junk was still there, right where I put it the day before the big storm."

"I'm not aware of Mr. Kane ever being in town after the storm," Mrs. Thompson said. "I can only assume that there wasn't anything he needed very badly in those things Coleman moved. Someone told me he got quite ill around that time and stopped traveling. It was probably that Mr.

Carlton who handled the details around here. I saw him once shortly after the storm, but never again after that."

"What a great story," Barstow said. "I appreciate this history lesson, Mr. Shanks, but I want to ask you about a certain item that we're interested in. Do you recall a large wooden box, like a trunk or a storage chest? We think it was painted black with red flowers on the top. Does that ring a bell?"

"Does it ring a bell?" Shanks said. "I'll say it does. When Flo called me in here to meet you, maybe you noticed me walk a little funny."

"I did notice that you seemed to have a bit of a limp, yes," Barstow said.

"Yes ma'am, ever since that day I have," Shanks said. "I remember that trunk because I dropped the end of it on my foot! Dang near broke it up—my foot I mean. The box was a sturdy thing. Lucky for me it was near the end of the work. My uncle had some doctor training so he fixed me up, but it sure did hurt for a long time and made me walk a little funny forever on from there. No big thing anymore, but heck, I remember that trunk. Only thing, remember I told you I peeked down there when I was with Billy Tatters that afternoon? I saw one or three things I think I remember, but I didn't see that trunk. I said that to Billy, and he said he knew that some of it had been moved to other parts down there. You know, other rooms. He said on account of some plumbing work had been done, they had to clear space in this room or that. I wanted to go look around some more, but right about then a lady running the place, the head nun lady I guess, scolded me and Billy for being down there and we went back upstairs."

"Do you remember what part of the building you originally put the trunk, and the rest of Mr. Kane's things?" Barstow said.

"Well, sort of I do," Shanks said. "It was in the middle part, like, closest to the lighthouse. I remember that because, when I went in and out, I passed a window each time, and there was the lighthouse just over there. I can't say which room or other for sure. Must be twenty or more rooms down there."

"And the things that you think were moved," Barstow said, "you don't know where they were moved to. Is that right?"

"Mmm-hmmm, that's right," Shanks said, shaking his head slowly. "One of the other rooms is all I could say. Billy Tatters did mention after that he thought it was up near the end of one of the sides, but he didn't know which one."

"It sounds to me, Sergeant," Mrs. Thompson said, "that there's a good chance the trunk you're looking for is still there in one of the basement rooms, even if not where Coleman put it initially. Are you going to go look for it?"

"I'll have to think about that," Barstow said. "I know there's been some back and forth for a few years now about that building and what to do with it, and I'm not sure of the legal status right now. Anyway, that's my problem. I just can't thank both of you enough for taking your time and giving me all this information. I really do appreciate it, and I know Chief Saxby will too."

"It's been our pleasure dear," Mrs. Thompson said. "Let

me put some cookies in a bag for you." She went off to the kitchen.

Coleman Shanks said his goodbyes and went back to his work. A few minutes later, Mrs. Thompson gave Barstow a supply of cookies and walked her to the door.

"One more question if you don't mind, Mrs. Thompson," Barstow said. "When you talked about South Cape May with your bridge friend Sandra Walsh, did the conversation get as far as things having been stored at Saint Mary's?"

"I do think I mentioned that, yes," Mrs. Thompson said. "Mind you, I didn't have all the colorful detail that Coleman just related, but I have known for some time about the offer from Saint Mary's and that items were moved there for safe keeping. I didn't know where in the building until this afternoon. I hope I haven't done any harm."

"Oh no, don't worry about that at all," Barstow said. "It's an interesting topic and I'm just filling in background information. If I could ask a small favor though, can we keep all this between you and me for the time being? Just as our secret?"

"Of course, dear," Mrs. Thompson said. "Our little secret, but only if you come back to visit some day after you finish the book, and let me know what you think. And do be careful out there today. I think that storm is finally coming."

22

A t the same time that Sergeant Barstow was sitting down to chat with Florence Thompson, back at the station, Deputy Chase Connor knocked on Chief Saxby's office door.

"Sorry to disturb, Chief," Connor said. "Got a few minutes?"

"Sure Three, come on in and have a seat," Saxby said. "I welcome the interruption. This pile of paperwork seems to magically expand every time I look away from it. I'm about ready to surrender for the day."

Connor sat down in one of the chairs across from Saxby's desk, notepad in hand. "I've spent most of the day looking at Phillip Starr for the Erik Kane killing, and I've been back and forth with Sea Isle. You remember that Sergeant Hannah from yesterday?"

"Yeah, I remember Hannah, good man as I recall. Do we have anything yet that puts Starr up there at the girlfriend's apartment Thursday night? He lives in Wildwood. If he drove up through the towns, and he has E-ZPass, that might show something."

"You're right Chief, that's what I was thinking too. If he took the Ocean Drive up through the towns, he'd have to take the Grassy Sound Bridge from North Wildwood to Stone Harbor, and then the Townsends Inlet Bridge from Avalon over to Sea Isle. Grassy Sound is a northbound toll and the other is a southbound. Anyway, we don't see anything there, but looks like we lucked out with a traffic cam on the causeway bridge into Sea Isle."

"Ah, good thinking," Saxby said, "so, do we have Phillip Starr's car going across that bridge?"

"I was disappointed at first Chief, because no, in the timeframe we've been looking at, none of the cars going over that bridge are Phillip Starr's. But, here's the thing— we do see one with an interesting corporate registration. There's a grey 2015 Ford F-150, registered to New Morning Investments. Crossed into Sea Isle at 9:17 and comes back out at 10:03. We don't get much of a look at the driver, other than what looks like a tall person in some kind of dark jacket or pullover. We can't read the plate on the way back out either, but it appears to be the same vehicle."

"That's a good break," Saxby said. "And that's almost exactly forty-five minutes, which would be enough time for him to get into town, turn north on either Central or Landis, and then the eight or ten blocks to the girlfriend's apartment."

"Right, and then back across the bridge and south on the Parkway or Route 9. My guess would be the Parkway, where he would be much less likely to be seen by anyone."

"Yeah, agreed, that makes sense," Saxby said. "But regardless, it looks like we may have him going in and out of town right around the time that Kane was killed. Do we have anything else?"

"Hannah and the other folks up in Sea Isle have talked with everyone they could find in Jackie Dillane's complex, and there's one thing that looks promising. One of the neighbors on the 2nd floor had gone down to her car to get something at about 9:45. She said that when she was coming back, she stepped aside to let a man come down the last few steps before she started up. She said he was wearing a black or dark blue hoodie with the hood up, so she didn't get much of a look at the guy. She described him as a white man, and a little over six feet. Apparently, she said hello to him and he responded with something muffled, that she thought was either 'hello' or 'how ya doin', something like that. The only other thing she remembered is that he was carrying a laptop under his arm. She thought it was odd that someone would carry a laptop outdoors in a light rain like that, you know, not in any kind of case or backpack. She did say that it was an HP laptop, because that's what her own is and she noticed the shiny 'HP' logo in the middle. So, that's not a lot to go on, but it does fit with the glance we get of the driver on the bridge."

"Correct me if I'm remembering this wrong," Saxby said, "but when they found Aaron Starr dead the other morning, didn't it look like his laptop was missing?"

"You've got that right Chief," Connor said. "There was no laptop at the scene, but there was an HP power adapter plugged in under the table. That, along with a matching shoulder bag at the back of his closet tells me that it probably belonged to him. If that's right, then, I'm thinking whoever killed him grabbed it and took off with it. Is that how you see it?"

"That sounds likely. Let's work with that until we find anything that says otherwise," Saxby said. "So, if Erik Kane is the one who took it, presumably to mine it for whatever he could find on the land deal, then it isn't much of a stretch to think that Phillip Starr took it back after perforating Kane the other night."

"That adds up Chief," Connor said. "And that's probably what Jackie Dillane's neighbor saw when he came down the steps. Everybody looking for what the other person knows about the land deal."

"Comes down to money and revenge. Two of the biggest criminal motivators in history. Well, seems to me when you put it all together," Saxby said, "we've certainly got enough to pull him in for some more questioning. Phillip Starr, I mean. Maybe we can put some scare into him. Funny, I said "we've got enough", but as you know it's Sea Isle's case. Not a lot of black and white with this one, is there Three? Lots of grey area. We think Starr, who lives in Wildwood, may have killed Erik Kane up in Sea Isle, possibly in retaliation for Kane killing his brother in North Wildwood. And we here in Cape May have an interest in all of it because we think Aaron Starr may have killed Jolene Kane over on Kearney Avenue. What are our friends in Sea Isle thinking about all this?"

"Pretty much what you said Chief," Connor said. "That there's enough to pick up Phillip Starr and bring him in for questioning. Sergeant Hannah plans to do just that this afternoon, and he's working with Wildwood to set it up. Hannah was trying to get hold of Detective Dooley also, so I guess he might be there too. Last I heard was that they're looking at two o'clock. You wanna come along for that?"

"Sure, why not. Put me down for that," Saxby said. He glanced at his watch. "I need to wrap up a few things, and then I've had about enough of riding this desk for the day. It's half-past noon now, so we've got about an hour. Give me a heads-up ten minutes before we need to leave."

————

It was forty minutes later when Sergeant Barstow appeared in Saxby's office doorway.

"Hey Vic, what's up?" Saxby said. "Did you get to meet with Florence Thompson?"

"I did Chief. Really good meeting," Barstow said. "Do you have time for me to tell you about it?"

Saxby looked at his watch and thought for a moment. "Is it still raining?"

"Not really, just kind of spitting right now," Barstow said. "But the sky over the water is looking pretty black. I have a feeling the rain is going to come down soon, and in a biblical way."

"Then walk with me over to Starla's Café," Saxby said, "just down at the end of the block. We can walk between the raindrops and talk on the way." He stood up and grabbed his coat from the stand by the door. "I'm headed over to Wildwood with Three soon, but I missed lunch and I think one of her super-protein smoothies will hit the spot."

They talked as they went down the stairs and started briskly down the block towards the outdoor pedestrian shopping mall that was the focus of the center of the town. Saxby summarized what he and Deputy Connor had discussed earlier, and how they were going to 'ride along' with the Sea Isle City police as they went to pick up Phillip Starr for questioning.

"Are you really thinking he's the guy who killed Erik Kane?" Barstow said.

"I am, yes," Saxby said. "After Marty and I talked to him yesterday, I was probably about sixty percent that he did it. Today, after learning about his car on the Sea Isle traffic cam, and that eyewitness, I'm raising my percentage. I don't think there's enough for them to arrest him, but damn sure enough to drag him in and put some pressure on him. See what happens from there. I'm sorry Vic, here we are already. The walk back will be for you to catch me up on your day."

Starla's Café, one of several coffee shops in Cape May, had a façade of no more than fifteen feet across, between a private home on one side and an antique shop on the other side. The interior was warm and softly lit, and filled with the intoxicating smells of coffee and baked goods. The young lady behind the counter was just cashing out a group of three people, who pulled their coat zippers up as they took their hot beverages back out into the rainy afternoon. Saxby was mildly relieved to see that Starla Sloan herself was not in evidence. He thought her to be a fun and interesting person, and always enjoyed chatting with her, but on this day, he was watching the clock. He ordered a smoothie that he had enjoyed on a recent visit, adding the extra boost of protein powder.

"What can I get for you Vic? Coffee and a cookie? They sure smell good."

"Thanks Chief, but as it happens, I've just been drinking coffee and eating chocolate chip cookies. I'll have one of those things you ordered. Sounds nutritious." She gave her order to the barista. Five minutes later they were back on the street outside, sipping their drinks through jumbo straws.

"Mmmm, this is really good Chief, good idea," Barstow said. "Feels like it's probably very good for you too. Unlike the last time I went with what you were drinking—last night."

"Oh, sorry about that Vic," Saxby said. "I know what you mean. I don't know what's in this thing, but I agree it's probably good for you. So, tell me about your meeting with Florence Thompson."

As succinctly as possible, Barstow related the gist of her meeting with Florence Thompson and Coleman Shanks. Near the end of her story, she stressed that they both had believed it to be likely that Anders Kane's old trunk was probably still somewhere in the basement of Saint Mary's. As they entered the police station, they stood in the hallway just inside the door to finish their conversation.

"So, as soon as I left her house, I drove out to the Point to have a look at the place—Saint Mary's. There wasn't much going on in the neighborhood, so I figure most of the houses are empty, but there was a car and a few pickups pulled up alongside the place. I found someone who turned out to be the caretaker, a guy named Deckard. He told me he was waiting for a couple workmen to finish up something they were doing inside, and then they were all going to clear out."

"Did he have an idea about what time that would be?" Saxby said. "And is it normal for them to leave the place totally empty?"

"I asked him both those questions," Barstow said. "He told me it was routine for the place to be empty for long stretches, but he and a few other people check on it regularly. There's something else interesting though. He told me he was planning to call us before he left, because he thought he'd seen the same black pickup cruise by really slow at least two or three times, like somebody was checking the place out."

"Interesting is right," Saxby said. "With a big, famous building like that place, having someone cruise by slowly to check it out doesn't seem strange at all, but three times is suspicious."

"Right, and way off season and in the pouring rain," Barstow said. "Anyway, he said he noticed it because he didn't have much to do, you know, waiting for the workmen. He was pretty sure it was a black Dodge Ram, not new, but no more than about five years old. He couldn't tell me anything about the driver or the plates. Oh—I almost forgot. He thought they'd all be out of there by eight at the latest. After that, the place will be empty until Tuesday morning."

"Hmmm, eight tonight," Saxby said. "And then the place is empty as a ghost town."

"Exactly," Barstow said, "there won't be anything but creaks and echoes in there for the last few hours of November 13th."

Saxby looked at his watch. "Hey, I'm sorry to cut this short, but Three's probably looking for me and we've gotta get over to Wildwood. Let's catch up later and we'll figure out next steps. Be careful out there."

23

By two o'clock in the afternoon, the storm had fully arrived. A drenching rain was pummeling the coastal towns of New Jersey, driven sideways by shifting wind gusts of over forty miles per hour. Birds and other animals had taken cover wherever they could find it, and most people with good sense or the luxury of being able to stay indoors were doing just that. The Kon-Tiki Motor Lodge, a block off the main commercial stretch of Pacific Avenue in Wildwood, was closed for the season, but the sheltered ground-level parking lot that made up two-thirds of the building's footprint hosted a busy scene.

When Saxby pulled his cruiser into the lot, he saw a grouping of police vehicles from several of the other seashore towns. Deputy Connor pulled in and stopped behind him, and they both got out of their cars and walked towards a cluster of poncho-clad figures standing together. Under the motel, the middle of the parking lot was a dry oasis of relative quiet, with the wind and rain whistling outside. Wildwood Police Chief Jean McGarry was the first to speak.

"Our friends from Cape May have arrived," McGarry said. "It's good to see you Tate, and you, Deputy Connor."

"Same to you as well Jean," Saxby said, taking Chief McGarry's outstretched hand. "Great idea to meet under here, whoever thought of that. I hope we haven't missed any of the fun."

"No fun missed yet," McGarry said. "You're just in time for a quick summary." She motioned for everyone's attention. "Okay folks, we are here today to assist officers from Sea Isle City with picking up a suspect for questioning in the matter of a fatal shooting that took place up in Sea Isle on Thursday night. Chief Milt Hawkins from that town is here today. Would you like to give us a little background, Milt, just so we're all on the same page?"

"Certainly Jean. Thank you," Chief Hawkins said. "So, we're here today in the lovely city of Wildwood because one of your residents, by the name of Phillip Starr, is our main suspect in the killing last Thursday of one Erik Kane. We have met with Mr. Starr already, and he denies any knowledge of the crime. He has an alibi for parts of Thursday evening, but not all of it. A traffic cam on the causeway bridge into Sea Isle shows a vehicle registered to Starr's company coming into town and then leaving in a timeframe that would have allowed him to commit the crime. In addition, we have an eyewitness that puts a man roughly matching his description in the immediate area of the crime at the right time. That's about what we have so far. Means, motive, and opportunity, but no hard evidence yet. It's my hope that if we bring him in for further questioning and apply some pressure, something might give. Questions?"

Officer Boynton from the Wildwood force raised a hand. "Do you plan to arrest him?"

"I'm hoping that he agrees to come in for questioning without that," Chief Hawkins said, "but I'm willing to do that if we need to. Either way, he's coming with us this afternoon. Anything else?"

Chief McGarry raised her hand in a quick wave. "Chief Hawkins, I already know the answer, but for the benefit of any of the other officers who might not, can you explain why our friends from North Wildwood and Cape May are here?"

"Absolutely," Chief Hawkins said. He looked across at Saxby. "But you know what, Tate, would you…"

"Sure Milt," Saxby said, stepping forward. "Be glad to, and I'll be brief, because it's miserable out and I'm sure we'd all like to get this done and get back indoors. We're here from Cape May, and Chief Banks over there down from North Wildwood, because we, along with Detective Dooley at County, have been working together on a tangled situation over the past few days…" He took two minutes to give the group of officers a condensed version of the series of crimes that had taken place over the past week, and how they involved the various shore towns, omitting anything about the land deal or the Parkway tolls. "As to why all of this started, I'll just say that it appears to revolve around some far-fetched scheme involving real estate and a chance at millions of dollars.

I'll be happy to answer questions about that another time, or you can ask your superior officers to fill you in. So Chief Banks, along with Deputy Connor and I are here as interested observers, or of course to help out however we can."

"All-righty then folks," Chief McGarry said, "if there's nothing else, here's the plan that Chief Hawkins and I worked out. Starr's address is 629 Pacific, which is on the bay side between Oak and Schellenger, not quite two blocks from here. The sign by the door says 'New Morning Investments'. There's an alley in back, which connects to a parking lot with an entrance on Oak. My officers Wright and Boynton will enter that parking lot in their two cars, and cover the alley in case anyone tries to run out the back. Once they tell me they're in place, I will accompany Chief Hawkins and Sergeant Hannah to Starr's door to speak with him. I will ask Chief Banks and our friends from Cape May to hang back a half-block away and watch. Mr. Starr has not yet been charged with a crime, and we will treat him respectfully, but let's also keep in mind that he is known to be a skilled user of firearms, and is suspected of shooting someone to death just two days ago. Questions?"

There were no further questions. After final checks and a few brief side conversations, the assembled officers took to their cars. Windshield wipers were turned to the highest setting as the cars left the parking lot to re-enter the raging storm. A few minutes later, Saxby and Chief Banks, along with Deputy Connor, were huddled under the aluminum awning of a bank building across the street and half a block away from New Morning Investments. They watched as three figures in dark ponchos convened in a doorway across the street, and then started towards the door.

As she walked, Chief McGarry reached up under her poncho to the radio near her shoulder, pressing the switch to send.

"Boynton and Wright, this is McGarry here. Are you in position in the alley?"

Almost immediately a voice squawked out of the radio speaker. "Wright here Chief. Yes, got here just now. As we pulled in, I thought I saw someone run away down the opposite alley, but I can't be sure. Visibility here is like being underwater. Could've been a trash can blowing over. Want us to stay put or try to check it out?"

"Stay put for now but be ready," McGarry said. "We're about to ring the bell."

"Hey Jean, look, the door's cracked," Hawkins said. "That doesn't look good. Not in this weather." They could see that the door to Starr's office was ajar by a few inches, with a dim column of light coming through and reflecting off the running water on the sidewalk. "Shit, look, that's a bullet hole up high in the glass there." Hawkins, McGarry, and Hannah all drew their pistols. Hawkins pushed the door open halfway and took a cautious look inside, calling out loudly to the interior. He pushed the door the rest of the way open as the other two covered him, guns at the ready. Between the coffee table and pair of chairs in the small sitting area across from the desk, a man's body was stretched out on the floor.

Chief Hawkins went over to the body as Chief McGarry

found the switch to turn the light on full. Hannah went off to check out the rest of the office and the connecting rooms.

McGarry keyed her radio to speak. "We are in the office and there is a man down here. Not sure yet if it's Starr. Possible recent gunfire. Wright and Boynton, be ready back there. Close on the back door and keep watch. Tate and Marty, you can come on in now."

Outside, Saxby, Banks, and Connor walked quickly across the street, sloshing through puddles as they approached Starr's office. As they entered, they saw Chief McGarry talking on the radio while Hawkins was across the room kneeling next to the body. Hawkins looked over his shoulder towards the door as the other three came in. "It's Starr. He's been shot at least twice but he's still alive. I think he's going into shock."

Saxby sniffed the air. "I'll bet it wasn't much more than a minute before we got here. I can still smell the gunpowder."

Sergeant Hannah came back into the room, holstering his pistol. "There's nobody else here on this floor, but the door to the back alley was cracked, and it looks like a little rain has come in recently, like somebody ran out just in the past few minutes. The door to the upstairs is locked."

"Starr lived in one of the apartments upstairs," Saxby said, looking at Hannah. "He's the landlord. And there's a couple of tenants also. Find a key and check them all out. Oh, sorry, Milt, that okay?"

"What? Oh, yes, of course," Hawkins said. He looked across at Sergeant Hannah. "Do what Chief Saxby suggested Neil. Has anyone called an ambulance?"

"Ambulance is on the way," McGarry said, crossing the room to hand a small white case to Hawkins. "And here, I found a first aid kit in the bathroom."

"Three, help Sergeant Hannah to check out the apartments please," Saxby said. "Spare keys are probably in his desk over there, or somewhere around. We need to secure the building. Even if nobody's home, in this situation we're fine to open the door and take a quick look around. Stay on your toes. Oh, and look around his place for any guns. We think he had a Colt Python and maybe a forty-five auto too."

Saxby went to kneel down next to Phillip Starr, as Hawkins pressed a thick wad of bandages against a wound in the man's side.

"He's shot twice, could be three times even, hard to tell," Hawkins said. "One's a through-and-through, and there's a big mess in the back. A .357 is my guess. Still breathing and I think he's tried to say something once or twice."

Saxby noticed a dark shape sticking out from under Starr's shoulder, and used a pen from his pocket to pull the object clear.

"Well, there's the forty-five," Saxby said. "Colt Government Model. And look, threaded for a suppressor. Dirty around the muzzle, probably just fired."

Chief Banks had come up behind them. "If that isn't the gun that killed Erik Kane, I'm Jiminy Cricket. I'll get a bag for it."

"I'll bet it's the one that put those holes up in the wall

over there too," Hawkins said. "Look Tate, he's trying to talk again."

Saxby saw that Starr's eyes had opened and he leaned in close to listen.

"You're the …Cape May…."

"Yes, I'm Chief Saxby from Cape May. You've been shot Mr. Starr. The ambulance will be here any minute."

Saxby could see that Starr was going to great effort to try to speak, but stifled his urge to tell the man to be quiet and relax.

"Doesn't look too good, does it?" Starr said. "I'm really cold. It's okay. I think I got him."

"You think you hit whoever shot you?" Saxby said. "Who shot you Mr. Starr? Tell us what you saw."

"I'll tell you…give me a minute. Do I have a minute? Sorry I lied about the gun."

"You killed Erik Kane the other night, didn't you Mr. Starr? You drove up to Sea Isle and shot him with this gun. Is that right?"

"I think I hear the ambulance," Hawkins said. "He's losing a lot of blood."

"He killed my brother… had it coming."

"Mr. Starr, did you kill Erik Kane?"

"I'm dying, aren't I? I'm done for."

Saxby and Hawkins exchanged a look. They heard the sirens getting closer. Saxby looked back down at Starr.

"You're hurt very bad, but the ambulance is almost here," Saxby said. "Tell me now, Mr. Starr. Did you kill Erik Kane?"

"Yeah, it was me. He killed Aaron. Guy had it coming."

They could see the color draining away from his face.

"Who shot you Mr. Starr?" Saxby said. "Who came here and shot you today?"

"Double-crossed me…very clever. He's going for it tonight. Try to get it…late. Point…"

They heard car doors slam and someone yelling outside.

"Who shot you Mr. Starr? Was it Jason Kane?" Saxby said, as he saw Starr fading away.

"The bastard shot me…It was him…tonight. Bastard."

Starr's eyes closed again just as Banks opened the door for the EMT crew, who came in and rushed over to Starr. Saxby and Hawkins stood and moved out of the way to let them do their work. Banks joined them across the room.

"Well, that's just great," Saxby said. "I really thought we were going to wrap this up tonight. Dammit. At least he admitted to killing Erik Kane. That's something. I'll go out on a limb and say we have an explanation for who killed who this week, except now this."

"Who's left then?" Banks said. "We're down to the last brother, right? Gotta be Jason Kane after all. He's the last man standing."

"Looks that way Marty," Saxby said. "He's the last of the descendants. The five kids. We've got to get the Crest folks involved now, see if they can bring him in. I couldn't make sense of everything Starr was saying, but he sure seemed to think Kane was still going to try to recover the document. You heard what I heard Milt, was that your take on it?"

"I'm with you on that Tate," Hawkins said. "He said something about 'tonight' more than once. I thought he also said something like 'get the point', or was he trying to say 'point' to something? Did that mean anything to you?"

"I think I have a good guess," Saxby said. "I bet he was trying to say something about 'The Point', as in Cape May Point. Sergeant Barstow had a very interesting meeting a few hours ago, with an expert on local history. Let me tell you what she found out, and then I think you'll 'get the point'."

24

The bells of a nearby church tolled the hour of four as Sergeant Barstow hurried from the door of the police station to her cruiser. The rain was a steady downpour, but the wind had let up just enough to make it possible for her to use an umbrella without it being torn from her grasp. With temperatures hovering around the mid-fifties, she was glad that at least icy roads and sidewalks weren't a problem. *This rain is enough to float the Ark, but it could be a lot worse,* she thought to herself.

When she called Chief Saxby to ask if he wanted to accompany her to meet with Sandra Walsh, he had suggested that she go ahead on her own. He told her about the events at Phillip Starr's office just an hour before.

"He died in the ambulance before they even got out of Wildwood," Saxby said. "Can't say I'm surprised, based on how he looked. Looks like we're down to Jason Kane after all. Martin Banks went to his place with the Crest crew but he wasn't home. They're talking to neighbors now. They'll find him soon enough."

"So, Kane it is then Chief, damn," Barstow said. "I don't know how I got that so wrong. He pulled my strings and played me like a harp. I am really surprised."

"Don't be too hard on yourself Vic," Saxby said. "We've run in to a bunch of stage-worthy actors this week. I was starting to lean towards someone other than Starr killing Erik Kane, until we got those pics of him crossing the bridge. Best we can do is to try to learn and move on."

"Should I still go to see this friend of Jolene Kane, then?" Barstow said. "Since at this point, we know it's got to be Jason Kane."

"Yes. Go ahead with what you're working on as if all this hadn't happened today," Saxby said. "Doesn't hurt to wrap up loose ends. But we don't have Kane in a cage yet, so be careful out there. In about eight hours it'll be midnight and that old document will be worthless, and I figure if anything else is going to happen it's going to happen before then. Let's meet up when you get back to the station."

———

It was a short drive over to Sandra Walsh's small house on the other side of town, and she answered the door on the first knock.

"Hello Mrs. Walsh," Barstow said, "Sergeant Vicki Barstow—I called earlier. May I come in to ask you a few questions?"

"Of course, Sergeant," Mrs. Walsh said. "It's terrible out

there, please come in. Wasn't it you I spoke with on the phone just yesterday?"

"Yes ma'am, that was me," Barstow said. She took off her coat, trying not to drip onto the rug just inside the door. "I was calling a number of Jolene Kane's friends to ask some general background questions. What were some of her habits, her interests—that kind of thing."

"Yes, I remember the conversation," Mrs. Walsh said. "It was all so terrible, you know, what happened to her. We weren't very close, but we were friends. She was a kind person. Here, let me hang up your coat so it can dry a bit."

Mrs. Walsh took Barstow's coat and hung it over the back of one of the chairs in the small dining room off the entryway. She then gestured to the other end of the dining table where she and Barstow took chairs at right angles to one another.

"Pardon me Mrs. Walsh," Barstow said, "but it looks like you've been crying. Is everything okay?"

"I have been doing some of that, yes," Mrs. Walsh said. "It's just that I've been thinking so much about Jolene, and how, you know, what happened to her. I thought I was over it, but when you called earlier and told me you wanted to talk to me, I guess that set me off again."

"I understand," Barstow said. "And I'll try not to take very much of your time. I wanted to talk with you again because of something that came up in the course of my investigation into Jolene Kane's death. I'm sure it's nothing at all, but as a police officer, I try to button things up as neatly as possible whenever I can. Really just to cross things off the list, if you know what I mean."

"Of course, Sergeant," Mrs. Walsh said. "But I hope I haven't become some sort of suspect in all this. Jolene was a friend of mine."

"Oh no, not at all Mrs. Walsh," Barstow said. "It's nothing like that. As I said, I'm just trying to tie up loose ends. This investigation has gone into several directions, and we think that one particular element may have something to do with a house that once stood in the area of town that used to be called South Cape May. That was a neighborhood that was largely destroyed by a hurricane in 1944. Are you familiar with the history of that part of town?"

"Oh, well, that is surprising," Mrs. Walsh said. "Only vaguely familiar. I must have read something about it years ago. More recently—in fact it was also yesterday—I realized that a friend of mine, who I play cards with, is something of an expert on the subject. We talked about it for a few minutes."

"Your friend, would that be Florence Thompson?" Barstow said. "I know that she wrote a book on the history of South Cape May."

"Yes, that's her. Flo Thompson," Mrs. Walsh said. "We get together for a bridge game most weeks, with a few other gals. Now how did that come up… Oh, I think I know what it was. One of the other ladies mentioned that she had been up to visit a friend in Margate, and they had gone for lunch at a place where there was a view of Lucy the Elephant right across the street. You know that historic wooden elephant? I think it was a hotel at some point. Anyway, Flo mentioned that there was a sort of 'sister elephant' out there in South Cape May for some years back in the late 1800s. I had no idea about that, and we talked about it for a while. Apparently, it was called 'The Light of Asia'."

"It's an interesting subject, isn't it?" Barstow said. "I've recently been learning about that lost part of town myself, so most of this is new to me as well. It was earlier today, in fact, that I met with Mrs. Thompson to talk about it. We talked for quite a while, and at one point she mentioned how you and she had just had a similar conversation. She thought that you had been particularly interested in how people were rushing around preparing for the big storm in 1944, and how many household items had been moved to safety in other parts of town. Do you recall that part of the conversation?"

"Oh now, let me see," Mrs. Walsh said. "I can't say I remember that specifically, but it could have come up. I found it a very interesting subject, and I suppose that when I realized Flo was an expert I may have gone on and on with too many questions. I hope I didn't pester her. Would you excuse me for a moment Sergeant? Let me just run to the powder room and then I'll get us a glass of water."

"Of course, Mrs. Walsh," Barstow said. "I'll be right here. Would you mind if I looked at your photos there, on the credenza?"

"Make yourself at home dear," Mrs. Walsh said. "I'll be right back."

Mrs. Walsh left the room and went down the hall. Barstow circled the dining table to get a closer look at the dozen or so neatly framed photographs that were arranged across the top of the credenza. She recognized both Jolene Kane and Mrs. Walsh, along with two other ladies sitting around a table that held several groupings of small white tiles that reminded Barstow of dominoes, if a little smaller. *Okay, there's the mahjong game.* Another picture, similarly posed, showed Mrs. Walsh with three different ladies, sitting around a square table that was strewn with playing cards. *And there's the bridge game.* Barstow recognized Florence Thompson as one of the bridge players. A third picture showed the bridge group smiling for the camera at a table in a local restaurant. There was a picture of a fair-skinned young teenager, maybe fourteen or fifteen, smiling and laughing while holding a small dog. Then a picture of just the dog, then a beautifully framed pic of...*wait...what... what's this?* Her gaze froze on a picture that looked very familiar, and she picked it up to look closely at it. It was black and white, grainy and clearly forty, fifty, or more years old. It took her a moment to recall why it looked so familiar. Two smiling young boys on a sunny beach, showing off their ice-cream cones.

Barstow's concentration was broken when she heard something across the room, and turned to see that Mrs. Walsh had returned, and was standing in the doorway, watching her. She had a hand to her face and Barstow could see that her eyes were filling with tears.

"Mrs. Walsh, I'm confused here," Barstow said. "I saw this picture earlier today—or one a lot like it, on Jason Kane's wall. Why would you have the same picture? Did you know them?"

Mrs. Walsh walked unsteadily to one of the chairs and sat down. "They were two fine boys. Erik and Jason. I loved taking care of them. But then, well, I had to leave." She dabbed at her eyes with a handkerchief.

"Taking care of them?" Barstow said, turning the picture around in her hands. "Jason Kane told me just this morning that his nanny was named Casey. Is that you, Mrs. Walsh? Is Casey short for Sandra?"

Barstow could see that Mrs. Walsh was trying to steady her breathing, as she dabbed again at her eyes. "No, but Casey and Sandra are both short for Cassandra, which is my real name. I'm so sorry for the deception Sergeant."

"So, you were nanny to Erik and Jason," Barstow said, "and you must have been also for Jolene, right? You were what, in your twenties?"

"Yes, I was twenty-five that day, when I took that picture," Mrs. Walsh said. "Jolene was about five years older than the twins. She wasn't feeling well and had already gone back to the house. She was very independent. I was hired mostly for the boys, and spent most of my time with them."

"Well, okay, this is a surprise," Barstow said. "So, your recent friendship with Jolene Kane...did she know that you were their former nanny?"

"No, she never did realize that, and I never told her," Mrs. Walsh said. "I mean, I wanted to at times, and came close more than once, but in the end, I was glad to be a small part of her life again and decided not to upset things. It felt a little bit like family to me, though I never told her that."

"But, how did you meet?" Barstow said. "Did you look for her, or track her down somehow?"

"No. I realize things might look that way Sergeant," Mrs. Walsh said. "But no. We met quite incidentally, through a mahjong group. I remembered the name and realized who she was almost immediately, but she never caught on to who I was. You see, back then, she knew me as 'Casey', and I haven't gone by that name in ages. My maiden name was O'Donnell, and I'm not even sure she ever knew that. A few years after I left the Kane family, I married a man named Walsh. That didn't work out at all—he left in less than a year—but I kept the name. I was just glad to have Jo for a friend, and enjoyed hearing the occasional bit of news about her brothers, although I made sure never to run into them, you know, in case they had a better memory than Jolene."

Still holding the picture of the young Kane brothers, Barstow picked up the picture of the teenage boy with the dog and studied it closely. *Something about the eyes. Yes, that's it—the set of the eyes in relation to the nose.* Her gaze went back and forth between the two pictures several times, as she nodded her head. "This is your son, isn't it, Mrs. Walsh?"

"Yes, that's him. That's my son Sean, my only child," Mrs. Walsh said. "He was fifteen in that picture."

"Jason Kane told me that you left suddenly, not long after this picture was taken. He said he was told that you had stolen something, but I don't think that was really it, was it, Mrs. Walsh? I think these three boys have the same father, don't they? You didn't leave because you stole something. You had to leave because you were pregnant. Isn't that it?"

Mrs. Walsh was crying openly at this point, but working to regain her composure. "He was so good to me—Mr. Kane was. Wendell Kane was his name. He was so nice to me, and his wife was sick for so long. I think he tried to do what he could, but he was so unhappy. It started with just talking, and then... well, you know how things happen. I was kicked out of the house, but it was mostly a show for his wife. He had someone find me an apartment in Philadelphia, and he set up a trust fund so I could have a small income. It wasn't a lot, but it was enough for us to live simply. I felt cheated but I know it could have been a lot worse. I hated that my son was 'the bastard' child, and didn't get to live in the big fancy house by the beach. But life isn't fair, is it?"

"So, these boys are all half-brothers," Barstow said, almost to herself. The possibilities were racing around in her head. *Her son is a direct male descendant of Anders Kane Sr.* "Mrs. Walsh, you told me that you weren't aware of anything in particular that Jolene Kane was researching, or excited about recently. That isn't true at all, is it?"

"No, it isn't. I'm so sorry," Mrs. Walsh said. She got up and started pacing up and down alongside the dining table. "Jo told me about something she found in her father's papers a few weeks ago. Some kind of land deal that her grandfather had made ages ago. No—it was his father actually. Anyway, at first it was just a curiosity, but then she found something else that made her think the whole thing could still be valid, and she got more excited. She said she had told her brothers about it but that they hadn't seemed very interested."

"And when was that," Barstow said, "that she found the further information?"

"Oh, I don't know," Mrs. Walsh said. "Maybe a week later? But she still didn't know what it was about."

"Mrs. Walsh," Barstow said, "think carefully now. Did she mention anyone named 'Aaron', or do you know anyone by that name?"

Mrs. Walsh stopped pacing to lean against the credenza with her face in her hands. "Oh my God, what have I done? Yes, she mentioned Aaron. She said something like 'I know who to call about this'."

"And did that name mean anything to you," Barstow said. "Aaron?"

"When I heard that," Mrs. Walsh said, "it did ring a bell. Not anyone I've ever met, mind you, but someone I heard about from Mr. Kane—Jo's father. I helped him clean out his office one afternoon. It was maybe a year before I left. There was a pile of old photographs and I asked him about a few of them. Who was this person, who was that person, you know? Mixed in that pile was a recent one that showed Erik and Jason along with two other boys of about the same age. I asked him about it and he told me that they were Aaron and Phillip Starr, and were the children of a man he had been meeting with that day. I think Jolene took the picture with her little Kodak camera while they were waiting for their fathers. That's when he told me a little about his grandfather and the family business. That's all I knew about them until Jo mentioned that she was going to contact Aaron."

"And we believe she did contact him," Barstow said, "and she was killed a few hours later, and then he was killed early Thursday morning. Presumably because of how he was involved in this whole thing."

A look of great shock had come over Mrs. Walsh's face, and Barstow reflected that it seemed genuine. "Oh my god Sergeant, I had no idea Aaron had been killed. You're sure it's Aaron Starr?"

"That's right, the same Aaron Starr in that old picture, and who Jolene Kane met with Monday evening. Mrs. Walsh, I can't stress strongly enough how important this is. A number of people have been killed, and others may still be in danger. How long has your son known about any of this?"

"My son…my son, it can't be. Not Sean," Mrs. Walsh said. She shook her head, as if to clear it. "Uh… when did… Wednesday. It was Wednesday dinner time. I remember because of what was on TV when he arrived. He only recently moved into an apartment in Wildwood, but he's been over to see me a few times. I told him what I knew from Jo, because it occurred to me that, if what she had found was real, he might be able to get a share of it. But Sergeant, you're saying Aaron Starr was killed Thursday morning, so my Sean couldn't have had anything to do with that."

"At the moment, I tend to agree with you on that Mrs. Walsh," Barstow said. "But there are numerous other aspects to the case that we're looking into. Right now, I'm most concerned about anyone who might be aware of that old land deal and who believes they might have a claim to it. In other words, any male blood relative." At that moment, Barstow's cell phone vibrated in her pocket, and she reached for it to look at the display. "Excuse me a moment please, I need to take this." She walked across to the foyer as she tapped the screen to answer, noting that Mrs. Walsh took the opportunity to walk back towards the powder room.

"Vicki Barstow here, hello Detective Dooley."

"Ah, Sergeant, hello. Glad I got you," Dooley said. "I tried Chief Saxby first but he didn't pick up. I just wanted to let you know that the folks in Wildwood Crest finally located Jason Kane, safe and sound at a friend's place down the street from his. Looks like he's got a rock-solid alibi since late morning. He says you encouraged him to lay low. He's still at his friend's and the Wildwood Crest folks are keeping a car outside for the time being."

"When I saw him this morning," Barstow said, "I had a gut feeling that he was on the level, but then when someone shot Phillip Starr, I figured it had to be Kane and I'd been as wrong as it gets. So, now, whew, I'm glad to hear that. I'm glad to hear he's safe too."

"Yeah, it sounds like your gut feeling wasn't too far off," Dooley said. "But the problem is, now there's only one brother left and he couldn't have been at Phillip Starr's office today."

"I'm not sure that's going to be a problem for long," Barstow said. "I think I found another blood relative." She quickly gave Detective Dooley a condensed version of what she'd learned in the past half hour, ringing off as Mrs. Walsh reappeared in the dining room.

"Mrs. Walsh," Barstow said, "I told you that Aaron Starr was killed on Thursday morning. What you wouldn't have any way of knowing is that Erik Kane was killed Thursday evening, and Phillip Starr was killed by an unknown assailant just a few hours ago. That call just now was from a county detective we're working with. He told me that Jason Kane has been located, and can account for his whereabouts all day. Right now, I am very interested in any possible, remaining blood relative. It's time for you to tell me everything you can about your son, Sean."

25

"That's a hell of a story, Vic," Saxby said. He glanced at his watch. "Just coming up on six now and already it seems like three days' worth of bad luck has happened since breakfast. And I've got a feeling there's more on the way. What's your overall read on Sandra Walsh?"

"I've been thinking a lot about that, Chief," Barstow said. "I think she's a proud mother, who was probably treated poorly way back when, but made the best of it. I think she's spent much of her life resenting that she wasn't allowed to be part of the privileged Kane family, and that her son was always going to be second class. And then, when she learned about this crazy land deal, she started to think it might be a chance for him to have his due. But as sure as I'm sitting here Chief, I don't believe she ever thought it would lead to violence. I left her just about balled up in tears with thinking that her son might have taken things that far."

Saxby and Barstow, along with Detective Dooley and Deputy Connor, had been going over the case in the conference room since Barstow had gotten back from seeing Sandra Walsh. With the realization that Jason Kane could not possibly have killed Phillip Starr earlier that afternoon, they had re-focused their attentions on Walsh and her son Sean.

"Now I realize what Starr was talking about right before he died," Saxby said. "He said 'it was the bastard'. He said that more than once. 'It was the bastard' or something like that. At the moment I thought he was talking about Jason Kane, who we all thought had shot him, but he wasn't. He was being more literal than that. He was talking about Kane's half-brother—the bastard son." Saxby looked across the table at Dooley. "Were your people able to find anything on Walsh yet?"

"Not a whole lot yet, Tate," Dooley said, "but we have an outline, and he doesn't exactly look like a boy scout. Matter of fact, because time is so tight, I put in a call to an old friend from town. You remember Joanne Belli, right? Grew up in Cape May. She's with Homeland now. I asked her for a fast favor and she was happy to help. You know we can't compete with the feds when it comes to getting info fast. Anyway, Sean Walsh, born 1966 in Philadelphia, which makes him fifty-four or fifty-five. What records there are point to him spending most of his life in or around the city. Several arrests ranging from late teens up to about ten years ago, mostly drug-related or petty theft. Assault with a deadly weapon—handgun—is the worst. Sounds like a drug-gang enforcer kind of thing. Nobody was shot, but there were threats. That one went away pretty quick, so I'm guessing he made a deal and ratted someone out. Joanne couldn't see what it was. Union carpenter job for a few years, and then with an industrial demolition company after that. My guess is he decided to clean up his act and take the steady paycheck. Other than that, he's six feet tall, with light brown hair and a fair complexion. New Jersey DMV says he drives a black 2017 Dodge Ram."

"Maybe he cleaned up his act until this week," Saxby said. "Hearing about the Parkway land deal from his mother probably gave him big ideas. But where exactly does he come into the picture? He first heard about the land deal Wednesday evening, isn't that what Mrs. Walsh told you Vic?"

"That's right," Barstow said. "About dinner time Wednesday is what she said, but it was just this morning that he learned about how Kane's stuff could still be in the basement at Saint Mary's, because she only got that from Florence Thompson at their bridge game yesterday."

"Got it. So, Wednesday night," Saxby said, "Jolene Kane had already been dead for almost forty-eight hours and Aaron Starr would be killed within eight hours or so. Three, summarize for us the evidence we have for Aaron Starr killing Jolene Kane please."

"Sure Chief," Connor said. "There's not much, and it mostly comes down to the fingerprints we found on that one window that opened onto her side porch, which appear to be Starr's. From what we understand about her, there doesn't seem to be any reason for his prints to be there apart from that night. Also, an E-ZPass registered to him went south over the Thorofare Bridge from the Crest at 8:20 Sunday night, and then again at 11:50. That fits with him coming into town to meet with her, and then coming back again later. There's her voice memo saying that he had been over to see her, but nothing about him coming back. That's really it, other than Jason Kane's belief that Starr killed his sister."

"Yeah, that's definitely not much to go on," Dooley said. "Although, I can't speak for the County Prosecutor, but unless something substantial turns up soon, I'd be surprised if he took Jolene Kane any further than Aaron Starr. And of course, the guy's dead, so that makes for a neat package."

"Agreed Tom, that's how I see it too," Saxby said. "Next up is Aaron Starr himself, who was found just after dawn on Wednesday morning. Three, what do we have on that?"

"Not much on that one either," Connor said, "but there's something in the works that could clinch it. As you know, our operating theory has been that it was Erik Kane who killed him, probably thinking that Starr had killed his sister. They haven't found his prints at the scene, but they did find traces of blood on Starr that wasn't his own. We only got the DNA sample from Kane yesterday, so it could be another day or two before we know if it's a match. Also, remember how it looked like an HP laptop was missing from Starr's place? Well, Wildwood tells me they found one under Phillip Starr's bed that looks like it belonged to his brother Aaron. Most of the prints on it are Aaron's, but there are a few from Phillip and also several partials that they think are from Erik Kane. One thing – the tech guy says that one of Phillip Starr's prints overlays one of the partials they think are from Erik Kane."

"Wait. Wow. so let me get this straight, Three," Barstow said. "Does this make sense? Erik Kane—who as far as we know hasn't had any contact with the Starr brothers for decades—somehow finds where Aaron Starr lives, kills him, and takes his laptop. Maybe thinking to find out whatever he may know about the land deal. Then, within about twenty-four hours, Phillip Starr tracks Kane to the apartment in Sea Isle, guns him down and takes the laptop back. Is that how you're seeing it?"

"That's how it looks to me Vic," Saxby said. "And remember, we have an eyewitness who saw a man matching Starr's description carrying an HP laptop outside the apartment where we think he shot Kane. What the hell is on that laptop anyway? Do you know if the tech guy in Wildwood found anything interesting on it, Three?"

"That's the funny thing Chief," Connor said. "Or the tragic thing, I should say. There doesn't appear to be anything on it relating to the land deal, or any communications between the Starrs and the Kanes."

"Let's not get too distracted by the laptop," Dooley said. "It may not have any value as far as what's on it, but it does fit in with the idea that these people were trying to find out what each other knew."

"You're right Tom," Saxby said. "It may be nothing more than an object, but it's an object that helps us put Erik Kane at the scene of Aaron Starr's killing, and then also helps us put Phillip Starr at the scene of Erik Kane's killing. Let's move on to Phillip Starr then. You stayed there after I left Three, can you sum up for us please?"

"Not much to sum up yet Chief," Connor said, "but I'll

tell you what I know. It appears that he was shot during some kind of struggle very shortly before we all arrived. He was shot two or three times with something that did a lot of damage, yet didn't leave shell casings behind, which is consistent with the .357 magnum revolver that you told me he owned. We didn't find that pistol on the premises, but we did find a cleaning kit and several boxes of ammo that would go with it."

"So maybe his killer somehow got his hands on it and he was killed with his own gun," Saxby said. "What about that forty-five auto we found?"

"Right, so, that was a Colt Government Model, and we found two ejected shell cases," Connor said. "We think Starr shot at his assailant, missing probably, but putting holes in the wall and one of the windows. As you noted earlier, that pistol had an extended barrel, threaded for an attachment, and we did find the matching suppressor upstairs in his room. Clearly hand-made but well-made, and recently used. So that's consistent with the weapon that we think killed Erik Kane. Looks like an argument, or a meeting maybe, that turned into a close-quarters shootout. We can't rule out the other guy being hit, but there didn't appear to be any evidence of that."

"I'm thinking of what Starr was saying to us when he knew he was dying," Saxby said. "He mentioned 'the bastard', and also something like 'double-crossed' me. I'm sure he said 'he's going for it tonight' and he did say the word 'point'. Here's what I think. Within a day or two after Sean Walsh found out about this land deal, somehow, he hooked up with Phillip Starr and they made some kind of deal to try to find the document. I'm betting that Walsh came into it after Starr had killed Erik Kane. Maybe he followed him or maybe he saw him do it. Maybe he was happy to see the brothers killing each other off so there'd be less people to share the loot. There's a lot we can only guess at until we have him in a cell."

"I'll buy your picture of it Tate," Dooley said. "That's as good as anything else we have. And then this morning he finds out about Saint Mary's from his mother. He takes that to Starr and they have a falling out. Or, better yet, he goes to see Starr thinking to kill him, because now he has everything he needs to know. Now, the only thing left is for him to get out to Saint Mary's and search the place for the document."

"But then what?" Barstow said. "What the heck does he think he's going to do with it at this point? I mean, there's a trail of bodies all over the shore towns, he just killed Starr this afternoon—does he think he's going to run into the police station waving the document and ask to see a judge?"

"Good questions Vic," Saxby said. "I can only guess that somehow, he thinks he's going to get away with it, and meanwhile, he's got visions of big money clouding his judgement. The Starr thing today appears to be a shootout. He might have a fair shot at self-defense. Even if he had to do some time, he may think he'll be super-rich when he gets out. Add that to the list of things we won't know until we get him."

"I just realized something," Dooley said. "Today is Saturday, the thirteenth, right?"

All the others around the table nodded at him.

"It's the second Saturday of the month," Dooley continued. "Remember last year when there was all that fuss in the
press about the backlog of cases at the county level? People
were fed up with all the delays with getting the simplest of
cases heard. The state put up some funding and they got a
few judges to volunteer for special shifts on a rotating
basis…"

"Of course, that's it," Saxby said, slapping the pile of
papers in front of him. "The second Saturday of every
month, there's a special night court that runs up to midnight.
There's a schedule in all the papers and on the Cape May
City website. I think it's Judge Zimmerman on duty
tonight."

"That's got to be it then," Barstow said. "Walsh is
hoping to find that document and get it up to the court
building before midnight. That's got to be his only chance."

"You're probably right Vic," Connor said. "But there
could be another possibility we should keep in mind. What I
heard is that he needs to get that document to 'an officer of
the court'. Unless I'm way off, any police officer, and
certainly a police chief, is considered an officer of the
court."

"You know, Three's right about that," Saxby said. "But
seeing as how he just killed someone, it's hard to imagine
that he's going to run up and try to hand a paper to a
uniformed cop. It's something to be aware of, but let's not
forget that he is armed and extremely dangerous. I don't
want any of us to see the loud end of that .357 magnum he's
got. Let's see, the caretaker out at Saint Mary's told Vic that
he and his people would be there till about 8:00, and from

there up to Cape May Courthouse is about a thirty-minute drive. Seems to me if Walsh is going to try to pull this off, he's got a two or three-hour window to work with."

"I'll call up to the courthouse and have them post a few cars around the area," Dooley said. "They can watch for Walsh's truck and take him down if that's how it goes. I'll also have them watching inside the building."

"Good. And we can have two of our patrol cars at the bottom of the bridge on the Parkway side," Saxby said. "There can't be much traffic going in and out now in this storm. And then we've got to get out there to the Point to watch over Saint Mary's. Hopefully this will all be over in a few more hours, and with nobody else hurt."

26

While Chief Saxby and the other officers were having their meeting at the police station, the rain continued unabated. In the several parts of town that were prone to flooding during the worst and wettest of storms, the water level rose by the minute. Soon, the few visitors who had come to town for the weekend despite earlier warnings about the approaching storm would begin to venture out from their inns and guesthouses to one of the taverns in the center of town, in search of food and drink. The TVs would be showing highlights of the latest football games, and all conversations would begin with talk about the weather.

The row of historic mansions that lined up along the last few blocks of Beach Avenue across from the seawall stood empty. The front yard of one of them was a construction zone surrounding a large pit that had been dug as part of a project to replace the water and sewer lines running between the house and the mains under the road. For several hours, as two of the storm drains in that part of the block had become clogged with debris, rainwater had been pooling along the side of the road and running over a low part of the curb and sidewalk into the yard. The pit had become a pool of churning, muddy water. Six feet from the pit sat a low wooden platform, similar in size and design to a common shipping palette. On the platform sat a diesel generator, which had been covered by a waterproof tarp until the cover had been torn away by the storm earlier in the day. On the ground next to the platform was a trio of five-gallon aluminum cans which held diesel fuel for the generator. As the rushing water continued to eat away at the ground between the platform and the pit, the whole thing began to tilt to one side, causing the heavy generator itself to tilt. As a particularly large mass of rock and dirt fell away from the side of the pit, the platform and the generator tilted further. Finally, the machine tumbled to its side, sliding off the platform and mangling and puncturing the fuel cans. Much of the fuel spilled into the pit, where it floated on the surface of the water, while more still rode a stream of water down a slight grade towards the huge Victorian house.

The only car in sight on the dark block was a late model Ford Taurus sedan that was parked in the driveway of the house next door. Resting on top of the tire inside the right front wheel well was a cloth-wrapped bundle roughly the size and shape of a jumbo package of carrots from the grocery store. At precisely 7:15, as the storm continued to rage, a small timer at one end of the package made an electrical connection, closing a relay switch that was connected to a blasting cap. In a fraction of a second, the front half of the car disintegrated in a violent explosion, launching jagged pieces of red-hot metal in all directions at the speed of rifle bullets. A large chunk of the car's radiator slammed squarely into a utility pole near the border of the two properties, almost cutting through it five feet above the ground. The pole leaned immediately towards and over the construction zone, the sounds of the tearing wood lost in the storm. In less than a minute, the combined force of the wind and the rain completed the job, and the pole broke in two, falling over the construction area. As the pole fell, ripping the heavy cables it supported from the neighboring poles on either side, the transformer mounted at the top broke partly away from its mounts. A shower of sparks went in all directions, igniting the spilled diesel fuel at a half-dozen points on the yard. Within a very few minutes, the cedar shingles on the front of the house had caught fire, and the flames spread quickly up the outer walls.

Five minutes after the initial explosion, the burning car's gas tank blew up, sending jets of fire splashing across the front of the neighboring house. In short order, the front porches and facades of both of the immense wooden homes were covered in flames.

———

Back at the police station, Chief Saxby, Sergeant Barstow, and Deputy Conner along with Sergeant Brody, had been going over their plans for the next hours. Detective Dooley had left to assist the Wildwood police with staging a raid on the apartment of Sean Walsh.

"Okay gang, if everyone's clear on their part," Saxby said, "I'm going to find the best poncho and umbrella I can rustle up and let's get out there to the Point before those workmen leave. Roy, were you able to call all the guys in?"

"Affirmative Chief," Brody said. "Dunnigan and Redding are here now, and the others should be here within ten or fifteen. Davis will be a little later, but he's on his way."

"Good," Saxby said. "Let's remember tonight, whether we're on roadblocks or staking out Saint Mary's, this Walsh guy is armed, dangerous, and willing to kill. The stakes couldn't be higher for him. I want everyone to be ready as can be."

The officers around the room nodded their understanding and agreement.

"And before we leave the station," Saxby said, "Let's make sure we all do a weapons check, and also…"

And then the lights went out.

27

"Shouldn't be more than about twenty seconds for the generator to kick in," Saxby said, as the several wall-mounted emergency lights around the station switched on. Ten seconds later the lights turned themselves off again as the full power of the building's twin generators came on line. The office was once again fully illuminated and a series of beeps and clicks could be heard as PCs, printers, and other devices rebooted themselves.

"Roy, take a couple of the guys and do a quick sweep of the building please," Saxby said, looking at Sergeant Brody. "Let's find out if anyone else is here and what they're doing. Make sure they're okay. Check with the fire department too, they may know what happened. Probably a line down or something like that."

"We're on it Chief," Brody said. "Give me a few minutes to find out what I can."

Saxby's cell phone rang, and he answered right away, seeing that the call was from Detective Dooley.

"Hey Tom," Saxby said, "that was quick. Did you get to Walsh's apartment?"

"We did, and I'm actually calling from there," Dooley said. "I think we're on to something with the night court idea. He's got a copy of the paper folded over to the page with the court schedule. There's also a box of shells for that revolver, but it's empty, so maybe he has his pockets full. Not much else here that jumps out at me. And they're talking about some kind of fire up by the boardwalk. What's that? Hang on a sec Tate, someone's talking to me."

Saxby listened while he waited for Dooley to come back on the line, hearing the muffled sounds of several people talking excitedly. Dooley was back after a minute. "Sorry Tate, I'm getting some mixed signals, but some people are saying that fire up by the boardwalk is actually a car that blew up. Like, exploded, they're saying. I'm skeptical of that, but we'll see. How are things going with your road-blocks and everything else?"

"Well, I'm not sure at the moment," Saxby said. "We're on generator now because we're in a power failure. I don't know what happened or how bad it is yet, but people are looking into it. As a matter of fact, the fire station is just across the parking lot, and I'm starting to hear sirens. I've got a feeling we're about to be stretched thinner than thin really soon, but we've still got to get out there to Saint Mary's and try to nab that guy."

"Roger that Tate," Dooley said. "As soon as I can get freed up, I'll try to get there to help out however I can. I'll be in touch."

Sergeant Brody and two patrolmen came back into the

station just as Saxby was ending the call. "Let's hear it Roy, what the hell is happening?"

"There were two people in the clerk's office," Brody said, "working on some special project, but they decided to wrap up and go home. We saw them out to their cars. Other than that, nobody in the building but us. I walked over and talked to Rich at the fire station, and while I was with him, he got someone else on the radio who had gone out in one of the trucks. Looks like a pole went down between two of those giant old places on the east end of Beach. Started a fire and now both houses are burning. They're calling other towns for help. Funny though, the guy said there's a car burning in the driveway, but, thing is, he said it looked like it had blown up. He said the whole front half wasn't there. I don't know what to make of that one, but anyway, it looks like the power's out across much of the town."

"Okay folks, things are starting to happen," Saxby said. "Roy, take your guys up to the fire on Beach and see how you can help out. At a minimum, they're going to need a perimeter, but check in with the fire chief and see what else. Also, eyeball that burning car as soon as you get there and get back to me with your observations. I need to know if that was an explosion or what." Saxby turned to Connor. "Three, I want you to go up there and check it out also, including that car. Once Roy and his guys are settled, take a tour through town and see what you can learn about what's open and who's got power. Come back after that unless you're really needed up at the fire."

As Brody and Connor went out with the junior officers, Saxby turned his attention to Barstow. "Do you have a number for that caretaker you talked to out at Saint Mary's?"

"I do, yes. Deckard," Barstow said. "Want me to see if I can get a status on him and the workers?"

"Yes, that'd be great," Saxby said. "I'll be in my office. I'm going to see if I can get through to Angela at the Mug and see what's going on there."

Saxby was just hanging up when Barstow came into his office a few minutes later. "I think we might have caught a little break," she said. "He says they're running behind but should be out of there right about nine. I asked him to text me a heads-up ten minutes before they leave. Did you get Angela? How are things at the Mug?"

"She says they've still got power there," Saxby said. "And she's heard from people coming in that most of the mall area does too. The customers are coming in dripping wet, but otherwise no problem. I just took a quick call from Roy too. That's an inferno of old wooden house up there, but they've got the car fire out. He says he's pretty sure there was a bomb in it. Metal fragments blown clear across to the beach and even imbedded in the seawall. I haven't told you this yet Vic, but when I talked to Dooley over in Wildwood, he told me that they were dealing with a car fire over there too, up by the boardwalk, and people were saying it looked like a bomb."

"Whoa, that's heavy stuff Chief. Really? If that's true, could these be diversions?"

"That's where my mind is starting to go," Saxby said. "Seems unbelievable, but we have to consider it. We don't know much about Walsh, but we do know he worked for a demolition company for a few years. Not a stretch to think he might have learned how to handle explosives." He looked at his watch and rubbed a hand through his hair. "Man, we've really got to get that guy tonight. It's a few minutes after eight. Looks like we have some sudden staffing issues, to put it mildly, but let's you and I plan to leave for the Point at 8:30 sharp. We'll take two cars, unmarked, and we'll park on Lehigh near the junction with Lighthouse Avenue. If my mental picture isn't too far off, I think there's a few houses along there with covered carports. That could give us a good view of the main entrance and two sides of the building. Dooley said he'll join us if he can. We're going to get soaked to the bone, but at least it's not that cold. At this point, I'll take what I can get."

28

The digital clock on Saxby's personal Ford Explorer ticked over to 8:43 as he drove slowly up Lighthouse Avenue towards the massive bulk of Saint Mary by the Sea. A block and a half short of the building, he pulled into the driveway of a darkened house that had a spacious breezeway between the main house and a detached two-car garage. He thought the carport, along with the row of mature spruce trees that lined the front of the yard, would offer good cover for a stakeout. After first checking that the Ford's overhead light was switched off, he got out and walked to the rear of the car. Looking back the way he had come, he saw a flash of blue light. He lifted a flashlight that had an attached gel filter, and answered Barstow's signal with his own flash of blue. She approached on foot, having parked her own personal car two blocks away on a side street.

"I just spoke with Deckard," Barstow said, once she had joined Saxby in the shelter of the breezeway. They both kept their voices to a whisper. "He's right on time and should be out just a few minutes after nine. I told him to leave normally without doing anything special, and not to acknowledge us in any way if he happens to see us. He said he's been watching for that black Dodge Ram, but hasn't seen it. He did see one car go by slowly about twenty minutes ago, but it was a small SUV, like a RAV4 or maybe a Honda CR-V. He thought it was red."

"Okay, good to know," Saxby said. "In a little while I'll take a walk around, three or four blocks out and see what I can see. I'll keep an eye out for anything that fits that description. Have you spoken with Three since he went back up to the fire?"

"Just real quick Chief. He said when he stopped in at the station, he picked up a call from someone who just noticed their car was stolen within the last few hours. He was going over to check that out. That was just before I got here."

"Interesting time to steal a car," Saxby said, "if that's really what happened. Did he say where?"

"Few blocks behind Congress Hall," Barstow said. "Around Windsor and North Street. That would be a quiet part of town at this time of year."

"I think I see them coming out of the main door now," Saxby said. He had been surveying the area with binoculars as they were talking. "Three men carrying a bunch of stuff —tools or supplies I guess—and then a fourth guy holding the door for them. That must be your friend Deckard. Yeah, that's him, because he's lagging behind to lock the door. Here, have a look." Saxby handed the binoculars to Barstow.

"Yeah, that's the guy I talked to earlier," Barstow said. "Deckard. Now he's walking back to check the middle door. That's it then Chief. Shouldn't be anyone in there now but spiders and ghosts."

"And mice. Don't forget them. Rats too, maybe," Saxby said "Big old place like that. Who knows what's in there."

"Gee thanks Chief, rats. I'll bear that in mind. It looks like there's probably a few emergency lights on inside somewhere, maybe in the main hallways running up each wing. We can't see it from here, but I think there's a flood-light or two in the middle courtyard. Other than that, those few little lights along the porch are it."

"And now we wait," Saxby said. "After nine now, so we should know soon enough if this is all a wild goose chase."

The stop sign at the end of the block before Saint Mary's caught a flash of light for a few seconds, and they both turned to look back in the opposite direction. A car with high beams on was getting slowly nearer, but then turned off down one of the perpendicular streets away from them.

"I couldn't tell what that was," Saxby said, "but I don't think it was big enough to be a Dodge Ram. When it went under the streetlight, I thought I saw red, but I'm not sure. Very common color anyway."

After a further fifteen minutes of watching from the shelter of the carport, taking turns with the binoculars, Saxby said, "quiet so far. I think I'll take that walk around now, and see what I can see. Call me if you need to, and I'll let you know when I'm coming back. Let's keep radios low and phones on vibrate." He zipped his poncho up and set out across the yard towards the nearest cross street. Barstow continued her watch, occasionally using the binoculars for a closer look.

Saxby walked slowly, keeping to one side of the street and away from streetlights. By the time he had gone a full three blocks, he had passed no more than two or three homes that appeared to be occupied. The neighborhood was quite dark overall, but he did what he could to protect his night vision whenever he had to pass by a lighted area. At one point he looked down a side street as he crossed at the corner and was sure that he saw a figure walking away from him near the other end of the block. *He's going towards Vic and Saint Mary's*! He thought to himself, as he started to run in that direction. Reaching the corner, he paused to look carefully around a tall hedge, in time to see the figure crossing the street near the middle of the block. As the person neared the far side of the street, a motion-sensor activated light on the front of a garage building came on, and he saw the person raise a hand to their eyes in defense against the sudden brightness. As the new pool of light spilled out across the edge of the street, Saxby could now see that the mysterious person was wearing a bright green raincoat and purple boots, carried a black golf umbrella, and was walking a large Labrador Retriever. He let out the deep breath he'd been holding, and laughed silently to himself with a shake of his head. He watched from the corner, unnoticed, as the blissfully soaked dog sniffed around the base of a telephone poll before continuing on his way, owner in tow.

After an uneventful tour of several more blocks, Saxby keyed his radio to tell Barstow that he was on his way back.

"Three or four minutes. I'll be approaching the same way you came in."

"Anything going on around here?" Saxby said, once he was again out of the rain in the carport. He looked at his watch, seeing that it was two minutes to ten.

"Nothing much Chief. Two cars went by that weren't anything like what we're looking for, and anyway they both had at least two people in them. At one point I thought I saw somebody up by the building, but it turned out to be a pair of deer walking around below the porch. Probably came out of the nature preserve over by the lighthouse. That's it. How about you?"

"Same here," Saxby said. "I went three blocks west and then back and forth. Only a handful of houses had any signs of life. I saw someone I thought could have been him, but it turned out to be one of the locals walking a big dog. No Dodge Rams, and nothing that looked like a CR-V or a RAV4. Not out on the street anyway. Well, it's ten o'clock, and I'd really like to know what's going on in town. How about you take a little break from the watch and see if you can get an update from Brody and Three. Use the radio in my car, it's dryer and quieter in there."

Saxby lifted the binoculars to survey the area while Barstow walked to the rear of the driveway to get into his Explorer. He was watching a raccoon amble down the long side porch of Saint Mary's when he felt his cell phone vibrate in one of his cargo pockets. Seeing that the call was from Detective Dooley, he answered, after stepping farther back to lessen the possibility of the light from the screen being spotted. He kept his voice low. "Hey Tom, what's up? You on your way?"

"I am," Dooley said. "I'm about twenty minutes from Saint Mary's. They've got everything under control in Wildwood and they don't need me hanging around. They're sure that car explosion was deliberate. One of the firemen has some experience with explosives, and he thought it smelled like good old dynamite."

"That must be what we have in Cape May too," Saxby said. "Dammit. That guy's blowing up cars as a diversion, and we don't have any way to know there won't be more."

"We really don't," Dooley said, "but my guess is that's it. He's achieved his goal of distracting the cops and keeping them busy, and the storm's doing the rest. The state boys are busy with a big pileup on the Parkway, some lines went down in Avalon and caused a bunch of small fires, and the list goes on Tate. At least it's raining. That'll help with the fires."

Saxby told Dooley where to find them, and they agreed that Dooley would park several blocks out and approach the carport on foot, announcing his arrival with a quick squawk on the radio. Saxby returned to watching Saint Mary's, and a few minutes later Barstow got out of the car and came up beside him.

"Looks like there's some more damage in town, Chief, but it's mostly under control," Barstow said. "Another power line down along the beachfront, near Convention Hall. Nobody's hurt and no sign of foul play, but the restroom trailer's on fire. Brody's sent two of the deputies to help out with that. He's got two of them still with him at the house fires, which are contained, but still burning. And he's got Lathrop and Dunnigan out on patrol in two cars."

"Good, sounds like he's on top of all that," Saxby said. "And how about Three? What's he up to?"

"He was caught up with that car theft for a while," Barstow said, "and he says it's legit, as in, somebody helped themselves to Gene Fenster's 2019 Hyundai Tucson. It's cranberry red, and the left front turn signal lens is broken, with a patch of primer paint just below it. He has company using the driveway, so his car was on the street, halfway down the block. Gene's pissed off, but dealing with it."

"Interesting," Saxby said. "That could be what the caretaker saw out here earlier. A dark night, pouring rain, sure, a Tucson could look like a CR-V or a RAV4. Yes, we will need to keep an eye out for any of those. This guy shot a man dead and probably set off a few bombs—hey, why not throw car theft into the mix."

Just then Saxby's cell phone buzzed again in his pocket, and he stepped back farther in the driveway to answer, gesturing to Barstow to keep up the watch. He saw that the call was from Deputy Connor.

"Hey Three, we're trying to stay off the phone as much as we can out here. What's up?"

"I know Chief," Connor said, "sorry about that, but I found something right after I talked to Vic and I knew you would want to hear it right away. I think it's connected to the car theft—you know—Gene Fenster's Hyundai."

"You found it already?" Saxby said.

"No Chief, but I found something better," Connor said.

"I found a black Dodge Ram, and it's registered to one Sean Walsh."

"Three, be careful there," Saxby said, alarm in his voice. "That guy's a killer."

"Got it Chief, and don't worry, I'm not there right now," Connor said. "I'm pulled over up by the Victorian Motel. So, right after I talked to Vic, I'm going around the block, and there's a house with a Boston Whaler on a trailer in the side yard, with a pickup parked right up next to it, partly covered by a big tarp. I guess first time I saw it I figured it looked all normal, you know—boat on a trailer, pickup truck, house closed up for the season. There's a lot of that around here. But this time, my headlights caught it just right, and the tarp had been mostly blown off by the wind. And then I'm thinking, wait, why is that tarp on the truck and not over the boat? Sorry Chief, I'll wrap it up. So, I run the plate and it comes up Sean Walsh. No connection to the house where it's parked. I figure he pulled it in there next to the boat, and tried to do a quick camo by ripping the tarp off the Whaler and tossing it over the truck."

"This is good stuff Three, really good," Saxby said. "How close is this yard to Gene Fenster's place?"

"It's close Chief. Less than two blocks away," Connor said. "My guess is that he was cruising around looking for a car to steal, settled on Fenster's Hyundai, and did what he could to stash the Dodge out of sight."

"Yeah, I think you've got that right," Saxby said. "And now we know we aren't looking for that Dodge Ram anymore, and we need to watch out for a dark red Hyundai Tucson. Good work Three. Get this out to the other officers in town, and keep doing what you're doing. Coordinate with Brody as needed and keep on patrolling the town. I'll fill Vic in on all of this. Keep sharp and be careful."

Before re-joining Barstow, Saxby called Detective Dooley on his cell phone to tell him what he had learned about the red Hyundai. Dooley said he should be in the neighborhood within five minutes, and would take a tour through the area on foot to see if he could spot it before meeting up with them.

They continued their watch for another fifteen minutes before Detective Dooley joined them under the carport, after giving the agreed-upon radio signal. Just like Saxby and Barstow, he wore a dark, hooded rain poncho, which, also like them, had only partially protected him from getting soaking wet.

"I found the car—the Hyundai," Dooley said. "It's about two blocks over on Princeton. The house is empty, and it's way back in the driveway, broken turn signal and primer paint, just like you said. The hood was still warm, but I'd say it's been there for a while. Hard to tell in this weather, a half-hour maybe. I ran back to my car and blocked it in. No way he's getting out of there."

"Good move Tom, and it's great to see you," Saxby said. "Very quiet out here. Most of the neighborhood's empty, as you saw. We've seen a few deer, and a racoon, and someone walking a dog, but that's about it so far. It's going to be eleven in a few minutes, so if he's going to go for it, it's gotta be soon."

"Hey, wait a sec, did either of you see that?" Barstow said, as if on cue. "A flash of light, up at the end of the wing near the beach. It seemed like it came from inside though, not out on the porch. I don't know. With everything dripping wet, it could have been a reflection."

"No, I just saw it too, or something," Saxby said. He wiped water off the lenses of the binoculars and lifted them to his eyes. "It looks like someone's moving along inside. Probably looking for a way down to the basement. He must have circled around on the beach and came over the dunes to the center courtyard. That's why we missed him."

Saxby motioned the other two into a huddle by the rear of his car. He opened the Explorer's hatchback and tossed aside a heavy blanket to reveal a pair of pump shotguns and several boxes of shells. "If he's in there, we've got at least a few minutes before he tries to come out, so we need to move. I wish we had a tactical team, but what we have to work with is the three of us. Tom, you don't have to take orders from me, but I'm hoping you'll agree to make your way around to the ocean side of the west wing and see if you can find where he got in. I'm going to go up on the porch and make my way up to one of the side doors over there. I'll see what I can see and I may decide to go in. With me so far?"

"Your plan's as good as any I can think of," Dooley said. "Maybe I can flush him towards you, or vice versa. Where's Barstow in this?"

"We need someone to watch from outside, but closer than here," Saxby said. "Vic, I want you to move up to the next corner, and find some cover where you can see across to the main entrance and along the two sides. Use the binoculars to watch for any more lights inside. That way, you can help us know if you think he's come up from the basement, or where he is on the main level. I expect him to be careful with his flashlight, but maybe he'll slip up. Tom, I suggest you get going as soon as you're ready. You can have one of the shotguns."

"Thanks, but you two can have the scatter guns," Dooley said. "I've always been more of a handgun sort of a guy. I've got fifteen rounds in my Beretta plus two spare mags. If that doesn't handle things, then I guess I'm up shit's creek anyway. I'll keep in touch. Let's do this."

With a quick check of his pistol and radio, and a final poncho adjustment, he went out along the road towards Saint Mary's, under cover of the well-treed yards that lined up across from the huge old building.

"You clear on what to do Vic?" Saxby said, picking up one of the shotguns and checking its status.

"I'm down with the plan Chief," Barstow said. She picked up the second shotgun to check it out herself, making sure it was fully loaded and the safety was engaged. "I see a good spot right up there at the corner, beside that big oak tree. That should give me a good view. With all that lattice along the ground, I don't think I'm going to be able to see into the basement, but I'll keep an eye out. Like you said, maybe he'll get careless and run his flashlight across a window."

A minute later they set out into the rain with Saxby in the lead. Barstow took up her position by the oak tree in the corner yard, and, with a nod, Saxby continued across the street to the building and went up the stairs onto the porch of Saint Mary's. To his left, set into the corner of the building, was the set of double doors that served as the building's main public entrance, and was the door that the workmen and caretaker had recently left from. Quietly, Saxby tested the handle, finding it locked up tight. Stretching out ahead of him on the right was the porch that ran the length of the west wing, at least a hundred and twenty feet long and about eight feet wide. In addition to the set of stairs Saxby had just used to come up from the sidewalk, there was a matching set at the far end of the porch, just before the dunes, and a smaller, more narrow set at roughly the porch's halfway point. Below the porch and farther to the right was a long strip of grass, then the sidewalk, and the street.

He started to move slowly along the wall of windows, pausing at each one to look and listen before moving quickly past. The raindrops splattered loudly against the roof that extended out from the side of the building to cover the long porch. Every twenty or thirty seconds the howl of the wind rose in volume as powerful gusts came in off the ocean and raced inland down the street and between the buildings. Between these moments, it seemed to Saxby, there were brief periods of relative quiet. He tried to take advantage of them by freezing in place and straining to listen. At one point, while he paused against the wall between two of the windows, he heard Barstow's voice on his radio, which he had turned down to a minimum volume. He pressed the button to speak.

"Saxby here, come in."

"Barstow here Chief. I thought I saw a flicker of light that must have come out of one of the basement windows under the porch, like roughly below where you are now. A minute after that, I'm sure I saw something at the rear, closer to the lighthouse, but on the main level. Putting it together, I'm thinking maybe what I just saw was him coming back upstairs from the basement."

Dooley's voice came on the line next. "Dooley here. I found where he got in. There's a door that's been broken in, on the end of the west wing facing the ocean. I'll keep watch and give him a warm welcome if he comes back out this way."

"Saxby here, careful Tom. Makes sense that he'd come back out your way. I'm here by the side door of the same wing, down from your position. Vic, keep watch and be ready. If he comes out your way, do not let him get near you. Just please don't shoot either of us. Saxby out."

Half-way down the long west wing porch, Saxby stood against the wall between the side door and one of the windows. During the next slight lull in the wind, he moved closer to the window and leaned in to look inside. The room he looked into appeared to be some sort of spartan office space, with a dark wooden desk and two matching chairs facing it. The door was open to the corridor beyond, and he was momentarily startled to see a narrow beam of light move along the floor and past the door. *I knew it—he's on his way back to the door where he got in!*

Saxby keyed his radio. "Saxby here. I think he's headed your way Tom, moving up the main hallway. I'm starting towards you on the porch now."

"Dooley here. Got it, I think I see a light coming…"

The transmission was interrupted by the sound of gunshots. Saxby could tell that they came from inside the building, not far from where he was. There were two shots, and he recognized the distinctive tearing boom of a magnum pistol. Immediately, the shots were answered by a rapid volley of five or six different sounding booms, and Saxby realized with relief that Dooley must be firing back at Walsh with his automatic. As he raced towards the end of the porch, he heard a third shot from Walsh's gun, followed again by a returning volley from Dooley.

Saxby reached the corner, ducking low, and looked around at the shorter porch at the end of the wing, where a figure was crumpled against the railing. A screen door into the building was clearly broken and hanging off one hinge. He recognized the figure as Dooley, who saw him at the corner and waved.

"I took one in the vest, but I'm okay," Dooley said, gasping out his words between heavy breaths. He groaned as he moved to raise himself into more of a sitting position. "I think I hit him at least once, and he ran back inside. Must be going back to one of the other doors. I've got this one covered. I'm good here. Go get him Tate."

Saxby nodded as Dooley gave him a thumbs up, and turned to run back in the direction of the main entrance and Barstow's position. Thinking of the clatter he would make running down the porch, he detoured slightly to take the end stairs down to street level. As he started to run down the street, he heard Dooley's voice come over the radio.

"Tate, Barstow, almost forgot. He's wearing a tan jacket. Not a raincoat. More like a bomber style. Probably coming towards one of the doors down near your end." Saxby was glad to hear Barstow acknowledge, and he added his own comment to tell her that he was headed her way in the street.

Thirty feet short of her position on the corner, he stopped to turn and look across the street at the porch. At that moment, there was a great crash, and one of the side windows nearest to the main door shattered outward. As a heavy wooden chair skidded across the porch to slam into the railing, he realized what had happened. Shoving the remaining shards of glass aside, the figure of a man stepped through the window onto the porch. With the scant illumination from the nearest streetlight that cut through the rain and spilled onto the porch, Saxby could see that the man was wearing dark pants and a light-colored jacket. His left arm cradled something against his body. His right arm, which was pointed loosely towards the street below, held something shiny.

As loudly as he could, Saxby yelled across the street to the porch. "Sean Walsh – this is the police! Drop your gun immediately and put your hands up!"

Walsh's answer was to raise his gun and fire. The shot missed Saxby, hitting the road surface in front of him, sending sharp fragments of asphalt up into his face. This caused him to flinch just as he fired his shotgun. The blast shattered another window to the right of his target, but Saxby could see that some of the pellets must have hit home, because Walsh recoiled and jerked one leg backward. Whatever items he'd been carrying dropped to the wet floor and slid off in all directions. Regaining control with surprising speed, Walsh fired again, the roar of the magnum echoing across the street. This time, what felt like a giant white-hot blade sliced across Saxby's right side, causing him to drop the shotgun and grab at the side of his chest.

At that moment, he heard Barstow yelling something from off to his left, and saw that she was now in the middle of the road raising her shotgun. As Walsh turned towards her, she fired, knocking him down. She continued to move across the street towards the stairs, but Saxby was closer and had a clearer view of Walsh from his position. Having momentarily lost track of the dropped shotgun, he struggled to draw his pistol from deep within the folds of his poncho as he saw Walsh trying to stand. He heard Barstow yell again, and saw that she was now up on the porch about thirty feet from Walsh. Saxby managed to get his pistol clear just as it looked like Walsh was about to fire at Barstow. He aimed as well as he could through the dark and the rain, mentally telling himself to put the front site on the target, and fired. As Walsh staggered backwards, still standing, he fired again, and then again four more times, finally seeing the man drop flat onto the porch floor and lie still.

Barstow got to him first, approaching cautiously with the shotgun ready. She saw the gun on the floor beside him and kicked it away as Saxby came up beside her. Dooley appeared from the other end of the porch, moving awkwardly and rubbing his middle, as Saxby knelt down beside Walsh just as he croaked out a few words. The wind rose suddenly, whistling down the porch and drowning out part of whatever it was he was trying to say.

"What was that? All I could hear was 'mother' something," Saxby said. "Did either of you catch it?"

"I heard it," Barstow said. "He said 'it was for my mother...' or something close to that. Maybe it was 'I did it for my mother'."

With that, Walsh lifted his head off the floor for a moment to look up at Saxby, before falling back. With the slow release of a last breath, his body relaxed and he was still.

Barstow raised a hand to her mouth, watching his face as the life left him. "The nose, the jawline...and his eyes. The eyes of Jason and Erik Kane."

Saxby stood up and put a hand on her shoulder. "He really is the spitting image, isn't he?" He looked around at the debris spread across the porch floor. A thick parcel of folders and loose papers had torn open, partially spilling its contents. The top flap of an ancient leather satchel had come loose, with several bundles of papers and envelopes falling out all around it. Bits of paper stuck here and there to the wet woodwork of the porch.

"You're hurt Chief," Barstow said, returning her focus to the living. "How bad do you think?"

"Feels like it just grazed me along my right side," Saxby said. "I guess I didn't have my vest cinched up right. Nothing that bad, but man, it hurts. A few stitches and a pint of whiskey oughtta do it. How about you Tom?"

"I feel like I've been kick-boxing with a kangaroo," Dooley said, "but I'm damn glad I decided to dust off the vest today. I'm moving slow, but I'll start gathering up these papers before they all blow away. Be interesting to see what's here, after all the blood and sweat that's gone in to finding it."

. . .

"Thanks Tom. Vic, let's get a call in for an ambulance," Saxby said. "And after that, it would be great if we could get Three or Brody, and a couple of the deputies out here on the double. We'll need to clear this building and close it up. Speaking of which, you should probably give your caretaker friend a call too. You know, sorry we shot up the place, but you might want to get down here—something like that."

29

Saxby was propped up in his hospital bed sipping the coffee that Angela had brought from the cafeteria when a cough came from the open doorway.

"Knock knock," Barstow said. "Ready for visitors Chief?" Detective Dooley was smiling behind her. They were both dressed casually and similarly in jeans, pullovers, and loose jackets. As they entered the room, Angela moved to a perch on the edge of the bed, freeing up the two guest chairs for the new arrivals. Dooley's face showed a slight grimace as he lowered himself into one of the chairs.

"I must say I'm surprised they managed to convince you to spend the night," Dooley said, "but I'm glad you did. In my case, they took a few x-rays, wrote a prescription, and tossed me out on my ass."

"Somehow I think you're exaggerating a bit Tom," Saxby said. "But I'm glad you got away with a few cracked ribs. A half-dozen stitches for me, and by the time they were done with that, it must have been two or two-thirty, and I was doped up enough that a hospital bed sounded just fine. Anyway, Angela's busting me out this morning after I see the doctor. But I'm dying to know—were you able to go through all those papers that he got out of the basement?"

"Yeah, that's what we've just been doing at our breakfast meeting," Dooley said, gesturing to himself and Barstow. "But there's nothing there that looks like the thing everyone's been looking for. Not a trace of it," Dooley said. "And after they took you away last night, a couple of us went down into the basement ourselves, and we found Kane's old chest. There was still some junk in it but no sign of any secret land deal paperwork. A week of blood and trouble for nothing, is what it looks like to me."

"Is it possible that the whole thing was never real at all?" Angela said. "Like, everyone running after it but it doesn't really exist? Like the Maltese Falcon or something like that?"

"I don't think that's a crazy thought, Ang," Saxby said. "But we've heard a lot this week that supported the idea that it was all for real. Having said that, it's fair to say that we never did have any hard evidence. I don't know. I might believe anything at this point."

"And in any case," Dooley said, "if it actually was real, it's been worthless since midnight, which was about ten hours ago."

"You know what guys," Angela said, standing up. "I know the three of you went through some serious stuff last night, so I'll go for a walk and give you some privacy to talk about it. I could use the time to make a few calls anyway. Be back in a few." The other three nodded their understanding and she took her coffee and left the room.

"I'm assuming there were some people working through the night while I was sleeping off my Demerol," Saxby said. "What else have either of you heard? Anything interesting with Walsh's apartment in Wildwood?"

"Oh yeah, sorry," Dooley said. "I missed a call from them while we were running around in the rain last night. He had clearly moved in not more than a few months ago, and didn't have a lot in the way of personal possessions. One thing they found was a will that he had made out just the other day, Friday morning actually. It was handwritten and witnessed, so should be legal in New Jersey. Left everything to his mother, Cassandra Walsh."

"Hmmm, he must have thrown that together real fast when he got into all this," Saxby said. "Fits with his last words, right? He was doing it all for his mother."

"In Cape May, Brody and one of his guys turned Walsh's truck inside out," Barstow said. "The main thing they found was most of a case of commercial dynamite. There were eight sticks missing, and the county guys who took it away thought that would account for the two car bombs."

"So, the car bombs were obviously intended as diversions then," Saxby said. "In Cape May he was trying to keep us busy and away from the Point or the way in and out of town. The one in Wildwood must have been meant to keep them from coming to Cape May to help us out."

"And if you're right about all that," Dooley said, "it accomplished what he needed it to do, didn't it? The guy was good. Shame he was a criminal who went maniac on us."

"The fire department guys think the two big houses that burnt down on Beach Avenue were collateral damage," Barstow said. "That's what they told Brody. A chunk of the car cut down a utility pole, and it fell onto a couple of cans of diesel in the neighbor's yard. Up in flames they went. That's really sad. Those houses along there have always been my favorites in town."

"I agree Vic, it's a shame to lose those beautiful old places," Saxby said. "At least nobody was hurt. I mean, not forgetting the fact that he shot two of us and tried to shoot you."

"One thing I still can't get my head around," Barstow said, "is, with everything that happened last night, and leading up to it, how did he think he was ever going to get away with it? Could he possibly have thought that he could shoot a few cops and then drive up to the courthouse and ask to meet with a judge? It's crazy."

"It's a head-shaker Vic," Saxby said. "That's for damn sure. We may have to file this case under 'Things we'll never be sure about'. The theory that works for me is that he got caught up in the momentum of it. One thing led to another, and then another, and then all he could think of was getting his hands on that document and finding any way he could to get it to someone in authority. That's the best I can figure."

"Let's not forget his last words," Dooley said. "He said 'I did it for my mother', right? And he rushed to make a will leaving everything to her. He may have known he was either going to be killed or was going to do jail time, but at least if he got that document to a judge, his mother would be taken care of. Wrongs would be righted. I agree with Tate that we probably aren't ever going to know for sure on this one."

"I think I'm going to be on the couch for most of the day," Dooley said, rising stiffly from his chair, "with a few of the doctor's good pills, but I'll start on my report at some point today. I know you both will also, as soon as you can. In terms of the shooting, I'm crystal clear on what went down last night, but we all know there's going to be the standard investigation. It's a pain in the neck, but it shouldn't take too long. Another thing is, well…look, the fact is, we killed a man last night, justifiably of course, but still, it's normal to have a reaction to that. I went through it once before, years ago, and I felt terrible for a long time. Look, I'll shut up, but all I mean is don't ignore it, okay? Talk to someone, take a week and go sit on a beach, have a stiff drink, eat a box of chocolates, whatever works for you, but don't pretend it's nothing."

"That's good advice Tom, thanks," Saxby said. "I hear you and I appreciate it. I'll start on my report later today too and I'll make sure you get a copy of everything from our department."

"Same for me too," Barstow said. "And I agree, thanks for the advice on that. I have no doubt that we did what we had to do, but yeah, it's still a lot to process."

Goodbyes were said all around, and Saxby was alone for a few minutes before Angela would be back. The storm had finally blown itself out overnight and bright sunshine streamed through the hospital windows. Some of it fell across the bed and he could feel its warmth on his legs. He reflected on Dooley's advice for dealing with the aftermath of last night's gunplay, and the lives that had been suddenly ended over the past week. Four people? No, it was five. Five dead inside six days, and close calls for a few more. There was so much work to do. The stiff drink Dooley had mentioned sounded really good. Going to sit on a sunny beach sounded even better. *Ah, of course. Sitting on a sunny beach with a stiff drink—that's the ticket.*

"I see your friends have left you to drift off to some mysterious place," Angela said, coming back into the room. "Maybe later you'll tell me where you were. I ran into your doctor just now at the nurse's station. He said he'd be here in a minute and then we can get you out of here. I bought you a 'Visit New Jersey' sweatshirt in the gift shop. It's lovely. I think it'll be a real keeper."

30

I t was eight o'clock in the evening, several days later, that Saxby and Angela had just finished dinner at the Ugly Mug Tavern and were nearing the bottom of an old-vine zinfandel that the wine merchant had dropped off as a sample earlier in the day.

"This is very nice," Saxby said, holding up his glass and inhaling deeply. "I thought it was just good at first, but after we got our food and starting eating, it got better. Amazing how food can change the whole experience. Are you planning to get some?"

"It might be a little fancy," Angela said, "but sure, I'll get a case and we'll just put it on the board as a special on Winey Wednesday and see how it goes."

"That sounds like a good plan," Saxby said. "When you order, get a case for us too. I really like it."

It was a typical small crowd for a Tuesday evening in the middle of November, but there was a guest DJ whose special program of eighties new-wave music seemed to be popular with the customers and added to an overall lively mood. The hottest conversation in Cape May, as well as the other shore towns, was Saturday night's dramatic showdown in the rain out at Cape May Point that capped an apparent week-long murder spree. Saxby was sure that he'd caught more than one interested stranger looking his way from across the bar.

"I don't think I told you," Angela said, "but I ran into Vic in the Acme today and I invited her to join us tonight if she felt like getting out. I hope that's okay."

"Sure, that's fine," Saxby said. "Just don't let me feed her any whiskey. She yelled at me last time I did that. Ah, and there she is. Hair down and all."

"Hey Angela, Chief, okay to join?" Barstow said, as she took off her coat and slid into the booth next to Angela without waiting for a reply.

"Glad you could make it Vic," Angela said. "The boss just ordered me not to serve you any whiskey though. How about a glass of wine?"

"That'd be good, something white and cold," Barstow said. Angela signaled to a waitress, who came over and took Barstow's order for a glass of Chardonnay.

"How are you holding up Vic?" Saxby said. "Haven't spoken with you much since Sunday. You okay?"

"I'm fine Chief," Barstow said. "Really, I'm good. I mean it. How about you? You healing up okay?"

"All in all, on track far as I can tell," Saxby said. "It gets sore when I wait too long to take my pills, but it's no big deal. I have a good nurse."

"Oh my god, it can't be, can it?" Barstow said. Her

attention was focused across the room, over Saxby's shoulder. "Easton Sinclair just walked in. What on earth…"

She waved and flashed a big smile as Easton Sinclair approached the table, resplendent in a double-breasted overcoat and a matching bowler hat. His right hand held a polished black walking stick topped with what appeared to be a sterling silver wolf's head.

"Good evening, I hope you'll pardon the interruption," Sinclair said, as he beamed a bright smile across the table. "Sergeant Barstow, Chief Saxby, good to see you. And this must be the proprietor of this fine establishment, Angela Andrews. Very nice to finally make your acquaintance, miss Andrews."

"Please sit down and join us for a drink," Saxby said. "I don't think we have any brandy as fine as what you have at home, but we have some good Scotch."

"I will take you up on your offer of a drink if you're sure I'm not gate crashing," Sinclair said. "But just one, and then I'll leave you to your own devices."

"It's settled then, have a seat," Angela said. The waitress arrived with Barstow's wine, and looked at Sinclair as he hung his outerwear on the tall rack beside the booth and sat down next to Saxby.

"Thank you, young lady," Sinclair said. "A glass of Scotch please. I believe I saw a MaCallan 12 when I passed the bar just now, is that correct?"

"Yes sir, that's correct," the waitress said. "Would you like a glass of that on the rocks?"

"Yes, but don't run away just yet," Sinclair said. "Tell me, do you have a glass that is four inches tall?"

"Ah..., I believe our old-fashioned glass is four and a quarter," Angela said. "Will that do?"

"Yes, I think that will be close enough," Sinclair said. He turned back to the waitress, who had been waiting patiently, and wore a slightly amused expression on her face. "I'll have exactly four ounces of that MaCallan, in the type of glass we've just discussed, with four ice cubes please."

The waitress nodded and went off to the bar to place the order.

"The drink is on us of course, Mr. Sinclair," Angela said. "But, now you're going to have to explain yourself. Are you in some sort of a mood for everything to be 'four' today?"

"Oh, yes, well, it's nothing really," Sinclair said. "And thank you for your patience with my peculiarities. The 'four' just came to me when I walked in. Inside the door over there you have a chalkboard that advertises, among other notions, a short list of dinner specials that someone with a creative sense of humor has entitled 'Square Meals for Nov. 16th'. At the top of the list is a pot roast dinner with 'root vegetables'. Today is the 16th, four is the square root, we are in a square room. Naturally, I decided as I walked towards the table that I should have a drink that would give me four fours."

"Ah, that makes perfect sense then," Saxby said. "Four ounces of Scotch, in a four-inch glass, with four ice cubes, but what is the other four?"

"Really now Chief Saxby," Sinclair said. "And just as I was beginning to admire your powers of deduction. I myself, am the other four. There are three of you at the table, I come in and sit down, and now we are four."

The waitress returned with his drink, which appeared to be precisely as ordered. He lifted the glass and took a sip, savoring the liquor with eyes closed, before breaking into a broad smile. "Delicious. A trip to the highlands in a glass, with just the right touch of grass and heather. The nectar of the gods."

"What brings you out on the town tonight?" Saxby said. "I don't think I've ever seen you here before."

"This place is pleasing to the eye," Sinclair said. "I've decided that you may see me again from time to time. But to answer your question, I've just come from a delicious dinner at the Pier House. Unusually for me, I accepted an invitation to join a small group of occasional friends, and I found the experience to be surprisingly enjoyable. After dinner, I had the idea to call on you at the police station, where a young officer suggested that I might find you here. I wanted to compliment you and Sergeant Barstow on your handling of the recent case. You did well, and I was glad to learn that your injury was not life threatening. I spoke with a Detective Dooley this morning, when he called me with a few questions about my slight involvement in the case, and I was glad to hear that he also had a narrow escape from grave injury. He was kind enough to provide me with a few details related to the case." Sinclair raised his glass in a toast. "So, cheers to your skillful resolution of this complex and dangerous matter, and to your service to the community."

"Thank you, Mr. Sinclair," Barstow said, after they had

all set their glasses down. "That's very kind of you. I'd like to ask you something about the case, if you don't mind. As the keen observer of people that you are, do you think Sean Walsh was just insane? I can't see how he could have had any hope of getting away with it and getting any of that Parkway money. It seems like he was a very intelligent person, but so much of what he did doesn't make any sense."

"It's an interesting question indeed, Sergeant," Sinclair said. "And I fear that there won't be a clear and definitive answer. Money can cast a very powerful spell over people. There are people who don't have much interest in the stuff, once their basic needs are met, and then there are many more who lust after it with all their energy. I was born to wealth and have lived my life with it. I have enjoyed its benefits, but beyond that, it has never been a focus for me. I suspect that Sean Walsh may have become entranced by this possibility of wealth that he came across—however unlikely —and it very quickly consumed him. And yes, it probably drove him in short order to a certain level of insanity, where all he could think of was getting that pot of gold for himself and his mother. I'm afraid that is the best I can offer you Sergeant, but I hope I've been of some help to you."

"That will have to do, won't it?" Barstow said. "Not everything makes sense. But yes, thank you. I appreciate your sharing your thoughts on that."

"My pleasure. There was one other thing," Sinclair continued, "I understand that quite some damage was done to the Saint Mary by the Sea building, which as you know, is no more than a few blocks from my house. Bullet holes and broken glass, that sort of thing. I heard somewhere that a charitable fund has been established to help with repairs, and I would like to make a donation to that. Someone suggested that you might know something about that fund, Chief Saxby. Is that correct?"

"I do know something about the Saint Mary's fund, yes," Saxby said, "and thank you for considering a donation. It's run by the same fine lady who manages a different charitable fund that my late uncle started years ago. Pat Younglove is her name. Call the Harbor House Fisheries main line and ask for her. She's the only Pat in the office. Feel free to mention me, but I know she'll take good care of you."

"I'll do that first thing tomorrow then," Sinclair said. "It would be great to see that old building returned to its former glory."

"That's kind of you Mr. Sinclair," Angela said. "And you've inspired me. I think I'll call Pat tomorrow myself to pledge a donation from The Ugly Mug."

"Excellent then." Sinclair said. He consulted his watch and then stood to reach for his coat and hat. "Bramford should be outside with the car in eighty seconds. Thank you very much for the fine drink and the conversation. I hope you will call on me, Chief Saxby, for an occasional visit or whenever it is that we can work on our next case together. I bid you goodnight."

He turned and walked to the door. As soon as it had closed behind him, Barstow leaned forward excitedly. "That guy may be halfway down the road to crazy town, but I think he's fantastic! I don't know when I'll see him again but I can't wait."

"I get you Vic, he sure is a character," Saxby said, laughing out loud. "And by the way, he really was a help with the case. We'll try to find a reason for you to consult with him again soon, though I hope it isn't another string of murders. So, what do you guys think, another one and then make it an early night?"

They ordered another round and settled up with the waitress. They had just gotten to discussing the abstract idea of sunny beach vacations when they were interrupted again as Mark Allen walked by, with coat on and clearly on his way out.

"Hello Tate, and Angela," Allen said, "and this young lady… oh, I'm sorry, It's Sergeant Barstow, isn't it? I didn't recognize you in street clothes."

"That's okay Mr. Allen," Barstow said, "I get that a lot, nice to see you. I enjoy your show whenever I can catch it."

"Evening Mark," Saxby said. "We're on our way out ourselves, but do you want to sit down for a few?"

"No, no, thanks Tate," Allen said. "It's time for me to get home and I won't keep you. You guys broke a pretty big deal of a case around here in the past week. It really is something out of the movies. I was thinking of doing a special segment about it on my radio show next Friday. What would you think of coming on and talking about it, you know, to the extent that you can, of course. You could think of it as your chance to tell the real facts while also reassuring people about their safety. That whole Parkway toll angle is riveting. What do you think?"

"You should do it Tate," Angela said. "It would be good PR. For the town and the police department."

Barstow was nodding vigorously.

"Well, I guess that's a consensus then," Saxby said. "Sure Mark, why not. I'll need to run it by the mayor first, but I can't see why he would object. Call Doreen and we'll set up a time to go over it. What are you going to call the segment? I know you like to come up with a catchy name for when you have a guest on."

"Yeah, I do," Allen said, "and I don't know, we'll think of something fun, but maybe a little bit sinister. Hey, how about 'The Parkway Murders'. What do you think of that?"

"No, the problem with that," Barstow said, "is that implies that crimes were actually committed on the Parkway, which is misleading. Unless you count speeding and tailgating anyway."

"I've got it," Angela said. "This is it. 'Murder Takes a Toll'."

"I like it," Saxby said.

"I don't like it," Allen said. "I love it. 'Murder Takes a Toll'. You get the okay from Mayor Torrance, I'll call Doreen tomorrow. You folks have a good evening."

"It does take a toll on ya, doesn't it?" Saxby said. "Even when you aren't the one who gets murdered."

"Yes, it does Chief," Barstow said. "It sure does."

EPILOGUE

Cassandra Walsh sat on a bench on the Cape May promenade, looking across the low dunes at the wind-blown expanse of beach and the endless ocean beyond. Bundled up in a sweater and winter coat, topped neatly with a wool scarf, she smiled and murmured a quiet greeting to the occasional stroller or dog walker. Every few minutes, when none of the passers-by could see her, she took a hand out of a pocket and dabbed at her eyes with an old cotton handkerchief. It was the Tuesday before Thanksgiving, and four days since she had buried her only child after a snowy funeral attended by herself and four other people. *And now the holidays. Wonderful. Just what I need right now.* She thought to herself.

Out on the beach, here and there, miniature tornadoes appeared for a few seconds at a time as the wind lifted sand and other marine detritus up into its chilly, spinning grasp. Looking out to the sand, she remembered long, hot summers from a lifetime ago. Was it a lifetime ago? *Can this still be the same lifetime?* The sand could burn your feet if you weren't careful, but then the ocean was so cool and refreshing. *What would it be like to go straight down there right now and walk right in? No, that would be too cold.* She shivered at the image.

She suddenly realized that one of the dog walkers had stopped beside her bench. She looked up at the man, but the sun behind him made it difficult to see much of him. And she realized that there was no dog after all.

"Hello Casey," the man said. "It's been a long time. I hope I didn't startle you."

She lifted a hand to shade her eyes in order to get a view of his face. *The face...those eyes...no, it couldn't be... Sean. Could it be Sean?*

"I'm sorry, I've caught you off guard," the man said. "Let me change sides so you're not looking into the sun. It's Jason, Casey. Jason Kane. I guess it's been what, about fifty years?"

"Oh Jason, oh my God," she said. "For a minute, I don't know...there's such a resemblance. It's been so long; I just don't know..."

She started to sob openly, and he rushed to sit next to her. He held her with both arms for a full minute as she cried into his shoulder. Straightening herself, she pulled out the handkerchief and wiped at her tears.

"I only heard about the funeral after it happened," he said. "I would have liked to be there. I'm very sorry for your loss."

"For my loss," she said, shaking her head and dabbing again at her eyes. "And your family has lost so much. Jolene was my friend. And Erik. The police told me about poor Erik. I'm so sorry Jason. I should never have told Sean anything. He did so much harm. I'm so sorry."

"You're right Casey, he did." He put his arm around her again. "But what he did here in this town isn't the whole story of his life. A bunch of people did terrible things, and caused a lot of harm. You lost a good friend, and then your son. I've lost my sister and then my brother within a few days, and then I lost a half-brother I never knew. I'm no philosopher Casey, but one thing I know is that life is going to go on. I know there's a ton of thinking to do, and healing to do, crying probably, but I'd like to hang on to the last bit of family I have left."

She pulled away enough to turn and look at him. She looked into his eyes. Her unspoken questions hung in the air.

"Yes, I mean that," he said. "You're all the family I have now, if that sounds good to you. Take some time if you need to. You're the mother of my half-brother, so we could call it 'aunt' if you like, but I don't think it matters. You can call me Jason, and I'll call you Casey, like the old days, but the important thing is that this is our family now. What do you say?"

"I say that's all grand Jason. Just grand. I'd be thrilled to be part of your life and to have you as part of mine if you really mean all this."

"Okay, that's it then," he said. "And just in time, because all of a sudden I've got more houses and more money than I know what to do with."

They sat together and looked across the swirling sand at

the ocean for a while. A man went by with a trio of little terriers wearing matching dog sweaters. As he passed, they looked at each other and exchanged a stifled laugh as they realized that the man himself wore a fourth matching sweater.

"You know, sitting here with you," he said, "and looking at the beach after all these years, I keep having the feeling that an ice cream cone would be nice."

"I don't know about that," she said. "It's a little cold for ice cream. How about next summer?"

"Next summer sounds great," he said. "It's a date. Say, I don't suppose you're any good with turkey, are you? I haven't had that for about a year."

"Actually, I'm very good with turkey," she said. "I was planning to skip it, but maybe now that I have a family…"

"Thursday it is then," he said. "Thursday at your place. I'll bring the ice cream."

———

The next day was almost as windy, though substantially warmer and with an abundance of bright sun. It was a perfect fall day—sunny and crisp, and warm enough for people to get out of the house and 'do things' before the day of the big feast.

It had been almost two weeks since bullets and shotgun pellets had torn into the woodwork of Saint Mary by the Sea, and much of the repair work had been completed. Most of the substantial repainting that was needed would be waiting for the following spring. On this beautiful day, the nearby nature reserve and visitor's center, under the shadow of the Cape May Lighthouse, was alive with activity.

After climbing the lighthouse, and browsing the gift shop, Margo Byrne led her grandson Jacob across the parking lot to the elevated bird watch platform that stood at the edge of the large pond that was a major feature of the Cape May Point State Park. Sturdily built of pressure-treated lumber, the platform stood eight feet off the ground and was a favorite of the bird watchers and other nature lovers who accounted for a large percentage of the fall visitors to Cape May County.

At just twelve years old, Jacob Byrne was a thoughtful young man, and stopped twice as they climbed the wooden ramp to pick up a few items of discarded trash, which he deposited in the trash can at the top.

"That's very good of you Jacob," his grandmother said. "Maybe you'll work outside someday, like an environmentalist or something like that. You know what, I bet we'll see some swans out on the pond, and then we can walk through the trails if you want to."

"Oh, look Grandma," Jacob said, almost as soon as they'd gone to stand by the wooden rail closest to the pond. "You were right, look at the swans! And those ducks over there—those are Mallards."

Just then a gust of wind rose up and blew over them and out over the pond. Jacob felt something on the back of his leg, and he looked down to see that another scrap of paper trash—a letter or something—was clinging to him. He realized that the wind must have picked it up from way across the parking lot, maybe from outside an overflowing trash can. As he grabbed at it, another strong gust tried to tear it from his fingers. He watched as the clump of paper flew out over the water of the pond, where it landed on the surface near a pair of graceful swans. They immediately started to peck at the paper, tearing the sheets to shreds.

"Darn!" Jacob said aloud, realizing he had only managed to save one of the pages, which he still held, crumpled up in his hand.

"What is that?" his grandmother said, coming over to look at the paper with him. "It looks really old. What does it say?"

"Just a bunch of names," Jacob said. "I think this one on the right says 'Morgenstern'. Yeah, that's right. I can't read this other one, but underneath it says 'Attorney General'. And the one at the bottom looks like Grant. U-something Grant, but the rest is all worn off. It must be one of those replica things, like that copy of the Declaration of Independence I got when you and Grandpa took us to Independence Hall."

"You're probably right Jacob," his grandmother said, "but it could be a page from someone's will too, or some other legal paper. Tear it up before you put it in the trash. Want to do one of the nature trails now?"

"Yeah, let's do that, maybe we'll see a snake again," Jacob said, as he started to tear the paper into small pieces before depositing it responsibly into the nearby trash can.

ALSO BY MILES NELSON

The Privilege of The Dead (2018)

Dean Boudreau has been going through a rough patch.

After twenty years with a Fortune 500 company, he is laid off as part of a campaign to hire younger, cheaper workers. Six months later, in an incredible case of mistaken identity, he draws on long-dormant skills to blast his way out of a bloody home invasion. Hurled into a strange new world, he struggles to find his path forward. When he is contacted by a childhood friend and her wealthy family asking for his help with breaking up a corporate embezzling ring, he decides to take the job, teaming up with his old Special Forces buddy, the charming but lethal Tommy Unser. As they begin to investigate, they find that all roads lead back to Dean's old boss.

Dean and Tommy embark on a mission of justice and revenge. Together, they will deliver a hot lead gut-punch to the greed and corruption of corporate America. As they cross the country from Philadelphia to Seattle, Chicago, Atlanta, New Jersey, and a tranquil island off the coast of Rhode Island, their success is anything but certain.

What is certain though, is that whiskey will be poured, bullets will fly, and rivers of blood will flow.

To Die No More (2019)

A year after the blood-spattered events of The Privilege of The Dead, Dean Boudreau and his old Special Forces buddy Tommy Unser are again working together. As part of an elite and top-secret team of government assassins, they report to a mysterious man known only as "The Colonel".

As the country sizzles in the summer sun, and tensions come to a boil, the team races the clock to uncover and crush a murderous domestic terrorism plot that reaches to the highest levels of power. The body count rises with the temperature as Dean, Tommy, and their lethal friends cross the country to dish out extra helpings of blazing hot lead in the name of justice.

From the strange landscape of the California desert, to deep inside our largest cities, and back out to the lush countryside of Kentucky, the whiskey…and the blood, will flow freely.

Murder at Exit 0 (2020)

In a small beach town, isolated from the mainland and in the grip of a harsh winter, death is stalking the streets…

As the snow falls and the body count rises, Police Chief

Tate Saxby and his small band of deputies race to catch the killer. Between a powerful local businessman, an ambitious mayor, and a mysterious visitor with a deadly past - who can Saxby trust?

In the dark of night, with a blizzard moving in, old friends, old secrets, and old sins will come together for a final, violent showdown. *And mugs will be turned towards the sea.*

* Clive Cussler Adventure Writers Competition 2020 - Top Ten Semi-Finalist.

Made in the USA
Middletown, DE
14 May 2025

75451185R00175